FEAR AND FORTITUDE

BOW STREET WALLFLOWERS
BOOK ONE

CHERI CHAMPAGNE

Cover design and illustrations by Cheri Champagne; image inspiration purchased from PeriodImages.com

Editing by Jen Graybeal and Amanda Bidnall

Logo design and creation by Rachel Champagne

Edition: 2

ISBN: 978-1-7386935-3-5

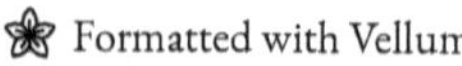 Formatted with Vellum

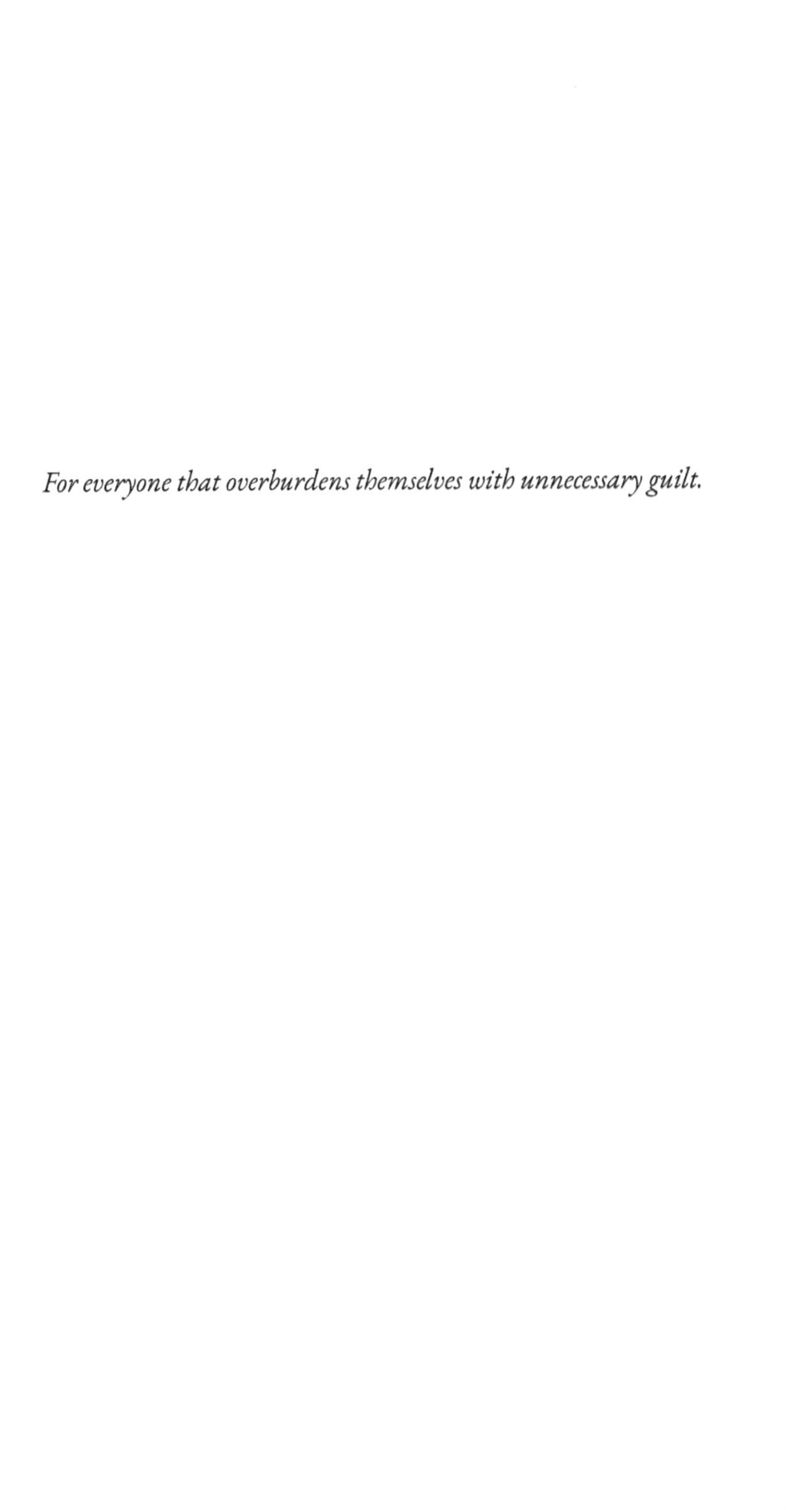

For everyone that overburdens themselves with unnecessary guilt.

CONTENT WARNINGS

Dear reader,
There are certain aspects of this novel that might be triggering to
some readers. (Spoilers ahead)
They are as follows:
** Villain boasting about harming an animal*
** Body shaming by the villain*
** Traumatic carriage accident*
** Claustrophobia*
** Accidental death*
** Poisoning*
** Dealing with loss*
** Swearing*
** Violence—particularly hand-to-hand combat and use of*
daggers and pistols
** Abusive family members*
** Threats*
** Discussions on death*
** Explicit sex*
** Sex without a condom (without pregnancy)*

FEAR AND FORTITUDE

PROLOGUE

*D*erby, 1797

A BUMBLEBEE BUZZED NEARBY, its little wings catching the summer sunlight, and Juliana Sinclair, granddaughter to the Duke of Derby, observed—carefully *not* looking at the carnage behind the stables.

"Touch it, Juliana," Miles Sinclair taunted, his golden hair brightened by the sun.

Juliana wrinkled her nose, her stomach wobbling in disgust at her older cousin's suggestion. She couldn't even look at the poor creature. It was the third in a sennight that her cousins had boasted about torturing.

"Leave her alone." Jasper gripped Juliana's shoulder and pushed her behind him.

Her big brother was fourteen, and even though he was younger than Miles and Francis Sinclair, he would protect her.

"It's just a bloody cat," Jean Sinclair sighed, rolling her eyes skyward.

Juliana gasped. "You said a bad word!"

"*I'm* eleven. *I* can say whatever I want." She huffed, notching her chin higher and carefully adjusting the brown curls at her temple.

Was it true? Were eleven-year-olds allowed to say such words? Juliana's governess had told her that she oughtn't use foul language at *any* age, but Jean was six years older than Juliana and no one else said anything, so surely she must be correct.

"You're just too stupid to know that it can't hurt you now that it's dead," Francis intoned, running his hands through his thick, dark hair.

He was big, much larger than his younger brother. At eighteen years of age, he stood almost as tall as Papa, and his blue eyes were even meaner.

"Stupid," Francis continued, "and ugly. Look at your gangling limbs and frizzy hair."

"*Ugly*," Jean enunciated.

Hurt spread through Juliana's chest, but she still asked, "Does being ugly make me stupider?"

Francis sneered. "Yes."

"I said leave her alone!" Jasper shouted.

"We don't have to!" Miles shouted back. "Our father will be duke one day, and then Francis will be. *You* will have to do whatever *we* say."

"Your father will not become duke," Jasper returned.

"I'm going to be a duchess." Jean flounced, narrowly missing stepping on the deceased cat with one slippered toe.

"It doesn't work that way," Jasper corrected. "Your father might be older than ours, but he is illegitimate, so he will never become the duke."

"*I'm going to be a duchess*!" Jean screeched.

Jasper shook his head. "Not unless you marry a duke. You'll not inherit a title."

"She can be whatever she wants to be," Miles snarled, shoving Jasper.

Jasper shoved their cousin back, and Juliana's heart skittered, fear prickling along the back of her neck. She didn't really understand their argument, but she didn't like that they were fighting.

"Stop!" She tried to pull at Jasper's coat, but he moved out of her reach.

With a shout of alarm, he was hauled bodily from his feet and pressed hard against the back wall of the stables, a blade pressed to his throat. His feet kicked wildly, and he clutched at Francis' hands where they held him firm.

"I could slit your throat from here..." Francis pointed the tip of the blade just under one of Jasper's ears and slid it along the curve of his neck until he reached the other ear. "...to here. I could let you bleed out, crying, sputtering for breath, and pissing yourself—"

"Stop it," Juliana begged, her body trembling. "Put him down."

Francis glared at her. "Our father is speaking with the duke right now. He's confident that he can convince the old fool to correct his mistake and make Father's birth legally valid. And then he will take his rightful place as heir apparent." He sent a scathing glance over her person, and then did the same to Jasper. "There can only be one true heir."

CHAPTER 1

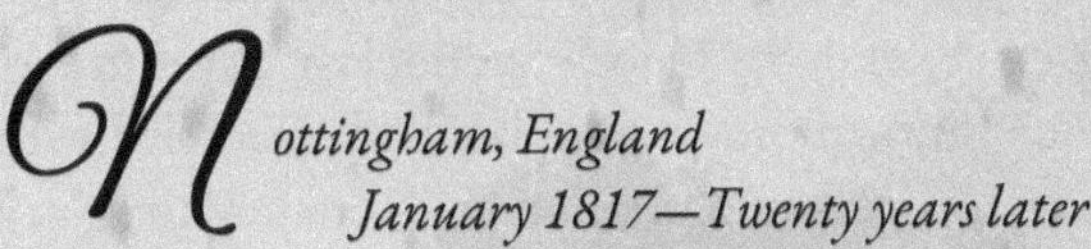

Nottingham, England
January 1817—Twenty years later

A BEAD of icy perspiration trembled from the tip of Lady Juliana Sinclair's nose as she took aim. Her arms shook with fear and hunger, and her raw fingers, numb with cold, wrapped around the loaded pistol's handle. Tears blurred her vision and her breath hitched, but she sighted her target through the forest's trees and slowly put her finger over the trigger.

Don't do this, her mind whispered. *Don't do this, Juliana. You're not a murderer.* Her thoughts rebelled and her stomach roiled with nausea and pain. *But I must. I haven't a choice.*

Tears burned twin trails down her frigid cheeks before catching the cold air and sending prickles of pain across her skin. With gritted teeth, she squeezed one eye tightly shut and pulled the trigger.

Bang!

Bang!

Her shot went wide, echoing through the forest, and the stag scampered off.

An overwhelming wave of simultaneous relief and regret washed over Juliana, bringing her to her knees on the forest's damp, spongy ground. And she wept. She'd not wished to harm the beastie, but now, without a source of food, she would surely die. For two days she'd been wandering the forest, and she was certain that she could not survive another night in the cold, covered only by moss that she'd torn from the ground. Her body was too weak, too cold.

Her mind's eye flashed with the memory of a warm carriage, the jostle, the flip...the searing pain to her scalp, the ear-splitting crack, and the blood. She looked down at her maid's costume, turned brown, and her body trembled with another shiver. Her pursuit of freedom had certainly come at a price.

BANG!

Bang!

A curse fell from the lips of Leonard Notley, the Marquess of Livingston, as he lowered his hunting rifle. His two greyhounds, Kitty and Boots, barked and sniffed the air, their ears perked.

His hunt had been foiled. "What the devil was that?" he growled at his best friend and man of all work, Percy Baxter.

The man's dark, well-trained, and well-practised gaze scanned the forest. "That sounded like a second shot."

"On *my* land?" Leo's eyebrows darted up. He'd never dealt with poachers before, and the prospect sent a shiver of dread down the backs of his legs, threatening to buckle them.

"I'll have a look, shall I, sir?" Percy gestured with his shaggy head of dark hair, a smirk on his lips.

While Leo appreciated his friend's avoidance of Leo's reviled title, he detested the unsubtle prod at his discomfort around people.

Leo growled. "Damn you."

His breath fogged around him, and his boots squished pleasantly into the mossy, silent earth as he marched determinedly toward the source of the other shot. He'd find the poacher, and he'd have the man removed from his land immediately, by God. No one would hunt on his land, and *no one* would wander about his estate just to gawk at him.

Noting his lack of a command, his dogs remained at his side, though Leo could sense the tension in the line of their backs, the stiff swing of their tails, and the taut bounce to their step. They were ready to spring into motion the moment he commanded it. He couldn't risk his dogs' lives, however, and sending them running toward a poacher was certainly a risk.

Low gasping sounds came from just beyond a curve of trees, and Leo's heart beat harder as he approached. Mentally shoring up his nerves to deliver a proper verbal thrashing, he scowled, inhaled, and...froze.

Sitting on the forest floor was a woman, her head bowed, her face in her hands as her shoulders shook. Her maid's uniform was filthy, and her dark, curling brown hair was half-pulled from its chignon. Leo's heart squeezed, his gaze falling on the pistol that lay on the ground several feet away. His anger evaporated. This woman wasn't a poacher in the vicious sense. She was merely trying to survive. And clearly losing the battle.

"Excuse me, madam," he said into the silence.

She gasped, her head snapping up before she scrambled away. Holy hell. The force of her wide, frightened gaze hit him hard in the gut. Her eyes, the colour of wet stone with green around the edges, stood out luminously against her filth-covered skin, and his heart punched once, hard, against his ribs in response.

"I'll not hurt you," he vowed, his breath fogging in the air.

The woman's gaze flicked down to the rifle hanging from his left arm, and he cursed under his breath before turning and handing the damned thing to Percy, who stood silently behind him.

"My name is Leonard Notley, and this is my land." His dogs whimpered, but he ignored them. He wouldn't overwhelm the poor woman with their attention.

How in the hell could she possibly have come to be there? Did she work in the home of one of his neighbours? If so, why in the devil was she so filthy, and why had no one come looking for her? And what had happened to cause her to be so frightened of him? The woman was full of mysteries that Leo wished to have solved, but he could scarcely interrogate her when she appeared to be so near to fainting.

She swiped at the tears on her face, leaving streaks of dirt on her cheekbones. Her breath was coming fast, her small, oval face obscured by each foggy puff. "My name is Juliana S- Smith."

Another painful squeeze gripped his stomach. "You must be frozen through," he observed, stepping closer. "Won't you come to my estate and warm yourself by the fire? I've food and water, as well."

What the devil are you doing, Leo? his inner voice rebuked. Indeed, inviting a woman—a *stranger*—into his home was the very last thing that he ought to be doing. *But such an intriguing puzzle.* A shiver shook her body, and his mind was made up, no matter how ill-advised. He would not let her remain out there, alone, cold, and hungry.

He closed the distance between them and extended his hand to her.

JULIANA'S HEART skittered wildly in her chest. She wouldn't, *couldn't* trust him. However... Her stomach growled plaintively, and her mouth felt dry as cotton. As much as she hated to admit it, she was in desperate need of help.

As though timed by the heavens, the clouds parted above the trees and lent a shaft of light over his body, giving her a clear view of his features. His clean blond hair was thick and wavy, and it hung down past his shoulders. His blond beard was short beside his ears and lengthened along his jaw toward his chin, where it must be at least two inches long. It was clear to her that his facial hair was grown not merely out of indolence, but was carefully chosen and maintained. Indeed, the hair around his full, ruddy lips was shorn back, kept clean and neat so as not to fall in the way while he ate.

Above his beard, his cheeks were pinkened by the cold, and his thick brows were two shades darker than his golden hair. And his eyes... His eyes were a shocking shade of pale blue that looked almost grey.

This is it, Juliana. You've finally gone mad with hunger, for surely no man as large and hairy as this could ever be so beautiful. And nor would his faint cinnamon-and-coconut scent make you wish to press your nose to his skin just to get another smell.

If this was delirium, she would die happy, she supposed. But just to be safe... With jerky movements, Juliana crawled to her pistol and shoved it in her costume's pocket—safely among her other treasures—before she accepted Mr. Notley's hand.

"Christ," he muttered. "You're frozen stiff." He removed his greatcoat and wrapped it around her shoulders.

Coconut-soap-and-cinnamon-scented material engulfed her, and the warmth left over from his body nearly had her in a swoon. "Thank you." She was tempted to duck her head inside the coat's folds and absorb the heat and the absurdly comforting fragrance, but she resisted.

He called over his shoulder to his man, and several servants came from around a corner. "We will return on the morrow week to continue our hunt. For now, we have enough meat to sustain us, and this young woman—Miss Juliana Smith—requires sustenance and warmth."

There were murmurs of response before the men leapt into action. Time seemed to whirl past as she was guided toward the edge of the forest and whisked upon a mount to ride across great stretches of land. The man's two greyhounds broke into frenzied barks and sprinted away, over hills and alongside stretches of previously tilled earth. Juliana did not know with whom she rode, and she truthfully did not care; he was warm and solid, and despite the slight jostle of the horse, she found herself dozing off, her hand securely wrapped around her pistol.

HIS FAILURE WAS the bitch's fault entirely.

The fact that he was forced to spend his nights at this shit inn on the outskirts of Nottingham—the walls cracked, the paint stained and peeling, and the bed lumpy—was her fault, as well. At least the place didn't have lice.

With the tip of his toes, he dragged the table's other chair nearer and rested his bared heels on it, hissing at the pain jolting through his chest. He'd just redressed the wound that grazed his ribs, the stitching angry, and with every movement, every stab of pain, came a deeper hatred for Lady Juliana Sinclair.

Fresh determination rushed through him, and he reached for his pistol to begin cleaning. He would find her, just as he'd promised, and he would not only carry out his task, but he would make her pay for what she'd done.

Darkness lifted, but the fog in Juliana's mind remained. Pain jolted through her scalp and skittered down her spine to tingle in her legs. The staccato chattering of her teeth echoed in her ears, and a shiver wracked her. A beam of sunlight shone through the ceiling of her enclosure, highlighting dust motes that drifted lazily through the air.

How long had it been since the accident? How long had she been lying thusly?

Air. She needed air.

The door's handle was frozen shut, and the more she pushed at it, the more her pulse sped. Trapped. Her nails caught on the wooden frame, ripping and bleeding. But she couldn't get out.

The air around her became too light. She couldn't breathe.

A scream wrenched from Juliana's throat, and her eyes snapped open as she woke. Her chest heaved as the nightmare memory faded from her mind's eye. Sweat saturated her night rail and the hair that framed her face, and shivers shook her frame, fresh fear and anxiousness washing over her.

"It's quite all right, miss." An elderly gentleman appeared at the edge of her vision, and she moved to shift away from him on the... *On the bed?*

When had she gone to bed, and in whose bed was she lying? And why couldn't she move?

"I am Doctor Benson," he continued. "I was summoned to Woodhaven Hall to care for you." His voice was gentle and soothing, but Juliana had been fooled into trusting before, and would certainly not be so again.

"Where are my things?" Was that her voice? It sounded scarcely above a whisper. "I must leave at once." *If I could but move.*

The doctor shook his head and gazed at her with pity in his eyes. "I would not recommend that, my dear. You have been abed with the fever for three days, and—"

"Three days?" *But I left the forest only moments ago!* Speaking was entirely draining her energy. She laboured for each breath as though she'd been running, and the room began to twirl around her.

"Rest now, Miss Smith."

The doctor smiled kindly at her, and despite his apparent compassion, a strong urge to flee raced through her veins. But logic won the day: she would not survive a night alone out of doors, and she must recuperate before she continued on to London. Hers was a standing appointment, after all.

Juliana nodded, and allowed the doctor to spoon some foul liquid between her lips. She coughed, but was grateful for the bit of fluid to soothe her parched tongue.

LEO PUSHED AWAY from the guest bedchamber's doorframe, and with a parting nod to the doctor, strode out into the wide corridor.

He wanted to know more about his guest, wanted to learn what had happened to her, what had caused her to become so frightened. And, curse it, he wanted to know what it was about her that made him feel...*something*. Hell if he knew what it was.

You don't deserve to know, his conscience whispered at him. Right. There was that.

"Leo." Percy hurried to match Leo's pace, their footfalls muffled on the hall's thick carpet runner. "I've had men search all of the roads bordering the estate, and there are no signs of a carriage accident on any of them."

It was in moments such as these that Leonard genuinely appreciated his friend's shared history in His Majesty's Navy —despite its grim beginning on the high seas. Percy was young —five years Leo's junior at nine-and-twenty—and clever, with a keen sense of duty and loyalty. He was entirely invaluable.

"Then what the devil happened?" Leo asked in an undertone.

Percy shrugged one shoulder as they rounded the corner into another hall. "Hell if I know. But we'll find out." He nodded once. "When Miss Smith is sensible again, I'll make some inquiries. Mayhap someone cleared the accident and hid any evidence."

"No." The word was pulled from Leo before he'd had a moment to consider it. His man gave him a raised eyebrow, and Leo gritted his teeth. If the man wasn't such a good friend and bloody talented employee, he'd have been dismissed years ago for impertinence. "I'd prefer to ask the questions myself, if you don't mind, Percy. Something is haunting her and, I confess, I'm being drawn into the mystery of it."

He truly was. It had only been three days, but once he'd had her under the bright candlelight in his home, he'd seen immediately that it wasn't dirt staining her maid's uniform— it was blood. And not only could her own wounds not have produced so much blood, but her pockets had been lined with bank notes, jewels, and trinkets, in addition to the pistol. The woman—maid?—had either witnessed or been involved in someone's injury, and possible death, and had somehow come into a fair sum of money. A carriage accident had been his and Percy's first assumption, but with no signs along the nearby roads, it was highly unlikely. What did she know? What had she *done*?

Leo knew better than to assume anyone's guilt, so before

he summoned the magistrate, he wanted to be absolutely certain of his convictions.

"Of course, sir." Percy's voice shook Leo from his reverie.

"Let me know when she is awake and lucid, will you?" Leo ground out, finally reaching his home's library, where his life felt like it fit back into place. "See that I am undisturbed until then."

CHAPTER 2

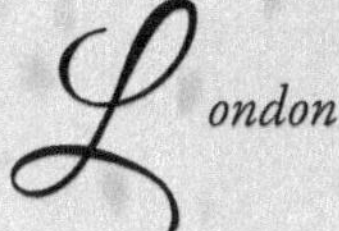

London

HER STOMACH FLUTTERING WITH NERVES, Miss Maria Roberts paced her familial town house's drawing room. Once-comforting walls of half white-painted wood panelling and half pale-pink paint surrounded her, the furniture delicate but strong and upholstered in a light-green stripe. She couldn't countenance sitting, however, with worry twisting around inside her.

Carriage wheels had stopped out front only moments before, and she would give her friend time to remove her cloak, bonnet, and gloves. The elaborately carved clock on the white mantel chimed the hour of ten, and Maria's stomach quivered once more.

At last, the door opened and Miss Heather Morgan entered, her brow puckered over green eyes. "Oh, Maria." She came forward and pulled Maria into an embrace. "Did you receive Juliana's letter?"

Maria pulled away and guided Heather to the chaise. "I did. And I'm worried for her. The weather has turned; I fear that her timing is poor."

"From what Juliana has said, her inducement was clear." Heather shook her head sadly. "Jasper was forcing her hand; she hadn't a choice."

"But to leave at such a time!" Maria's stomach felt weighted with a stone, and her throat thickened. "It is a standing appointment. Surely she must know that there is no need to rush. Her plan was not thoroughly thought out. And what will happen once her brother learns of it?"

Heather clasped Maria's hand in both of hers, and gently squeezed. "Juliana understands the risks of what she is doing. Indeed, the outcome would be the same at any time of the year. You are allowing your concern to run away with you."

Maria shook her head. "You are correct, of course. The result will be the same for us once we have joined, as well."

Peals of laughter echoed from the floor above, and Maria refrained from rolling her eyes. Her sisters were silly, indeed… and cared for naught but their reputations and ability to ensnare a husband. And in the privacy of their home, they were cruel purveyors of gossip.

"The *haut ton* will care less about *our* involvement than Juliana's," Heather noted. "Truthfully, I rather fear my family's reaction. The urge to simply abandon them is overwhelming."

Eyes wide, Maria's gaze snapped up to meet her friend's, mirth and recrimination filling her simultaneously. "*Heather*!"

Heather's green gaze remained steady on Maria's, no small amount of resigned sadness hidden behind it. "Come now. You must acknowledge that given any opportunity, I would wash my hands of them."

"And so you should." Outrage filled Maria on behalf of her friend. "We must keep a level head, however; bide our time until we have concluded our first tasks. *Then* you may abandon your appalling family."

"So I shall." Heather's gaze turned shrewd. "All of us have our secrets; this is merely one among them."

It was true, of course, but why did Heather have to be so dashed perceptive and calm when Maria only felt panic? No, not panic: a healthy amount of logic.

She burst out, "Juliana is a young woman travelling alone to London—with pockets full of coin and jewels, no less. How are you not more concerned, Heather? What if her carriage overturns, or there is a highwayman, or—" Maria broke off, unable to voice the horrible thoughts going through her mind as her stomach knotted painfully.

"She pilfered her brother's pistol," Heather reminded her soothingly. "If anything untoward occurs, she is capable of defending herself."

Maria threw her free hand in the air with a noise of exasperation and fear. "Precisely! She has Jasper's pistol! Do you not see what a disaster it could be if something frightened her and she *did* hurt someone?" She paused, but her friend said nothing, and Maria gave another growl of frustration. "*Murder*, Heather. Lady Juliana Sinclair, the daughter of the late Duke of Derby, would hang for murder."

"Blimey," Heather muttered. "Then let's hope that Juliana doesn't murder anyone."

Nottingham

Light shone through the library's large windows over Leonard's shoulders. Parchment littered his desk and crinkled between his thumbs and forefingers. His chest tightened.

Another rejection. There'd been countless, and this one was from sodding Scotland. How had his reputation spread that far?

The guilt that had made a home in his heart for the past years twisted painfully, and he ground his teeth.

He pulled the spectacles from his face, dropped them upon a pile of correspondence, and pinched the bridge of his nose. His library was ordinarily the only place in which he felt truly at home, but at the moment, he wanted nothing but to get away.

Something poked at his shoe, then worked its way up his stocking-clad calf beneath his grand, oaken desk. His skin twitched and his muscles bunched, but he pointedly ignored it.

"Good morning, sir." Percy sauntered into the large space through the adjoining drawing room. "Your breakfast has been served next door. And, as I understand it, Miss Smith is awake and out of bed."

Despite himself, Leo's stomach gave a quick squeeze. Five days had passed since they had happened across Miss Smith in the forest, and they still had no answers as to how she'd found herself there. He wanted answers, yes, but he also wanted to know if her eyes were as luminous—with that curious mixture of grey and green—as he recalled.

"Thank you, Percy," he muttered, gathering the correspondence on his desk into a pile to be burned.

"Any luck?"

Leo raked his fingers through his hair then scratched at his beard in an anxious gesture. "Afraid not. If I could but put the applications under a different name—"

There was a soft knock at the door, and Leo's gaze snapped upward. Standing in the opened doorway was Miss Smith. His gaze roamed her pale face, now clean of dirt and just as smooth as he remembered, despite being marred by bruising at her temple and jaw. Her dark curls were tightly pinned back, most likely to tame them, for he imagined that they had a mind of their own when let free.

She wore her maid's uniform, which his staff had cleaned several times though the stains were still visible. She'd been gifted new underclothes, as hers had been ruined, but looking at her now, he doubted they fit her properly. Good God, but her hips and breasts strained the uniform.

Leo's stomach wobbled alarmingly as she stepped into the room. Her eyes were indeed split colours as he recalled. And utterly brilliant. Lord, but he could stare at her for hours and never become bored.

His tongue suddenly stuck to the roof of his mouth. Sweet Jesus, she was taller than he remembered. Leo was a large man at over six feet and three inches, and—when and if he was ever forced to leave his estate—he usually towered over other Englishmen. But Miss Juliana Smith would surely reach the height of his nose. Hell's tits, he found that attractive; he wouldn't have to slouch to kiss her.

Where did that thought come from?

He cleared his throat and stood, silently cursing his delayed reaction. "Good morning, Miss Smith. I'm pleased to see that you are recovered."

The woman smiled hesitantly, her gaze flicking toward Percy before meeting Leo's. "Thank you, sir, for your hospitality. I feel much improved."

More tickling skittered over Leo's ankle, slowly tugging down his stocking. He shook his foot and cleared his throat. "Won't you sit down, Miss Smith?"

TALL. The word travelled through Juliana's mind as she approached Mr. Notley's desk and sat in the chair facing it.

She'd been on the marriage mart for years after her come-out before she'd given up hope and permanently affixed herself to the proverbial wall. In the early years, she'd been approached by countless men, but they had wanted either her family's fortune or her brother's favour; they never wanted *her*. As time had passed, she'd become known as a woman who said no, and men had lost interest.

"If only you'd been born a man," her papa had said. *"I've no use for a female; I needed my spare before your mother died."*

"But, Papa," Juliana had cried. *"Think of the grandchildren that I could give you to dote upon."*

"I could scarcely ask you for grandchildren. Look at you! Much too tall, and awkward like a giraffe... What kind of man would have you without taking my money with him? Do have more intelligence, Juliana, like your brother. He is precisely the sort of child that I require: obedient, good natured, and sensible."

Her chest tightened at the memory, and a keen sense of discomfort threatened to permeate the protective shell that she'd erected around her heart. *Not anymore, Papa.* He was dead, and so were his opinions.

But Jasper isn't, and clearly he thinks so little of you as to force you into—no. She would not allow herself to think on it. Jasper's betrayal was still so painful, so fresh, despite the fact that she'd learned of it a month ago. If only he'd told her of the ducal financial woes!

Juliana swallowed the emotion that had abruptly thickened her throat as Mr. Notley gave his man a nod and sat at his desk.

"I have some questions for you, if you don't mind, Miss Smith."

She inclined her head, knowing that this would happen at some point but dreading it all the same.

"How did you come to be stranded in the forest?"

Prickles of fear darted down the back of her neck, making her want to squirm or scratch at it, but she held her hands tightly together in her lap. She didn't want to tell him, didn't want to reveal any of the painful moments that, more than anything, she wished to forget. He couldn't know who she was, *what* she was.

Adjusting her hands in her lap, Juliana cleared her throat and prepared to say the half-truth that she'd been rehearsing in her mind for the past hour.

"I was travelling at night by carriage." Her voice was hollow, devoid of the agony the words caused her. "There was a shout, and the carriage was dragged into the forest by the horses. We hit something—perhaps a rock, or tree—and over-turned, rolling several times before stopping. I—" Her voice cracked, and she cleared her throat. "I was stuck in the carriage for more than a day, I'm certain. I'd tried to get out, but—"

She was silent for several long moments when Mr. Notley prompted, "But you weren't able to?"

Juliana shook her head. "Once I was finally free, I'd lost my sense of direction—the snow covered any tracks that we'd made—and I began to wander. You found me after that."

"I'm sorry." Mr. Notley raked his fingers through his glorious blond hair, then scratched at his beard. It was a capti-vating movement that Juliana suspected was oft-repeated. "Did you not have a chaperone, Miss Smith? Was your family not concerned for your safety?" He tapped a short stack of blank parchment on his desk. "I've writing materials if there are persons to whom you wish to write."

Her gaze dropped to her tightly laced fingers, her knuckles white in her effort to quell their trembling. A persistent ache had settled in her chest, and she breathed deeply against it. "My parents are dead," she said truthfully. "I have no family that would worry for my safety." *And I cannot write to my friends, for they will worry, and Jasper will surely pull the truth from them.* "I am well and truly alone."

"I see," Mr. Notley hurried to say. "My apologies, Miss Smith."

She licked her lips, nerves eating away at her abdomen. Returning home was not an option. Jasper would be furious. There would be shouting, and he would unquestionably lock her away like a prisoner until the day he saw her wed to the elderly Viscount Rivers. Sold like his mother's baubles for some pound notes to fill his coffers.

Juliana wouldn't stand for it. Instead, she'd rallied her friends and made her appointment in London. It would be a far cry from the life that she'd known, but it would be *hers*. And that was better than being a piece of property. The appointment would hold while she fully regained her strength and the storm passed. But for the moment, she required this man's aid.

The tale came to her in a moment of brilliance and, truthfully, it was her only option now.

"I was on my way to interview for a position as a governess," she lied, "but I fear that I missed that opportunity days ago. If you wouldn't mind, I would be very grateful for a copy of a recent newspaper." Juliana did not enjoy the company of strangers, and she most certainly did not enjoy the thought of prolonged company with a man. But children... Children were honest, even when adults sometimes wished they weren't. It made them trustworthy, which was precisely what Juliana needed. If she could but find a home in which to hide while she recovered, she could continue on to London once the weather improved.

Mr. Notley's eyes widened slightly, and the room fell silent. She blinked. No, it wasn't silent. There was a soft, muffled humming coming from somewhere—

"Miss Smith, do you know who I am?" Mr. Notley asked

bluntly, the blue of his eyes dimming slightly with what appeared to be remorse.

She blinked again, taken aback. "My pardon, but you're Mr. Notley, are you not? Is that not what you said when we were introduced?" She lifted her hands to her cheeks. "I'm so sorry, sir, if I've made an error. I scarcely recall much of that day's events."

There was a snort and a stifled giggle, and Juliana's eyes widened.

Mr. Notley pinched the bridge of his nose before turning an apologetic glance her way. "Yes, you have the right of it, Miss Smith."

He stood, giving her another view of his impeccably tailored—if slightly dated—suit of clothes. His grey woollen coat matched the grey of his breeches, and his blue waistcoat brightened his eyes. Beneath his blond, bearded chin was a starched white collar and elaborately tied cravat. The man was striking.

"Please allow me to introduce Miss Elizabeth Notley." He stepped out from behind the desk, dragging his right foot behind himself. And there, was a petite girl with bouncing blonde ringlets, cherub cheeks, and a laughing bow-shaped mouth, clinging to his bare, muscular, and hair-smattered calf.

CHAPTER 3

It was not the introduction Leo had imagined, but he supposed it would have to suffice. In fact, he'd not imagined introducing them at all, but after the last batch of school rejections and with no one coming to interview for his posted position, how could he not at least try with the governess that had fallen into his lap?

The woman didn't know his title or his past, and while the thought of deceiving her sparked guilt, it didn't compare to the guilt he felt for dooming Elizabeth's future with his mere presence. Damn, but he could scarcely look at Lizzy without images of death flashing in his mind's eye. What could he possibly say to her that would make up for what he'd done?

Despite everything, however, the girl seemed drawn to him. She would appear at his side, play in his study... It was all the more reason that she must go to school: she deserved so much better than he could give.

With a giggle, Lizzy released him and bounded toward Miss Smith's chair, lifting on her toes to examine the woman. *Shite*. Would that it was socially acceptable for Leo to do the same. He'd study the precise shade of her eyes, the arch of her brows, touch the underside of her wrists and feel her pulse there... Hell, he would devote himself to learning all of her.

Returning to his seat, Leo surreptitiously bent to tug up his stocking and fasten the ribbon, then watched as the little sprite touched the woman's hands and skirts. Her fingertips grazed Miss Smith's skin, circling each knuckle and trailing along the slender line of her fingers.

A slow, warm smile bloomed on Miss Smith's lips, revealing perfect white teeth, delicate dimples on both cheeks, and a pleasing crinkle at the corner of her eyes as she observed Lizzy's exploration. It was as though her demeanour had changed in an instant. As though she was charmed by—even welcomed—the child's curiosity. Hell if Leo didn't feel slightly charmed, himself. It took a great strength of will for him to not urge the child aside and demand answers from Miss Smith. Like precisely *why* he felt so damned...*off* when he was around her.

Leo caught Percy's glance from where the man stood against the dark wood bookcases along the far wall, and twitched his lips. Percy's one raised eyebrow spoke volumes. Miss Smith's story had answered only some of their questions, while raising several more.

"Your hair is darker than mine," Lizzy observed, her words slightly slurred by excess saliva.

Leo opened his mouth to rebuke the waif, but she continued quickly. "It's very pretty," she said wistfully, while absently stroking Miss Smith's wrist. "It's curly, like mine."

He cleared his throat. "One ought never to grab at a person's...er...person, Lizzy. It isn't polite." But he damned well agreed with her.

"It's quite all right," Miss Smith returned, her gaze flicking upward momentarily. "It's natural for her to be curious, and I rather enjoy children's honesty."

Interesting. Another piece to her proverbial puzzle. He would think on that later.

"Were you born'd here, like me?" Elizabeth asked.

Miss Smith smiled. "I was born here in England. I resemble my father and my mother in different ways, but the curls in my hair are all from my mama."

"I knowed it," Lizzy breathed. "My mama was English and went into the sky when I was born'd."

A small indentation appeared between Miss Smith's eyebrows. "I'm sorry to hear that, Miss Elizabeth. Mine did, as well."

Lizzy gripped the chair's handle and hoisted herself up onto Miss Smith's lap. A twist of apprehension tightened in Leo's stomach. "Lizzy, we mustn't crawl upon Miss Sm—"

"You have marks on your face," Elizabeth noted, pointing at Miss Smith's bruising with extended index finger.

The woman's smile turned sad. "Yes, I do. I was in an accident."

"And it hurted?"

"It did hurt, yes."

"I growed up to four," Elizabeth announced, holding up four fingers. "How old are you?"

Miss Smith laughed and held a hand behind Lizzy's back to keep her from falling. "I am five-and-twenty."

Leo's gaze darted toward Percy again, confusion filling him while Lizzy asked more questions. How could this woman be on the shelf? Hell, even if she'd been born into a poor family, some landowner or parson's son would have surely found a way to begin courting her. And yet she remained unwed. *And in my home.*

"Are you going to be my new governess?" Lizzy's small voice brought his attention back to the woman across from him.

Leo cleared his throat and opened his mouth, but Miss Smith spoke first.

"I have not yet interviewed with your father, nor has a position been offered. So, no, sweeting, I'm afraid not."

Elizabeth giggled, her ringlets bouncing. "Leo's not my father, he's my uncle!" She turned and hopped to the floor, approaching Leonard with a skip, then inexplicably slid her petite hand into the cuff of his coat sleeve, leaving it there while her fingertips stroked his arm hair.

Shame washed over him, and he swallowed hard against the sudden lump in his throat.

"My apologies, Mr. Notley, for presuming," Miss Smith hurried to say.

Leonard gave her a tight smile, the fist of pain that had been lodged in his chest for the past three years giving him a sharp jab. "It is quite all right, Miss Smith. Elizabeth is my ward, and has been for over two years. We share a resemblance, so it is a natural conclusion."

She smiled back, and his heart gave a responding *thwump*, which was swiftly followed by a tumult of regret, fear, and sadness. *Christ*, this was going to be difficult.

The woman had appeared on his land covered in blood—which presented an admittedly curious puzzle. And without knowing the full truth of what transpired, his trust in her was heavily tainted. Her genuine fear and reluctance to discuss the matter, however, seemed to confirm a carriage accident—in which *someone* had been gravely injured. This could lead to countless conclusions.

Perhaps she and another governess journeyed together in search of positions in the countryside. Or, mayhap she had been travelling alone with a man and withheld the truth to preserve her reputation—fuck knows why *that* thought made him ill at ease. The possibilities, as they say, were endless.

Despite his tainted trust, he was wont to give her the

benefit of the doubt while they awaited confirmation, for Christ knew not everyone that *appeared* guilty of something *was*.

Additionally, the woman had a good rapport with Lizzy. As evidenced by her comportment, mannerisms, and speech, she had, herself, been trained by the very best governesses. He would request proof of her qualifications, but truthfully, the utter relief at having found someone to teach his niece surpassed the need for proof. And, the possibility of her learning the truth of *his* identity in the exchange was too perilous.

He avoided looking at Percy, for he was sure that the man could read his expression. This was *Leo's* decision, damn it, and he was doing it for Elizabeth, who deserved a hell of a lot better than to be stuck alone with him.

"As for the governess position," he said, his voice slightly lower than he'd intended, "your timing is rather fortuitous, as we have need of one. If you would care for a position here, it is yours to claim."

A KNOT CAUGHT in Juliana's throat, and she swallowed against it. It was what she'd wanted: a temporary position in a safe place to wait out the storm. But *was* it safe? She'd told Mr. Notley about the carriage accident; what if he decided to search for the wreckage? Then he would know what she'd done...

Her gaze fell on the small child, innocently tugging at her uncle's blond wrist hair.

No matter how tempting, she would not—*could* not—come to care for the man sitting before her. The position was simply there to fill the time before she was able to continue her journey to London—and complete her rendezvous. Of course, teaching the darling Miss Notley would be but an added pleasure to her stay.

She inhaled deeply, filling her lungs with a steadying, cinnamon-and-coconut-scented breath before smiling at Mr. Notley on an exhale. While she would never come to fully trust another man, she had been insensible in this estate for five days and neither her belongings purloined, nor her person assailed. So, she conceded this once. Little Miss Notley needed her, after all.

"I would be delighted to accept the position," Juliana said.

The man's striking blue eyes crinkled in the corners and his lips widened in a smile, revealing clean white teeth. Good heavens, but the man had a wonderful smile.

"Thank you, Miss Smith. My man-of-all-work, Percy, will explain the particulars of the position to you, and once I have concluded with some correspondence, I will show you around the estate."

"That sounds lovely, thank you."

"Do you know where you were on the road before your horses ran into the forest?" he asked. "I would like to be specific in my letter to the magistrate."

Juliana's lungs froze, and every muscle in her body seized. Where...? *Good God, no.* He couldn't... No one could... But someone might one day, and they would know. Not that it had been *her*, though. Mr. Notley and the magistrate, however, would know if they saw...

Where was Notley's estate located, precisely? Without knowing her exact location, she couldn't even lie about the carriage's direction to save herself. If she *did* know, however, would she reveal the truth? *No.* The horrid, honest word crept from the depth of her soul. What she'd done was... Lord, but she despised thinking on it. *The blood...*

The corners of her vision began to quiver, and her lungs—no longer frozen—seemed incapable of taking in enough air. She gripped the chair's arms in an effort to ground herself as the room began to swim. Her chest constricted. Oh, heavens, was she about to faint? She was certain that she would either faint or perish; no other option was viable.

Mr. Notley and his man, Percy, were at her sides, gripping her arms, and before she'd even truly realized that she was walking, they had moved her through an adjoining drawing room and out a pair of French windows into a blast of frigid air. Juliana gasped and her body trembled. She blinked, her gaze focusing past the vapour of her rapid breaths.

The portico's cover provided protection enough for her to observe without being snowed upon, and she took it in. White, fluffy snow fell from the sky in clumps, sticking to the collection already layered upon the ground.

Her breathing gradually slowed, and the unrelenting quivering turned into an occasional tremble from the chill.

"Thank you," she said, her breath a cloud that quickly dispersed.

Percy nodded once. "Of course, miss."

"How did you know what to...do?"

He looked over her head at Mr. Notley, then returned his dark gaze to hers. "I've seen this previously. A distraction will not always help, but I'm glad that it did, this once."

"How do you feel?" Mr. Notley asked.

Juliana met his curious blue gaze, and despite the cautious alarm in her chest, her heart warmed at his inquiry. "Better, thank you."

He nodded, and a moment of silence passed before Mr. Notley offered his arm. "Come. Let us return inside to Miss Notley."

❦

CLUNK. He lowered his tankard back to the taproom's table, the ale sloshing over one side and splattering onto the roughened tabletop, as he eyed the other patrons. There were only three others there tonight, each alone and hunched over their drinks. The place stank of sour ale and old potato pies, but it was somewhere warm to rest after spending five days trudging over fields and hills, and through the freezing fucking forest.

Bloody hell. Somehow, the bitch had evaded him. It wouldn't, however, stop him from searching. In fact, it made him more determined to find her.

The familiar tingling heat reignited in his chest, and his lips curved upward in a wicked sneer.

He was reasonably certain that since he had not discovered her corpse among the snow—yet—that she must have inspired some sap's pity and been permitted into their home. It was why he'd begun inquiring after her at every shop in Nottingham. *Someone* must know where she was.

He took another gulp of his ale and grimaced before placing the tankard back on the table. *Thunk.*

The taproom's door swung open on creaky hinges, and a jovial-looking man strode in, bringing with him a haze of powder on the air.

He hated him on sight. Too sodding happy.

"Martha!" the big man behind the bar shouted over his shoulder. "Flour man's here."

A petite woman with dark hair came to the front and greeted the large flour merchant. They exchanged goods while he watched in idle curiosity.

"Did you 'ear that Lord Livingston 'as a woman at 'is 'ouse?" the flour merchant asked.

Ears suddenly perked, he set aside his tankard and stiffened his spine.

"Does he, now?" the woman purred, clearly interested in the gossip.

The big man nodded eagerly. "I 'eard it myself just this mornin'. The woman came into some trouble, like. 'Eard 'e's fixin' 'er up; 'ad the doctor in and everythin'."

Juliana. Blood rushed in his ears as anticipation flooded him. It was her. It had to be.

When he found her, he would right a wrong and take the bitch; it was what was agreed upon and what was best for the dukedom.

At long last, a smile tugged at his lips.

WITH A SOFT *CLICK*, the library door closed behind Miss Smith and Elizabeth as they walked with a maid toward the nursery. Leo had promised to join her in a moment, but intended to give her time to acquaint herself with the space that would be hers.

He was also desperate to speak with Percy alone.

Footfalls, and the chatter of women's voices, floated away down the corridor, and Leo spun to face his friend. "What the devil was that?"

"Miss Smith evidently experienced something emotionally disturbing. It might take time for her to recover from whatever she witnessed in that accident. From your bedchamber in the familial wing you mightn't hear it, but she suffers from nightmares, often screaming in the night."

"The doctor and the maids have mentioned it, yes," Leo replied thoughtfully, shifting his stance from one foot to the other. "But what of her tale? We need to find that carriage and sort out what happened with the magistrate. Something does not feel quite right."

Percy nodded. "Yes, I concur."

"Did you get the sense that she was withholding a pertinent piece of information?" His man nodded again and Leo continued, "Mayhap she is protecting someone. Or she was travelling under duress."

"Under duress?" Percy's thick, dark eyebrows lifted in alarm.

"Come now, a woman travelling alone, at a pace that was undoubtedly too swift... Was she running? Is she frightened, or in danger?"

Percy shook his head. "You're far too quick to assume that everyone is innocent or in some need of rescuing."

Leo gestured wildly toward the door through which she'd just left before slumping in his seat. "Clearly she *was* in need of rescuing. The woman was one night away from dying in that forest."

The man watched him, his gaze unnervingly thorough and probing as it scanned Leo's face. It made Leo want to turn away or shield himself with his hands, but he held firm.

"You desire her," Percy noted bluntly.

Heat spread over Leo's chest and up his neck, which was mercifully hidden by his clothing and thick beard. "*Of course I bloody do*!" he hissed. There was no sense in denying it. "She is a dramatically handsome woman that very literally embodies everything that I physically desire. If we even remotely got along, I would be a fool not to marry the woman." *But I can't —and won't—put anyone through that.* "Under ordinary circumstances."

Percy shrugged. "I don't see why you couldn't."

"You don't see—?" Leo's shocked and bewildered and, damn it, *angry* gaze hardened on his friend. "To the devil with you, Percy. *You know why.*"

The man squared his shoulders and faced Leo directly. "I know why you *think* that you cannot marry, Leo, but that was more than two years ago, and it was not your fau—"

"Even removing that from the situation, Percy, I have a sordid past. What woman in her right mind would marry a... a..."

"A reformed pirate?" Percy offered, striding closer.

"*Reformed*." Leo spat the word, his face growing hotter. "Reformed or not, we were bloody pirates."

Percy's voice softened. "We were young, and—"

"Youth does not excuse piracy." He shifted in his seat, and the leather creaked.

The man scoffed. "Leo, you were the least *pirate* pirate of the lot. With the exception of the obvious looting, and murder in defence of our lives, you did little to even resemble the name. And now you have a title, which, according to society, wipes your history clean."

Leo lifted an eyebrow at his friend. The man was doing his utmost to convince Leo of his innocence, when Percy himself suffered from constant guilt and refused to even consider settling with a woman. The hypocrisy was overwhelming.

"You are not altering my stance," Leo said. "In the years after we returned to England, I did nothing to improve my reputation, particularly with women. It was *because* of my philandering that Walter—"

"That was *not* your fault—"

"*But it fucking happened*!" Leo threw his hands up in exasperation. "In that moment, I made a vow to be celibate. If my desires can kill, then I will do my best to not sodding have them!"

Percy shook his head. "That's irrational, Leo. And it oughtn't prevent you from having relations. You're attracted to the woman. What would be the harm—"

"For Christ's sake, Percy!" Leo hissed. "She's now under my protection as a member of my staff. It would be highly inappropriate for me to seek any sort of physical relationship with her—let alone marriage—even without my sordid past."

Leo cursed at the man and strode determinedly toward the door, not wanting to hear more.

Percy called after him, "Fucking can sometimes just be fucking, Leonard."

CHAPTER 4

"Another drawing room?" Juliana asked, somewhat dazed by the labyrinth that was Woodhaven Hall. Her family's ducal estate was rather grand, itself, but its design was practical and familiar, if opulent. Woodhaven Hall was a confusing composition of rooms and a maze of corridors that she would never become accustomed to.

Mr. Notley nodded once. "The one nearest to the dining room at the front of the home was originally for social occasions and for the ladies' withdrawing after a meal, while this one was reserved for the family."

She could certainly believe that. The other room was designed with image in mind: each piece of furniture perfectly aligned, no trinket out of place. Whereas this room felt warm and welcoming, with rich shades of burgundy and pink, thickly stuffed furniture meant for relaxing, and a fireplace on either side of the room. It was uniquely lavish and comfortable.

"And the others?" she asked. "I believe this is the fourth that you've shown me."

"I haven't the foggiest. Some ancestor designed the place,

and while the rooms are routinely cleaned by my staff, I have little use for them."

Juliana hummed and continued down the hall. The tapers and sconces were lit, and the warm air carried the scent of costly beeswax, teasing her senses. His hands clasped behind his back, Mr. Notley matched her pace.

Beyond the candles swirled a fragrance that was uniquely *him*, and Juliana attempted to breathe past it, wishing that it didn't interest her so deeply. Cinnamon, coconut, and trees. It was bewildering to her how anyone could have such a warm Christmastide scent that was so appealing. Despite her efforts to remain unmoved, she found that it curled her toes in her threadbare slippers and quickened her pulse.

It was dangerous here for Juliana. *Mr. Notley* was dangerous. There was some unnameable quality about the man that made her want to be near him, and the longer she remained in his company, the stronger that sensation became. They'd only been touring his estate for three quarters of an hour, surely, and yet she felt almost entirely at ease in his company. Enough that she had the absurd urge to lean closer to better inhale his scent. Would that the housekeeper had given her the tour in his stead. Why *had* he chosen to take her?

She ought to put her guard up, to force herself to focus on what *really* mattered while she was under his roof: recovery, remaining hidden, and, of course, aiding the young Miss Elizabeth before the rendezvous in London. She most certainly oughtn't wonder if Mr. Notley's hair was as soft as it appeared, or what it would feel like to slide her hand inside his cuff like Elizabeth had done during their interview. Indeed, that would be scandalous.

"And this is the billiards room," Mr. Notley was saying.

Oh, dear. Juliana had missed the past several rooms at least while she was ruminating. Attempting to recover, she made a noncommittal humming noise in response and corrected the direction of her thoughts.

He guided her in another turn and gestured into an opened doorway. "That is the card room; it has an adjoining door at the rear to another card room and, beyond that, a music room, which opens into the ballroom on the left."

They approached a set of double doors next, and he swung them wide, preceding her into the grand space. Juliana's eyes widened in awe as she strode in behind him. The ceiling high above was embellished with gilt leaves and painted with cherubs and dancing cupids. The chandeliers hung high, glittering even in the dim light coming through the windows along the far wall. The room was magnificent, with creams and gilt, the floor a glossy cream marble. Furniture had been abandoned in one corner of the space and covered with sheets, and just beyond that was a balcony for an orchestra.

Having spent the past nine years gracing the walls of ballrooms, with little to do but converse with her friends and admire the fine spaces, Juliana considered herself rather proficient in the art of judging ballrooms. The ballroom in Juliana's familial home was beautiful in its own right: black and white with a checked marble floor, which was rather modern in style. But *this*. Mr. Notley's was an elegant masterpiece that was truly something to behold.

It was curious indeed that he, a seemingly modest gentleman farmer, would have so large a home—and the funds to keep every room clean and the seldom-used corridors lit with beeswax candles. He must have had fruitful crop yields and loyal tenant farmers, for certain.

Was he a busy man, always locked in his study conducting business, or did he spend time interacting with his niece? From what she'd witnessed earlier, he appeared nearly indifferent to—if not slightly irritated by—her presence. Did he know how to interact with her? That was something, perhaps, that Juliana would attempt to learn.

While her position in the home was temporary, she would be pleased to know that she'd made a difference in her time there. That perhaps, while she imparted her knowledge onto Miss Notley, she could also bring the girl joy and impart some knowledge on the gentleman of the house, as well.

The man waved a hand nonchalantly through the air. "I imagine that Lizzy will have dancing lessons in here at some time, but I rather doubt that it will be any time soon. I really ought to have it turned into a library or some such, for I doubt it will ever serve its purpose again."

Juliana gasped, and an objection burst from her mouth. "Oh, but you mustn't! I—I beg your pardon, Mr. Notley, but this room is far too beautiful to alter."

His gaze searched hers for a moment, before his lips curved and he looked away. "I've a room that might interest you, Miss Smith."

THEY STRODE in silence through a series of rooms and down several corridors, their footfalls muffled by the thick runner. Leonard walked with purpose, his body aching with need and his mind screaming at him to stop. No matter what his body —and bloody Percy—thought, he didn't deserve to be happy with a woman. Not again. No matter how damned tempting Miss Smith might be, not only was she under his employ— which would make him even more of a cad to contemplate— but he'd made a promise of celibacy. For the first time in a long while, his body just didn't want to listen.

She carried with her an aroma of flowers that he couldn't quite place: not roses, lilacs, or anything common, certainly. It was unique, as though she'd acquired a perfume from abroad.

He'd seen the bottle, too—blue, worn, and chipped on one side—when he'd examined the contents of her pockets while she was ill, but it was unlabelled. The mystery of it played over in his mind, and despite his efforts to the contrary, his musings grew increasingly libidinous. He burned to know what it was, and where and how she applied it. Did she use one drop at her throat, behind her ears, her wrists...or did she put it between her breasts? He imagined himself pressing his nose to each sensitive spot and inhaling, searching for the source of her scent.

Unconsciously quickening his pace down the corridor, Leo bit back a growl and resisted the urge to shake his shoulders free of their sudden tension. *You can't have her*, he reminded himself.

With relief, he noted that they'd arrived at the thick, unyielding door that he'd been racing toward, and he reached for its large handle. "Here we are."

With a small amount of effort, Leo swung the door wide, and was immediately struck with a wall of warmth, humidity, and the overwhelming scent of flowers.

"A conservatory!" Miss Smith exclaimed as she strode past him.

The large space was one long rectangle, with the floor and the bottom half of the walls made with a curious mixture of cemented pebbles and crushed brick, while the ceiling and upper walls were composed of large rectangular windows. Two wide fireplaces were built into the walls on either side of the conservatory's length, and both had fires burning in the hearth nearly all year round to keep the blooms at the desired temperature.

Miss Smith walked along the first of four rows of blooms, hidden by some plants that had been placed upon tall, narrow tables. Leo hurried to catch up, walking along the second row and catching glimpses of her between spots of vivid colour.

She paused to touch the petal of a bright-yellow flower. "I've a friend that would dearly love this place."

"Have you, indeed?"

Her lips curved, and Leo's cheek gave a responding twitch.

"She studies all manner of plants," Miss Smith continued, "and keeps a modest collection in a small conservatory that she's built at her home."

"There is an identical conservatory, as well, on the opposite end of Woodhaven Hall. It houses fruits and vegetables that are seasonal," Leo noted lamely. "I daresay your friend could come and enjoy the conservatories any time that she desires."

His chest tightened, and a faint sense of panic fluttered in his heart. Christ, why would he suggest such a thing? *More* guests? He'd been fortunate enough that Miss Smith hadn't recognized his name, but another might, and he couldn't stomach their reaction if they did. He turned and continued his walk, following the sound of trickling water toward the circular fountain that graced the centre of the conservatory.

Keeping both spaces filled and operating was costly, to be sure, and if they hadn't already been a fixture in his home, he wouldn't have added them, but they brought him peace and bloody good desserts. He was fortunate that his tenant farmers brought a steady income and both his sheep and crops proved prosperous. Lizzy would want for nothing. Except, perhaps, a life free from his tainted name.

"Have I your permission to bring Miss Notley into the conservatories so that she might begin learning the names of the plants?" Miss Smith asked, having resumed her walk, as well.

Leo clasped his hands behind his back, grateful that his offer was ignored. "Of course. This is her home; she has leave to learn any part of it that she wishes."

They reached the end of their rows and stopped at the

fountain, facing each other in the brightly lit space. Thick snowflakes fell beyond the panes of glass above them, but within, the air was heavy with warm humidity.

A soft sigh escaped her lips, attracting his gaze. They were full and smooth, despite having been chapped only days before. The abrupt need to know their taste gripped him. Would she be sweet, tart, or would she, perhaps, carry the flavour of the mysterious floral fragrance that hovered around her?

Hell. Turning his head away, he bit the inside of his cheek to quell the last of his desire before returning his attention to the woman. And caught her watching him. Her gaze lingered on the narrow bit of exposed neck below his ear, and along his beard. Her breath quickened, and Leo dug his fingertips into his palms in an effort to control the rush of triumph that rippled through him.

They were too close together, scarcely more than an arm's length apart, but he could still feel the heat from her body, could smell her unique floral scent... *Christ.*

This was ludicrous. He hadn't even come close to growing aroused since life had changed so drastically and Lizzy had come into his care, and yet this woman had him—

The door slammed open, and brusque footfalls entered. Leo swiftly stepped back, putting distance between himself and Miss Smith, silently urging the thrumming of his pulse to calm.

"Oh!" a woman gasped. "I'm right sorry, I am, Master Leonard. I didn't realize that the conservatory was occupied." Leo internally cringed at Mrs. Talbot's use of his childhood name, and silently hoped that Miss Smith hadn't noticed. "I just come in to add more fuel to the fire, as it were."

With another internal rebuke at his reckless behaviour, Leo smiled at the older woman. "It is quite all right." He swiftly made the introductions. "Miss Smith is to be Elizabeth's new governess, and Mrs. Talbot is our housekeeper."

The women greeted each other and Leo gritted his teeth, despising the position he'd put himself in.

"Oh dearie," Mrs. Talbot was saying. "That uniform is a far sight too small. I'll see to it that material is ordered at once."

"You're too kind."

The housekeeper smiled. "It might be some time, mind, due to the weather..."

The women continued their conversation, but Leo scarcely took notice.

He felt ill. They oughtn't be alone in a room together again, he and Miss Smith, for Lord knew, she stirred something within him that he shouldn't feel.

CHAPTER 5

The muffled pitter-patter of paws on carpet followed Juliana as she traversed the wide corridors of Woodhaven Hall. The tapers were lit, lending a warm glow to the grand space, but even though she could see, she was at sixes and sevens as to where the blasted deceitful Mr. Notley was.

Irritation and ire skittered over her nerves, sparking fire in her neck and across her chest. It had taken three days, but she'd come to realize what he'd done. *It was inevitable*, her mind whispered. *Men will always disappoint you if you let them.*

She glanced over her shoulder to eye the curious spotted greyhound. "The footman mentioned the library. Do you happen to know the way, Kitty?" The dog wagged her tail, her tongue lolling to one side, and Juliana gave the beastie an idle scratch with her free hand as she continued on.

In the three days since she'd begun lessons with Elizabeth —and since she'd last seen Mr. Notley—Juliana had come to realize that the little girl, while in dire need of aid in her speech, was uncommonly advanced in her letters, maths, Latin, and, surprisingly, geography. What Juliana had witnessed during her interview was merely evidence of the poor girl's desire for affection.

Her heart gave a sharp twist. What Miss Elizabeth Notley required was a mother, not a governess. And Juliana was most decidedly not that woman.

She and her greyhound shadow passed an empty, darkened room, and a chill swept over her. Woodhaven Hall must cost Mr. Notley an outrageous sum to heat in the winter, for with the high ceilings and grand windows, the drafts were unmistakable. She wondered how many maids it took to keep fires burning in the commonly used rooms. Come to that, she'd never before considered what it must take to keep her own home—

No, she corrected herself. It wasn't her home any longer. Jasper had seen to that.

Her brows drew together in a frown as she thought of her brother. Jasper had grown from an affectionate child into a protective young man. And yet, after the death of their father, he'd seemingly changed in the course of a day. Gone were their nightly games of chess, their conversations, and the smiles that he'd once offered so readily. He'd turned sour since the duke had died, always grumbling and snapping in constant irritation.

If only he'd have spoken to her, and not *sold* her to Viscount Rivers.

She had known that their inheritance had somehow been squandered, because Jasper had become so parsimonious that nearly all of their meals consisted of potato—and the rare pigeon. But she'd naively assumed that the estate's income would save them from insolvency, and that, perhaps, she could lend her aid by pursuing her interests and meeting with Grace Huntsbury.

The sparse collection of her mother's jewels, and the allowance that she'd saved, had been gathered just after her father's death. She'd succeeded in hiding them from Jasper—to protect them from being sold, and to prevent him from discovering her intentions. He would be furious, undoubtedly, but maybe he would come to see that she'd done it for *them*.

With a mental shake, she continued along the corridor, around a corner, and down yet another set of stairs.

In the three days since she'd been alone with Mr. Notley in the conservatory, Juliana had not left the confines of the nursery or her bedchamber. She was embarrassed by her open perusal of him, and she'd been busy performing her assessment of Miss Notley's knowledge and abilities.

During that time, she'd come to two clear conclusions. First, her desire for Mr. Notley, if not a hindrance to her goals, was certainly inconvenient; and second, Mr. Notley was hiding something. She ought to have known.

It was for that reason that she'd stolen out of the nursery after Elizabeth had fallen asleep that evening, and had gone in search of the dastardly man. Locating him, as it happened, was rather more difficult than she'd thought, for she'd all but entirely forgotten the location of the library in the labyrinth of a building.

Glancing into another opened door, she caught sight of a pianoforte. *The music room.* Despite the advanced hour, the pastel-blue room was bright. She had the sudden urge to plunk the pianoforte's keys, but she was on a mission.

A warm, flickering light shone from beneath a door around the next corner, and Juliana strode directly for it. She released a quiet breath and was silently grateful for the greyhound's calming, happy presence at her side. Squaring her shoulders and gathering her indignation, Juliana pressed the door's latch and stepped through the doorway. And nearly swallowed her tongue.

Mr. Notley stood near the shelves of books along the far

wall, his coat removed and his shirtsleeves rolled to his elbows, exposing the disconcertingly alluring hair on his forearms. He carefully examined a book that sat easily in one hand, a duster poised in the other, and his expression was a mask of focus behind his charming spectacles.

She wanted to remain angry—to hold fast to the emotion—but it became increasingly difficult as she noted the endearing smudge of dust on the bridge of his nose and the scent of coconut and cinnamon that coiled around her senses. The man was caring for his books, for pity's sake.

How many times did Jasper make me feel safe, comforted, and loved before he betrayed me? Abruptly, the warmth that had begun to bloom in her chest dispersed in a puff of smoke. No matter how much she might need the temporary position —and a place to hide from Jasper and avoid the perils of travelling in such weather—she wouldn't stand for trickery, falsehoods, and manipulation. The irony was not lost on her, but her false pretence was for her safety—her very *being*—not a ruse to acquire a spouse.

Straightening her shoulders once more, Juliana strode into the room.

THE SWISH of fabric and the soft patter of paws came from the entry of the library, and Leo paused before making the next swipe with the dusting rag. In the three days since he'd seen her, he'd almost managed to convince himself that she wasn't as striking as he'd recalled, but his body's instant reaction to her lent truth to his original assessment. There was something fundamentally... Christ, *attractive* wasn't even a strong enough adjective to describe what feelings she inspired in him.

The hair on his body, both fine and thick, stood on end.

His gut knotted, and a disconcerting tingling began at the base of his spine. He slid the tome back into its position on the shelf and turned to face her, coughing in an attempt to cover his discomfiture.

Several members of his staff had worked together to alter their tallest maids' uniforms, but even with the modifications, the material still pulled tightly across Miss Smith's generous bosom and was just a mite too small for her rounded hips. Never in his life had he found a maid's uniform the least bit attractive, but on Miss Smith he wanted nothing more than to—

"I'll not stand for prevaricating, sir," she said, mercifully snapping him out of his lewd thoughts.

He tossed the duster aside and removed his spectacles. "About what, pray tell?"

A charming little line appeared between her eyebrows as her brows puckered. "Miss Notley's education, of course!"

It was his turn to frown. He folded the spectacles and placed them carefully on a side table. "Explain," he grunted.

She huffed a breath and planted her fists on her waist, which he imagined was meant to express her wrath and irritation. Instead, he found it rather enchanting. *Stop it, man.*

"The young girl has knowledge far beyond her years, as you well know." She gestured exasperatedly, then shook a finger at him. "You merely require someone to offer affection while she continues to learn. A wife, perhaps?" Her spine stiffened. "I'll not stand for that sort of manipulation. If your maids and housekeeper are teaching her adequately, you can offer her the affection yourself, sir, and I'll be on my—"

"Now wait just a moment!" Leo stepped forward, suddenly not finding this so amusing. His gut churned with a nauseating combination of anger and guilt. Would yet another attempt of his to ensure Elizabeth's education collapse? He couldn't fail his brother again. This was his opportunity to provide for the girl, to work through part of his infinite debt to Walter. "Lizzy requires a proper education."

"She—"

"You've known her for only three days. How could you possibly—"

"I beg your pardon, Mr. Notley," she said stiffly, her green-and-grey eyes flashing, "but I've had sufficient time to test her knowledge in maths, Latin, geography—"

Leo scoffed. "You're telling me that a four-year-old child is well-versed in Latin, maths, and geography?"

Her lips pursed. "For her age, yes, as a matter of fact. She is able to recognize patterns, knows her numbers and some basic equa—"

"*Patterns*." He rubbed his hands together thoughtfully before letting them drop to his sides, the sense of impending disaster and guilt in his stomach twisting like a blade. "You believe that her elementary knowledge of some subjects is enough of an education to sustain her through life? Or do you mean to tell me that Elizabeth is capable of teaching herself in the future?" He paused, allowing her a moment to consider his words. "Because I'm certain that my maids and house-keeper have reached the end of their abilities to educate my niece."

Her eyes grew wide as he spoke, and her lips parted slightly before her expression grew pensive.

"You may put your fears to rest, Miss Smith," he contin-ued, enunciating the words carefully and speaking just above a whisper as his gaze bore into hers. "The very last thing that I want in my life is a wife." Once upon a time he'd imagined that he would do what was expected among the peerage, and marry and sire children, but that was before Walter...before he'd decided that celibacy was best for him.

"Oh, but Mr. Notley, I had not—" She bit her lips together, her gaze darting toward the window for several long moments before she cleared her throat. "You're correct, of course. I hadn't considered my argument with a clear mind. I beg your forgiveness, sir. I allowed personal feelings from my past to impact my judgement. If you will allow me, I would very much like to continue on as Miss Notley's governess."

Swift relief swept through him, the force of it nearly making him dizzy. His guilt remained, always hovering there in his heart, but for the moment, he felt comfort in the knowledge that his niece's education would be sorted. The muscles in his shoulders unclenched, and he discreetly released a long breath, searching the woman's uncertain expression.

Trust was difficult for many people, he realized, but with Miss Smith, something felt different. Whatever had influenced her to storm into his space and bluster at him, Leo very much wanted to know the story behind it.

"You may stay," he said.

The uncertainty in her gaze eased slightly. "Thank you, Mr. Notley."

They stood thusly for several long moments, the expression on Miss Smith's features turning first thoughtful, then hesitant.

He would very likely regret asking, but his mouth opened anyway. "Is there anything else that you wish to discuss?"

The dark curls perched precariously atop her head bounced as she gave a nod. "Yes. Miss Notley mentioned that she does not see you unless she visits you in your study. She wishes to improve your relationship, to know you better—"

"She does not know what she wants."

"I believe she does," Miss Smith replied in a voice that was somehow both soft and firm. "And I will ensure that she gets it."

His stomach clenched, and unease prickled up his neck. "I do not know how to interact with children," he confessed. Damn, but he sounded the fool.

A bright smile lit her lips and crinkled the corners of her eyes, and Leo's chest squeezed in response.

"I can help with that," she announced. "Commencing tomorrow, we shall begin each day by breaking our fast together, the three of us. She will learn comportment and table manners, and it will strengthen your bond."

His gaze caught on the sparkle in her eyes, and despite himself, he nodded. The tightness in his chest grew stronger as she flashed him a grin and slipped from the room. As he watched her go, he very much feared that he'd agreed to something that would hurt him more than she could possibly know.

EXULTATION FILLED his chest as he spied Juliana through a high window of a grand estate. He'd been searching for days, and had found the correct one, at last.

He shifted his seat, settling back against the trunk of a tree, sheltered from the falling snow. The darkness of the evening and the drooping branches shielded him from view; anyone who cared to look would see only shadows. But he... He could see Juliana clearly.

Her bruise-marred skin was pale against her drab uniform, but he knew what she truly was. She was a stain upon the ducal line. No matter how many people died in his wake, he would see his task completed. All he had to do, now, was decide whether to find his way inside or wait until she ventured out of doors.

CHAPTER 6

*E*yes slightly bleary from her night of restlessness, Juliana strode down the lengthy corridor, the everpresent pitter-patter of muffled paws and little feet moving alongside her. The owner of the aforementioned paws—and her brother, Boots—were the reason for Juliana's poor sleep. Lord, but it felt as though the dogs had spent the entirety of the night barking at shadows.

A small hand slid into her own, and she gave the girl a reassuring squeeze. She was nervous this morning, and truthfully, so was Juliana.

Her stomach was a mass of nerves, swirling and swooping unpleasantly. She'd made a fool of herself the previous day, intruding on Mr. Notley's solitude and accusing him of— Lord, she hated to even think on it. She ought to have thought through her assumptions before voicing them, but so many years of life with her father, and now her brother, had taught her some invaluable lessons. She merely required experience in learning other men's cues.

Living with her father had been a constant lesson in humility. His choice of tongue-lashing could come in the form of belittlement or direct insults. When he wasn't indifferent to her, Jasper had been there to comfort her, to disengage her mind with a silent game of chess when she was hurting. And then he'd inherited the title, learned of their father's debts, and changed into a man she scarcely recognized.

They descended the last staircase and rounded a corner.

Before Mr. Notley had the opportunity to show his true nature—and before the weather cleared for her journey—Juliana intended to begin the repair in the man's relationship with his niece. She would be the governess not only to the child, but to the man, as well. For while Lizzie had an uncle in Mr. Notley, she desperately needed a father.

Kitty let out a playful bark and bounded ahead of them down the hall. Elizabeth laughed and chased after her, a noticeable *crinkle* coming from her hands.

"Mind the parchment, Miss Notley!" Juliana called after the child.

The girl was a darling and, despite Juliana's previous assertion to the contrary, needed the guiding hand of a governess. While Juliana did not intend to remain for long, she hoped that she could aid the sprite in her decorum and speech while continuing the education that the staff had begun. All this, of course, while introducing her new agendum.

A low muttering nearly halted her steps, but she gamely continued on toward the opened door of the dining room.

Tightening her jaw against the disquieting ripple of emotions weaving through her, Juliana paused in the doorway. The man of the house was absently scratching behind Kitty's ears while Elizabeth pranced around the table with Boots. The man-of-all-work, Percy, leaned forward, his fists planted on the side of the long table, but his warm gaze was on Lizzy.

Juliana wondered at the men. Elizabeth and Kitty had obviously intruded upon a private discussion, but neither man appeared put out by the interruption. If Juliana had burst in on her father in such a way, even in the public space and when she was expected, a lashing of the tongue would not be the only sort she would have received.

"I beg your pardon, Mr. Notley," Juliana said, a slight nervous quaver in her voice as she dipped in a curtsey. "Mr. Percy."

The man-of-all-work straightened with a shallow bow, and Mr. Notley's hand stilled on Kitty's neck as he stood.

"Miss Smith," he acknowledged with a nod as the dog pawed at his arm.

An apology sprang to her lips, but she held it back. That was precisely the problem in this household: loneliness, estrangement, and guilt. The guilt, she would not play into, but the others...

Even Juliana's loveless home still had points of warmth. Her father's—and now, her brother's—staff had always been so lovely to her, so caring and generous where her father had been heartless and cruel.

She saw herself in the small child, but in Mr. Notley, she did not see the same cruelty as her father had shown. Mr. Notley might see Elizabeth as an obligation, but he looked at her with affection in his eyes. And that was something worth encouraging.

Juliana gestured to Elizabeth. "Do come along, Miss Notley, as we rehearsed, and before we break our fast."

The child skipped to Juliana's side, her blue eyes wide and uncertain. Juliana nodded encouragingly.

Lizzy scratched at her ear, then rose up and down on her toes as she faced her uncle. "Would you care to..." The child hesitated, tapping her chin as she considered her words. "...join us for tea this afternoon, Uncle Leo?" She hurried forward and extended the crinkled bit of parchment toward him.

Percy turned toward the sideboard, a small grin on his lips.

The buzzing of nerves intensified in Juliana's stomach. Mr. Notley wouldn't refuse, surely.

"I..." Mr. Notley gazed in confusion at his niece's hopeful features, and nodded. "Of course I will join you. I would be delighted. Thank you for the invitation."

Miss Notley lifted on her toes, her blonde ringlets bouncing, and Juliana beamed at her.

She guided the girl to the sideboard and selected food for their meal, then sat with her at the table. Mr. Notley resumed his seat and withdrew a newspaper, which obscured his face from view.

We'll have none of that, Mr. Notley.

"Have you the opportunity to read Walter Scott's new novel, *The Antiquary*, Mr. Notley?"

The paper rustled, and his face appeared behind one folded corner. "I haven't, no."

"I would recommend it, should you have the time." She spread some jam on a slice of toast.

One of his blond eyebrows crooked upward, and he closed the paper, folded it, and set it aside. "Do you read many novels, Miss Smith?"

"I do." She smiled at him as she took a bite of her toast. The tart and sweet burst of fruit on her tongue broadened her smile before she swallowed. "I've a particular fondness for adventure stories." Though she rarely had the pleasure of reading them, since her father would shout and bluster about the nonsense with which she filled her head.

Her vision grew unfocused as she thought wistfully of her favourite stories—particularly those novels written by the well-known Mr. Mystery—and how they made her feel. The longing that had always tugged at her was strong; perhaps that was one thing that had bonded her with Maria and Heather. The three of them were always searching for a way to break free not only from their families, but also from the staid lives that society would force upon them.

"Adventure," Mr. Notley said dubiously. "I imagine you now feel that you've had enough adventure in your life."

"Not at all," Juliana said truthfully. "My...*experience* frightened me, to be sure, but I intend to have many an adventure in my future."

The man's gaze turned assessing, and Mr. Percy lifted his coffee cup in salute, a twinkle of appreciation in his dark eyes. Juliana cleared her throat and turned to Miss Notley sitting beside her. They'd gone off course in their discussion.

"What of you, Miss Notley? Do you enjoy adventure? Perhaps a tale of daring and excitement is in our future?"

"Yes!" The girl bounced in her chair, her cheeks full near to bursting with eggs.

A sound perilously close to stifled laughter came from Mr. Percy, and Juliana suppressed a sigh. She corrected the girl's behaviour with a gentle reminder.

"Very good," Juliana encouraged with a nod. "We shall begin reading a new novel this evening. I've just the one in mind."

Miss Notley nodded eagerly, but the hot, tingling sensation of Mr. Notley's gaze boring into Juliana's profile shifted her attention away from the girl.

She cleared her throat once more, swallowing a sip of tea to ease the sudden tightness there. "Miss Notley, why do you not tell your uncle what you have been learning?"

Miss Notley's blue eyes lit with excitement. "I saw a book with drawings of pretty flowers..."

Soon, Juliana swallowed the last sip of her tea and escorted her charge back to the nursery. The meal progressed and concluded with pleasant conversation, Juliana prompting the girl in topics to discuss with her uncle, Miss Notley bursting with enthusiasm, Mr. Notley gamely playing his part, and Mr.

Percy quietly observing with mirth. It was an ideal first attempt.

WITH A SILENT CURSE and trembling hands, Leonard unknotted his cravat and attempted to tie it again. His curst fingers wouldn't sodding behave.

"A penny for your thoughts, Leo," Percy drawled behind him.

Leo glanced at the man's reflection in the mirror. Percy reclined in an armchair near the hearth in Leo's bedchamber, his legs outstretched and crossed at his ankles.

"I've nothing to say," Leo lied.

"Untrue. You're..." He tilted his head and eyed Leo thoughtfully. "You're nervous about going to tea because you can't bear the sight of your niece, as she bears a resemblance to Walter. And her governess threatens your self-imposed rules on sex."

Leo growled, a deep scowl on his face. "Bastard."

"True." He gestured vaguely toward himself. "I'm here to tell you, however, that your having sex with Miss Smith won't kill anyone."

"Leave it alone, will you?" *She's under my employ, and I just...can't*. He couldn't forget that.

"She is interested in you, as well." Percy shrugged. "But if you insist, I shall leave it."

Leo's gaze snapped upward to meet Percy's in the mirror, his pulse jumping.

"*There*," Percy accused, pointing his finger at Leo. "That heat in your gaze is matched in hers when she looks at you. Do not tell me that you have not noticed."

"I've noticed," Leo grumbled, returning his attention to tying his sodding cravat.

The man nodded and heaved a dramatic sigh.

"There was a disturbance outside last night."

Leonard blinked, adjusting to the abrupt change in topic. "So I surmised due to the dogs' incessant barking. Do you know what it was?" With one last tug on the fabric at his throat, he turned to face his friend.

Percy shrugged one shoulder. "Unknown. I will walk the perimeter of the building while you are at tea, but I remain unconcerned. It was likely a nocturnal animal sniffing about for food."

Leo nodded. "Wish me luck."

"Good luck." Percy smirked, his eyes challenging and filled with mirth.

"Sod off."

Percy's low laughter followed him out the door.

Tea. Leo could not recall the last time—if ever—that he'd joined anyone for tea in adulthood.

The corridor flickered brightly with candlelight as he marched swiftly toward the staircase.

Tea! he scoffed silently. And he'd said yes, of all things. *Not just yes*, he reminded himself. He'd said, "I would be delighted." Which, of course, he wasn't. But Lizzy had been watching him so hopefully with her large blue eyes, and Miss Smith had observed him with a knowing gaze that made him want to both prove her wrong *and* prove her right, whatever her assumption.

Damnation, his nerves were wrought.

He reached the nursery and softly knocked on the closed door. There were hushed voices and a bark within, before the door swung inward to reveal the greeting party. Miss Smith released the door and dipped in a curtsey, which Lizzy attempted to replicate, so Leo bowed appropriately.

Both of them had altered their attire. Lizzy wore a bright white dress with yellow ribbons around the bodice, sleeves, and hem, and Miss Smith had changed into a maid's uniform with capped sleeves, and had removed the white fichu. The frock was still modest, but the way the fabric strained against her breasts was veritably indecent. And positively delicious.

"Mr. Notley?"

Damn. He blinked, fighting the heat that he could feel blotching his chest. "I beg your pardon. I was momentarily distracted by Lizzy's beauty."

His niece's face lit up in a smile, and she twirled before gripping his hand and tugging him toward an armchair.

"Come along, Uncle Leo! You sit just there."

Miss Smith followed them, taking her seat on the settee to his left, leaving enough space for Lizzy to sit between them. The room was large and bright, the colours cheerful and child-like in their pale shades. There was a doll's house in the corner of the room, with the dolls posed similarly to their tea service, as though Miss Smith had used them to instruct Elizabeth before he'd arrived.

Miss Smith poured while Lizzy gathered sandwiches on a plate. Despite himself, Leo's gaze caught inappropriately on Miss Smith's inviting bosom before he hastily glanced away. His cock stirred, and he resisted the urge to shift its position. Curse his galling attraction to the woman.

"Milk or sugar, Mr. Notley?"

Stifling the urge to scowl—his mood soured by the past and his inability to satisfy his wants or needs—Leo rolled his shoulders and attempted a smile. "Both, please. Two lumps."

With a curious glance at him, she turned to her task.

"For you, Uncle Leo!" Elizabeth said brightly, thrusting the plate of sandwiches at him.

Something panged in his chest, and he suppressed another frown. "Thank you."

His little niece beamed at him, her gap-toothed smile full

and wide, and that dratted pang tightened his chest once more.

They lapsed into silence as Leo accepted his tea—and had a verbal jousting match with his inner demons. The girl seemed so sodding pleased by his attentions, and yet if she knew the truth of him, if she knew just how much her association with him was damaging her future, she would surely wish to be free of him. And this Machiavellian, interfering woman thought to force them together.

And he was bloody well falling in with her plans. Just one look at his niece's hopeful features had him entirely under her spell. *Blast it.*

Under her governess' watchful eye, Elizabeth stiffened her spine. "What do you think of the weather we are having, Uncle Leo?"

Leo hid a smirk behind his cup. His niece had clearly rehearsed the question, and he wondered briefly if their entire discussion would consist of similar inquiries.

"I think," he responded, "that it is cold, but also beautiful."

"Indeed." She nodded, a blonde ringlet falling loose over her brow. "And what do you think of the latest fashions?"

Just like that, a small piece of the wall erected around his heart was chipped away. With each one of his niece's questions throughout tea, with every one of her glances to Miss Smith, searching for reassurance, Leo's chest warmed just a little bit more.

It was precisely what he didn't want. *Damnation.*

He couldn't afford to grow attached to the girl, and she certainly wouldn't want such an attachment once she was old enough to understand... Leo gave her a tight smile as she offered her opinions on their horses.

The remainder of their tea progressed much the same. Leo ate the sandwiches and washed them down with tea while

Lizzy interrogated him. Miss Smith joined the discussion when addressed, her eyes glittering with amusement and pride as Lizzy held the reins. He was decidedly *not* charmed. No, indeed.

The organ in his chest fluttered. He was, he would admit, haunted, for it was the woman's amused eyes—crinkling in the corners—and the hint of dimples on her cheeks that he pictured for the remainder of the day.

JULIANA INHALED the familiar scent of books, ink, and parchment, the faint trace of burning wood from the hearth, and...beneath all of that, the hint of the wildly intriguing man sitting across from her: coconut, cinnamon, and trees.

She flipped the page in her book but recalled nothing of what she'd just read. Seated in a matching armchair on the hearth's other side was Mr. Notley, his chin resting in his hand, as though in contemplation, and a book open on his lap, his legs stretched toward the fire. He appeared for all the world a man at his ease. Would that Juliana felt that way. Instead, her muscles strained and her pulse skittered at his nearness.

When she'd entered the library, she'd sought a moment of solitude in which to read after Miss Notley had fallen asleep, but soon after she'd entered, so had Mr. Notley.

He cleared his throat, his gaze lifting from the pages of his book to meet hers.

A zing travelled down her spine, and Juliana suppressed a shiver. *Blimey.*

"Do you truly enjoy tales of adventure, or were you merely attempting to encourage Lizzy to read?" Mr. Notley asked, his eyes glittering with twin reflections of the firelight.

Juliana closed her book and set it on the round table at her elbow. "I crave adventure, Mr. Notley."

His left eyebrow lifted, but he remained silent. Somehow, she knew what he must be thinking, and she worried her bottom lip between her teeth. The truth of it was, she *had* experienced something that had...scarred her soul. But it hadn't diminished her anticipation of what was to come of her meeting with Grace Huntsbury. A new life awaited Juliana. *Adventure* awaited her.

"Lift that eyebrow all you please, Mr. Notley," she said. "My first adventure mightn't have gone to plan, but I intend to have others."

"And you're a governess," he drawled. "I find that astonishing."

"What is so astonishing? It is a perfectly respectable—"

"What I find astonishing, Miss Smith," he said, his eyes lit with interest, "is that no man has claimed you as his wife."

Despite herself, a frown pulled her brows together. "I resent the fact that my life mustn't have any meaning if I am not yet married and bred. What if I do not desire children? What if I despise men?"

His gaze seemed to bore into her, and heat flushed her chest. *Too bold? Drat.*

"*Do* you despise men?" His voice seemed to lower an octave, and her belly gave a responding quiver.

"I do not. But I might, and I detest the notion that a woman cannot make that choice."

"You, Miss Smith, are a radical." His gaze turned challenging.

"Is that a problem?"

His lips pursed as he considered her. "No. As for children, I daresay it ought to be your choice, since you must bear them."

"However?"

A sigh escaped him, and he lifted one shoulder in a shrug. "Rules in society dictate that a woman's choice be given to her husband. I imagine, therefore, it is prudent for a woman to make a superior match. If I were inclined to take a wife, I would not force the matter of children. But other men feel differently."

"And you are not inclined to take a wife?"

His lips thinned. "Indeed not." He blinked, and the playfulness returned to his gaze. "And what of you?"

Juliana huffed a breath. "I've had offers, but none I wished to accept. The...my father would—could—not offer a dowry for my hand." The duke had refused every political alliance, was not swayed by pretty words or promises, had stated that no man would truly wish to marry his mistake of a child, and had gambled her dowry away. He was not even willing to give her away, he'd said, wishing to keep the burden of her company on him. She cleared her throat. "He said that I was too tall to attract a good husband. I...am firmly on the shelf, sir."

Movement beyond the reflections on the window panes caught Juliana's eye, and for one heart-thundering moment, her breath froze in her throat. Twin tingles of terror travelled down the backs of her legs, and her heart began to race. *Could it be*—no. That had been dealt with.

She released a slow breath before she realized that Mr. Notley was speaking.

"What kind of father would—" He spun in his seat to glance over his shoulder at the window. "What is it?"

"N-nothing, I assure you." But the moment had been severed, and an unnatural stiffness had entered her posture. "I'd best retire for the evening. Good night, Mr. Notley."

His gaze was curious, but he asked nothing, merely notched his chin. "Good night, Miss Smith."

IF JULIANA HADN'T BEEN SO DRATTED distracted by Mr. Notley, she would not have forgotten to bring the book with her to her chambers. But the man had a quick mouth that inspired decidedly licentious thoughts.

Her slippered footfalls were muffled on the corridor's carpeted runner, the rooms dark beyond opened doorways, and the scent of coconut and beeswax drifted along the air as she made her way back to her bedchamber. A sharp bark sounded from somewhere deeper in the maze of Woodhaven Hall, and a prickle of unease lifted the hair upon her nape.

With an internal rebuke she forced her fingers to loosen on the book that she held tight against her chest. These feelings were surely borne of her nightmares, and she would do well to forget them. No one here knew the truth of her identity.

"We meet again," a rumbling voice said from behind her.

The book dropped to the floor with a muffled *thunk*. Her lungs froze on a squeak, her pulse skittering in her veins and her stomach twisting painfully as she spun to stare wild-eyed into the darkness beyond the ring of candlelight.

"Miss Smith?"

The voice penetrated the fear, and she released a slow, steadying breath to calm her racing heart. She knew that voice. "Mr. Notley."

He stepped closer and into the glow of the sconce's candlelight. "My apologies for frightening you." He scanned her with his hot, penetrating gaze, then bent to retrieve the book, extending it out to her.

"It was naught but a trifling startle, I assure you," she lied, accepting the proffered book with a tight smile. "But it is I who must apologize. I suppose I oughtn't wander the halls at night. I'd simply thought to—"

He made a soft grunt as he shook his head and stepped closer. "There is no need to be sorry, Miss Smith. This is your home; you are free to wander and explore as you please."

Another fit of barking came from somewhere in the darkness, sending the little hairs at Juliana's nape to stand on end.

With the exception of attending balls and fetes, she'd never been permitted out of her bedchamber at night. Lord knew from what her father thought he was protecting her, but whenever she'd been caught, she had been punished. For that reason, she'd grown accustomed to exploring in the dark, without the aid of a candle. The darker her surroundings, the less likely she was to be caught.

She'd since grown out of those fears, but something about her nightmares, and the eerie feeling that had been growing inside her since taking on this position, had her teeth on edge.

"Thank you," she said, her voice sounding all too loud to her ears. "I couldn't sleep, and thought to retrieve the book I had been reading earlier." She lifted it in one hand.

"I'd be glad to walk you back to your chambers, if you desire."

Her abdomen gave a wobble, and she inclined her head. She understood this feeling well enough, knew what it meant that she felt this pull toward Mr. Notley. It was, indeed, *desire.*

Continuing down the corridor, the man fell into step beside her. Lord, but his warmth radiated toward her, carrying his alluring scent. It made her want to lick him, just to see if his skin tasted as he smelled.

A quiver danced up the backs of her legs, and heat pooled in her belly. *Trouble,* her inner voice cautioned.

She slid a glance sideways at him as they walked silently through the corridors. His eyes glittered in the sparce light of the sconces. His nose was crooked slightly when viewed from this angle—it was utterly endearing—and his lips... His lips were full and pink, and made her heart flutter.

"Here we are," he murmured.

Juliana blinked, surprised to see that they had, in fact, already reached the nursery. "Th-thank you, Mr. Notley."

CHAPTER 7

Not for the first time, Leo cursed his trembling fingers as he attempted to knot his cravat. He glared into the looking glass, then glanced over his shoulder at Percy lounging on an armchair. "Are you not meant to act as my valet?"

Percy crossed one leg over the other, his legs outstretched. "Yes, but we would both find that demeaning."

"Mmm," Leo hummed. "Quite."

With a muttered curse, he returned his attentions to his cravat.

"The dogs were barking again last night," Leo noted. "I searched the halls, but saw naught that might disturb them. Were *you* able to learn the reason?"

Percy shook his head. "Afraid not. One of the footmen says he heard rustling in a shrubbery, but was not able to determine its source."

"Damn. Very well. Have the maids draw the drapery closed in the evening. Mayhap a neighbouring dog has gotten loose. You know how Kitty and Boots are around other dogs." He tightened the knot of his cravat with a satisfied huff, then tugged on his shirtsleeves before donning his blue coat.

"Worried what she will think of you?" Percy asked, an eyebrow raised.

"Sod off." Of course he'd been thinking about it, but he couldn't admit that aloud. Despite his best efforts, the little radical was under his skin.

Their discussion in his library last evening had roused more than his curiosity, and their meeting in the corridor had only amplified his feelings. He hid a smile as he glanced down at the buttons on his waistcoat. The woman was charming, to be sure. But something haunted her, and he was determined to discover what it was.

"Will Uncle Leo come, Miss Smith?" Elizabeth asked softly, her warm hand clutching Juliana's as they strode through the labyrinth of rooms.

Juliana gave the little girl a reassuring smile, resisting the urge to tug at her too-tight bodice. The housekeeper and maids had done their best to alter the uniform, but it was still not fitting correctly. Such was fine with Juliana; she wouldn't be here long, anyway.

"If he received my note, then I'm certain he will join us. But do not concern yourself, for we shall have an enjoyable time, just us two, if he does not attend."

Lizzy's little bow-shaped lips curved into a smile before she gave an excited hop. "May I have a treat?"

Despite Juliana's attempt to withhold it, a laugh escaped her. "I've spoken to the cook, and we've been given leave to sample."

The hand in hers squeezed tighter, and a delighted squeal echoed in the hall as Lizzy jumped again.

"But," Juliana hurried to add, "we mustn't indulge too much; the staff in the kitchens require the ingredients for their cooking."

"Yes, Miss Smith."

The moment they lapsed into silence, Juliana's thoughts wandered back to Mr. Notley. She'd scarcely slept at all the previous night, nor could she read the book she'd retrieved from the library. Instead, she lay awake, replaying her last exchanges with Mr. Notley in her mind.

His gaze had heated her through her frock during their tea, and it continued to heat her every time she thought on it. Their discussion in the library had been stimulating; she wanted more.

She'd very much wanted to discover what thoughts had been behind those looks of his. Had he thought of kissing her? Because imagining kissing him—and doing far more depraved things to him—had begun to consume her evenings...and her mornings...and whenever she had a moment to think.

His lips, she mused, would be soft, his beard coarse. She thought of running her hands through his long blond hair, of raking her fingers against his scalp and hearing him moan— *would* he moan?

Both dogs bounded toward them, having been released from a footman's care. The young man hurried forward with a contrite smile on his lips. "Me apologies, misses. I fink Boots and Kitty 'eard you coming." His thick east London accent was low and rough, but somehow pleasing.

"It is quite all right, I assure you."

"Vey'll keep you company on your walk, and tru'fully vey could burn off some energy."

Juliana smiled at him, and his ears pinkened slightly.

"Is vere anyfing else you be needin', Miss Smith?"

"No, thank you."

She smiled again, and he turned down another corridor with a deep bow.

The dogs pranced around them, and Lizzy released Juliana's hand so that she might join them.

"Is everything well with Samuel?" Mr. Notley asked gruffly from behind her.

Juliana halted and spun to face him, her absurd imaginings of the night before still hot and fresh in her memory, and she was struck dumb. No matter the dated fashion, the man was magnificent in matching grey waistcoat and breeches and deep-blue wool coat. His hair curled over his shoulders, and his shorn beard brushed the knot of his starched white cravat. Lord, but she wanted desperately to touch it.

"The man ran off with a crimson face," he continued.

Juliana's gaze met Mr. Notley's, and a puzzled frown pinched her brows together. "Goodness, I do hope that he wasn't upset. He'd just brought the dogs—"

"Uncle Leo!" Elizabeth skipped toward him and wrapped her arms about his leg. "I'm so happy that you came." She released him and bounced up on her toes.

Juliana's heart gave a squeeze at the softening of Mr. Notley's features, and she forced herself to turn away. In accepting the position as a governess, she had acknowledged a duty to educate Miss Notley. It was decidedly *not* an opportunity to lust after her uncle.

"Shall we continue on?" she asked brusquely, leading the way down the brightly lit hall.

THE DOGS RACED AHEAD of Miss Smith, and Lizzy gripped Leo's hand, chatting animatedly about all that she might sample during their walk. Leo listened with half an ear and responded when necessary, but his attention was unwaveringly fixed on Miss Smith's retreating form.

A wave of self-loathing rippled just beneath his skin but, Lucifer help him, he couldn't tear his gaze away from the rounded sway of her hips. He wanted to grip them and bury his face in the soft globes of her flesh, nibble at them, and have her squirm beneath him. Damn, but he wanted to see them bounce as he took her from behind. He—

"Here we are," Miss Smith said brightly, stopping before the conservatory's door.

Shite. Leo cleared his throat and stepped aside, allowing Lizzy and Miss Smith to precede him. Giving his cockstand a discreet pinch, he took a bracing breath and followed them inside.

The air was warm and humid, and carried the sweet and piquant scent of fruits and herbs. It was a point of pride for him that he'd managed to keep both of his ancestors' conservatories producing, and often had a surplus to give as offerings to his servants, the tenants, and their families.

"Oh, I love these!" Lizzy squealed as she plucked a blackberry from its bramble against one wall and popped it into her mouth.

Miss Smith's eyes had widened in wonder as she'd begun to explore, the column of her neck stretching delicately backward as she took in some of their taller trees.

"How did you amass such a collection?" she asked.

Leo clasped his hands behind his back and cleared his throat, forcing his mind to focus on her question and not on how he'd like to graze his lips along her neck. "In his youthful years, my father paid a substantial sum to have plants brought from around the world to the conservatories. I am uncertain what began his fascination, but he continued to collect until his death."

"Remarkable," she breathed. "How do you maintain them?"

"I have a horticulturist on staff, and pay for a pollination service with a man who keeps bees. The rest of my staff keep the fires alight and the fountains flowing."

"How fortunate for Miss Notley to have you for an uncle."

An immediate wave of icy guilt swept over Leo, and he frowned against it. No, his niece was not fortunate. Nothing about this sodding circumstance was fortunate. He was spending time in her company because Miss Smith had burst into their lives and demanded it, but the girl was better off without him.

Miss Smith's brow puckered. "Have I said something to...?"

Leo cleared his throat with a grunt. "Indeed not." Lord knew why he felt the need to comfort the maddening woman. "But Elizabeth's future will no doubt be difficult with me as her reclusive uncle. I have no desire to make it worse."

Her gaze thoughtful, she nodded. "I understand. Purchasing entrée into the House of Lords is enough of a challenge, but garnering society's approval?" She waved a hand through the air with a sympathetic roll of her eyes.

The woman was entirely wrong in her assumption, but Leo had no desire to correct her. Let her believe that he was attempting to buy his way into the *haut ton* with the purchase of a title; it was far more palatable than the truth.

Elizabeth darted toward them and gripped Miss Smith's hand. "I found the blueberries!" Her face was wreathed in smiles and soiled by wet spots of red, blue, and purple.

"Splendid!" Miss Smith returned Lizzy's grin. She withdrew a handkerchief from the sleeve of her uniform and bent to wipe at Lizzy's cheeks before straightening and gesturing at the trees behind her. "Can you name these fruits, Miss Elizabeth?"

His niece's lips twisted in thought as she studied the hanging fruit. "Apples?"

"That is a very good guess," Miss Smith commended, "but incorrect. These," she said, reaching up and testing the firmness of the fruit, "are pears. Observe their shape, how they taper toward the stem. These are not yet ready to be harvested, but they must be so before they are ripe, or they will all fall to the ground."

"How do you know so much about pears?" Lizzy asked.

I might ask the same, Leo thought, observing the exchange with interest.

Miss Smith grinned. "I've eaten many of them—as have you, dear—but I have also read about them in books about horticulture. Today, we've come so that I might see what plants are here, and then as part of our lessons, we will learn more about them. When we return, I expect that you will be able to tell me all about each fruit before you taste it."

A small pout puckered Lizzy's lower lip before a smile replaced it. "But I will get to taste everything?"

"Everything that you correctly identify, yes."

Lizzy laughed gleefully and skipped ahead, the dogs bounding after her.

Leo fell into step beside Miss Smith, his blood humming with awareness of her. She was still a mystery that he wished to solve, but there was also that illicit heat that she roused in him that had his full attention. He wanted to know more, wanted to spend more time in her company, wanted to... *Christ*, he wanted to touch her, to sodding *taste* her. It was all forbidden, of course, completely dangerous to the both of them.

She gasped softly, and he squeezed his eyes shut against the sudden tautness in his cods. Damn it, he was aching.

"Mangoes!" she breathed in awe.

His eyelids felt weighted, but he lifted them to watch the column of her neck arch delicately back. His gaze blazed a trail over her exposed skin, and a matching fire burned hotter in his blood with each inch that he inspected.

"I haven't seen these since I was a child," Miss Smith said wistfully.

Leo bit back a groan. "You are welcome to partake at your leisure, Miss Smith. Or I could have the cook include them in—"

"I found strawberries!" Lizzy squealed from the far end of the conservatory, her voice echoing through the large space.

His lips tugged in a grin. But his mirth swiftly fled, replaced by a low hum of awareness that seemed to vibrate just beneath his skin.

Miss Smith's sweet floral scent, coupled with the fragrance of fresh soap and the fruits that surrounded them, filled his senses, and the space between them was suddenly closed. He was uncertain which of them had taken the first step, and he didn't care.

Their gazes met and held and his pulse leapt. Their chests rose and fell with suddenly rapid breaths, the air between them growing nigh feverish. Miss Smith slid her hands up his arms, driving away every thought other than *her* and the feelings she inspired in him.

Rational thought aside, his aching body led the way.

ONE WOULD THINK that somewhere in Juliana's mind there would be a voice—likely one reminiscent of her father—telling her to back away from Mr. Notley, to abandon the desire surging through her, and to continue her walk through the conservatory. But no such voice came. All she felt was a bone-deep need to press her lips to his, to run her fingers through his beard, and his hair, to press her body flush against his...

The air was hot and sweet between them as Mr. Notley's gaze searched hers in question. Her hands tightened on his thick, hard shoulders as she pulled him toward her. Her pulse thumped through her veins, making her feel as though her whole body vibrated with the force of it. Until finally, his lips connected with hers.

Her breath caught in her throat, and a spark of some unnameable pleasure jolted through her centre. His beard was soft against her skin, not at all coarse as she'd imagined. Skimming her hands over his shoulders, Juliana raked her fingers through his hair. *Silken*, as though he'd recently brushed the locks.

A low moan rumbled through his chest, his arms coming around her waist. An answering ripple of desire wove its way down Juliana's spine, settling low in her belly. His palm cupped her jaw, and the added warmth almost made her groan. With coaxing lips and a gentle stroke of his thumb along her jaw, he was inside her.

Cinnamon. He tasted sweet and spicy, the lingering burn of cinnamon intoxicating as his tongue swiped devilishly over hers.

Juliana had kissed men before, but those kisses by comparison had been rushed and sloppy, whereas *this*... Oh, sweet merciful heavens, *this* was slow and heady, as though each moment were deliberately thought out with her pleasure in mind. And she wanted more.

His head tilted, allowing him to explore at a different angle, and a whimper found its way up her throat. She tightened her grip around his shoulders, raking her fingers against his skull.

He groaned, breaking the kiss to glide his lips along Juliana's jaw. She tilted her head to accommodate him, her eyes closed as gooseflesh spread over her skin, and her core throbbed with want.

Finding the spot just below her ear where she frequently put her favourite fragrance, he stopped and inhaled deeply.

"Right here," he whispered hoarsely, nudging the spot with his nose and lips.

Juliana shivered and pressed herself tighter against him. The hard ridge of his arousal strained insistently against her most sensitive area, and she gasped at the jolt of pleasure and anticipation that it caused. She moved her hips against him again, this time deliberately, and exulted in the heat that spread through her.

Mr. Notley groaned again and found her lips once more, his kiss growing insistent. His hands roamed her back before settling on her bottom, pressing her more firmly against his arousal.

Juliana's pulse was galloping wild through her veins, and she could not seem to keep her breathing under control, but she scarcely cared. She gave herself fully into the sensations rocking her, and she would gleefully take more.

The rapid footfalls of dogs and a child broke into Juliana's lust-fogged mind, and just as quickly as it had begun, their kiss ended. Mr. Notley spun and paced away, his spine stiff and his fists clenched.

"Please excuse me, Miss Smith," he muttered, slightly winded. "I will send Samuels to escort you in my stead." With that, he strode away, sparing her nary a glance.

Juliana's heart still raced, and her lips felt kiss-swollen, her body aching and frustrated. But what she felt most was hurt. Mr. Notley had abandoned her in a difficult circumstance, after sharing kisses that had her reeling.

"Miss Smith! Miss Smith!" Elizabeth reached her, rounded cheeks stained several shades of purple. "I found fruits that I can't reach. Can you help me, please?"

"Of course, dear," Juliana replied numbly.

She woodenly returned Lizzy's smile and followed her along the path, the dogs trotting alongside. Lizzy's blonde ringlets bounced with each step, as though the girl's excitement and exuberance could be expressed by each golden lock. And instantly, Juliana understood what had frightened Mr. Notley off. He'd been fearful of the repercussions.

Mr. Notley had his niece to consider in all of his actions and, mayhap, for just a moment, he'd been selfish. They'd also been close to discovery. But what would his reaction have been if they had shared those kisses in a more private setting? Would they have begun to explore each other's bodies?

The thought sent a wave of heat through her. Juliana mightn't have experienced lovemaking before, but she knew what it entailed...and she knew that it would ruin a woman for marriage.

Pulling her bottom lip between her teeth, she bit gently as she walked. Her position as Lizzy's governess would soon end, and she would resume her journey to London. What would become of her if she were discovered before then, or her rendezvous did not go as planned? Would she be forced to return to Jasper or the vile man to whom she'd been sold? What if someone discovered the carriage? She would be precisely back from where she'd fled.

If she was no longer a maiden, however, would her brother be able to sell her off? Would *any* man wish to marry her? Hope blossomed in her chest. It was a risk, certainly, but she was already on the shelf, and she was about to embark on a personal adventure from which she anticipated great fulfilment. And, truly, anything was better than marrying Viscount Rivers. It was worth the risk.

Impossible though the thought was, Juliana believed that she'd found just the man to take on the task.

CHAPTER 8

*L*eo paced in front of the large desk in his library, wishing that the scent of leather, parchment, and ink would calm his senses. But instead, the warm aroma of flowers remained in his nose, the taste of berries on his lips, and the sound of soft moans and sighs in his ears.

"*Christ*!" Leo shook out his hands before running them through his hair and beard. His heart still raced, and his cock-stand wouldn't sodding alleviate.

Given more time with Miss Smith, he might have taken her right there in the conservatory, and that was a bloody dangerous thing. The heavy hands of guilt and shame swarmed his chest and settled hard in his gut. He couldn't have her—or any woman—and he'd best remember that. He needed to clear his head, needed to think.

Why did Miss Smith affect him so? He wanted her so damned badly—there *must* be a reason why. Who was she, really? He knew very little about her, and that realization was rather alarming. Why did she make him feel such unwanted emotions? Hell, how was she educated? He'd not even requested references, for God's sake. Had she a family that missed her or days off in order to visit with them? Or, hell, was she in trouble with a magistrate for her radical views? Worst of all, he did not know why he missed her so badly when she was apart from him.

Spinning in his pacing, he punched a fist against his hip. He'd brought this woman into his home, and she'd grown close to his niece, had found her way under his skin...and he knew not the first thing about her. He didn't even know the truth of how she'd been left on his land, covered in blood and holding a pistol.

Frustration rode him, his heart tripping over in his chest and his gut buzzing.

He squeezed his eyes shut and pinched the bridge of his nose, uttering a string of curses under his breath.

He couldn't do this. Not again. Couldn't risk the lives of the ones he held dear for a woman. There were answers that he must have, and he wouldn't allow her to distract him this time.

"*Percy!*" Leo called, his voice sharp and abrupt against the silence. He strode toward the library's door, and pulled it open. "*Per—*"

"Oh!" Miss Smith jumped, her hand poised as if to knock.

Leo's shout died on his lips and his lungs deflated. Despite himself, something warm prickled just behind his ribs, and it made him want to snarl. This woman had indeed begun to crawl under his skin. And he didn't like it.

"I apologize for the interruption, Mr. Notley. I came to invite you on a walk out of doors with—"

With a grunt, he clasped her arm and guided her quickly inside, closing the door behind her. "We must speak."

She worried her bottom lip. "If this is about what occurred in the conservatory, I assure you—"

"Who are you?" he growled.

She blanched. "Wh-what?"

"All this time, and I've not learned a thing about you. What are you plotting? Do you aim to soften me up by forcing me together with my niece? Because it will not work." Her eyebrows snapped together, and he continued. "Who is your family? Where were you educated? How is it that you have not contacted a single soul since I found you? Who knows where you are, Miss Smith?"

Fear flashed in her eyes before she glanced away, and her pale skin grew increasingly ashen. Several long moments passed between them in silence, and Leonard grew increasingly agitated with each one.

"It is true, Mr. Notley; you know naught about me, and I've no intention of enlightening you. But understand this." She met his gaze once more, steely and determined. "Miss Notley is incredibly bright. She is observant and sensitive, and before I arrived, whenever you chose to dine, walk, or ride alone, that little girl was left alone, as well, craving your attention and affection."

Despite his best effort to stop it, a sickening, hollow feeling began in his chest and spread out his arms to tingle in his fingers. He irrationally blamed her for the pain, and absurdly wished to strike back. He fisted his hands, leaned a hip against the back of an armchair, and waited through a moment of heavy silence before he spoke. "Percy tells me that another search has begun, and as of yet your carriage has not been found."

Her cheeks paled further. "Wh-what?" Her voice came out a harsh whisper, and Leo knew that he'd hit his mark.

She ought never to have avoided my questions. "While you were recovering," he drawled, "an initial search of the surrounding roads was conducted, but after you mentioned driving into the forest, the search expanded further onto my land." He paused, holding her wide, frightened gaze. "I've been informed that as of yet, the search has not yielded any evidence of an accident. It has made me wonder if you spoke the truth."

"I-I did, but..." She wrung her hands, her gaze sliding sideways toward a window, and the darkness beyond.

"I've begun to wonder," he continued, wanting to provoke her further, "if there is a carriage to find at all. Mayhap you've fabricated the entire tale just to garner a position in my home."

She shook her head, her cheeks pale and her neck growing red. "How dare you accuse me of falsehoods, sir!" The pucker between her eyebrows deepened. "I *was* in an accident. The carriage rolled somewhere in the forest, and I was trapped. I did everything I could to get out!" Her eyes began to swim, and she rubbed at the back of her neck with trembling fingers.

Leo wanted to know more, to push her further. Even though he hadn't a doubt that her experience had been harrowing and disturbing, there was one large part of her tale that he knew she'd omitted. Something wasn't quite right. When he'd found her, she was covered in blood, but she'd not been the one to cause the stains. To whom did the blood belong?

"How did you escape the carriage, Miss Smith?" Leo asked bluntly.

Her eyes were like two-toned saucers glinting in the candlelight, with horror lurking in the corners. Part of him wanted to rescind the question and relieve her of the pain he knew she felt, but this mystery ate at him. He wanted to believe her innocent—refused to lay any blame at her feet without proof—but at the moment all he felt was suspicion.

Back stiff and her lips pursed, Miss Smith closed her eyes on a sigh. "Please accept my immediate resignation, Mr. Notley."

Alarm jolted through him, and he caught her arm as she began to turn away. "Miss Smith!"

"*I didn't!*" She whirled on him, pulling her arm from his slack grip. "I didn't escape that carriage!"

With a swish of her skirts, she marched from the room, his traitorous greyhound Kitty in her wake, and Leonard in a state of utter perplexity. "What in the bloody hell does *that* mean?"

CHAPTER 9

"Sir," Percy implored, holding Leo's robe out to him. Leonard continued to pace, unable to quell the anxious energy that ricocheted inside him. A soft yawn came from behind him, and he was once more silently grateful for the dog's company. Boots, the inaptly named black greyhound that sported a white patch of fur on his chest, was the only of the sibling beasties that had remained faithful.

An errant drop of residual bath water trickled over the hair on his chest, and he scratched it idly. He caught sight of himself in his bedchamber's mirror, and grimaced at the black tail of ink that curled over his shoulder and morphed into a dark, elaborately patterned sleeve that ended just above his elbow. Bloody insolent thing.

"She said that she didn't escape the carriage, Percy," Leo said, mentally shaking his mind free of cobwebs. "So how do you imagine she came to be wandering the forest when we found her?"

Percy's lips thinned. "I've men still searching, sir. When they find the carriage, I imagine we will have our answers."

With a nod, Leo strode to his friend and man-of-all-work

and slid his arms through the sleeves of his robe, tying the sash about his waist before he removed the towel from around his hips. "Has she left the estate?"

Percy accepted the towel. "No, sir. I believe she intends to do so in the morning."

Leo rubbed at his neatly trimmed beard hair, his gaze locked on the fire blazing in his bedchamber's hearth. The room was spacious and comfortable, painted in a pale green and decorated far more lavishly than he truly required. He scarcely spent any time in the space, preferring to ride, walk, or convalesce in his comfortable library. He'd not thought that he would spend time languishing within these walls, wondering about such a confounding woman, but there you have it.

He cursed and sat upon the chaise by his fire, Boots taking a cushion left conveniently on the floor near the hearth. "Truthfully, I have no wish for her to leave. Hell, but we've waited so sodding long for a governess to accept the position. I'd merely hoped to question her. To get some bloody answers. I just..." He sighed, scratching his fingers through his beard. He'd grown frustrated by his feelings for her, and he'd reacted irrationally.

Percy moved about the room behind Leo. "As I've said, you desire her. Why not get it over with?"

Leo scoffed, selected a cinnamon drop from the tray that Percy held out to him, and popped it into his mouth. The sweet spice burst sharply on his tongue as he rolled it back and forth, letting the heat sizzle through his senses.

A dish of coconut oil appeared in front of him, and he dipped his index finger in, before massaging it into his beard.

"Thank you. I'll not debauch a woman merely for the sake of one pleasing night, Percy."

Memories of their heated kisses in the conservatory raced through his mind, and he gritted his teeth against the surge of desire and guilt that they wrought. He was grateful that they'd been interrupted, for the devil knew what he would have done if given the opportunity.

At one time, Leonard would have happily taken Miss Smith to his bed without compunction, but after... He cleared his throat and refocused his wandering thoughts. Put simply, he hadn't slept with a woman in just over three years, and he didn't know when—or *if*—he would do so again.

As out of touch as he was with the world beyond his estate, Leo was acutely aware of his discomfort and awkwardness around others. Before now, however, he hadn't considered that a problem. In fact, he'd rather relished his isolation and detested the thought of engaging with others. Hell, he even avoided meetings with his steward, preferring to conduct business through letters. He couldn't...*abide* this struggle against his self-imposed—and befitting—restraints.

He rolled the slowly shrinking cinnamon drop over his tongue, relishing the spicy flavour.

Since she'd entered his home and his life, Miss Smith's presence had him wanting things that he could not have, such as her body and her trust. Even should she be inclined to give them, he did not deserve them. For Leonard was not a man to be trusted.

NERVES RACED up and down Juliana's spine as she paced her small bedchamber.

Click-clack, click-clack... Heavens knew what Kitty thought they were doing, but she was along for the walk, and Juliana appreciated the silent support.

Despite her avowal to remain unmoved by Mr. Notley's presence, she had somehow let him in. It made her furious with herself that she'd gone against her promise. She'd known that if she allowed her heart to trust a man, he would find a way to break that trust. *And what happened, Juliana?*

"He searched for the carriage and used it to hurt me," she whispered, steeling her nerves.

Kitty bounced and licked at Juliana's fingers. Despite her ill feelings, she grinned down at the dog.

There was no hope for it. Her time in Woodhaven Hall was at an end. Soon, Mr. Notley's men would find the wreckage and would learn the truth of what she'd done. Her only option now was to continue on to London, despite the ill weather, and hope that the journey did not prove too treacherous...or that her brother did not happen upon her first.

She would use her pitiful funds to change horses along the journey and garner rooms at nearby inns when the sky grew too dark to continue. It would only be a few days—five at most—before she reached the comforts of London.

Her fingertips tingled, and she shook out her hands. The hour notwithstanding, she'd requested that a horse be saddled —no matter the snow, she could not countenance being alone in a carriage at the moment—but there was one task that she must carry out before she left—*if* her quarry was amenable, of course.

What she required was something to protect her from her brother's machinations, something that would provide a more permanent barrier between her and the viscount's attentions, so that she might pursue the future that she desired.

While the feelings that Mr. Notley had inspired in Juliana had undeniably been irksome, she could not deny the attraction she felt toward him. He was indeed the ideal man to divest her of the one thing holding back her life: her maidenhead.

JULIANA LIFTED her fist to knock, but lowered it again.

Goodness, Juliana. Just knock.

Nerves danced along her hips and thighs, feeling both hot and cold at once. Frowning, she rubbed a hand over her waist and discreetly shook out her legs beneath her skirts. Kitty reacted animatedly, leaping back as though Juliana intended to play. She suppressed a sigh. *I can do this.*

She raised her fist to knock, and the door swung swiftly inward. A gasp caught in her throat, the scent of cinnamon and coconut so strong it made her knees wobble.

"Miss Smith is here to see you, sir," Percy announced, stepping aside.

Kitty barked, and Juliana started as the greyhound bounded gaily into the room.

Mr. Notley jolted upright, spinning to face her as he stood from his position by a comfortable hearth. "Miss Smith!"

Kitty and her brother, Boots, raced toward one another, leaping together in circles before darting past Percy and Juliana out of the room.

Very aware of Mr. Notley's expectant gaze, heat spread over Juliana's chest and neck. And suddenly the words refused to come. The man wore a green silk robe that showed enough of his neck and chest to make her stomach swoop and the skin behind her knees tingle. *Oh, Lord, am I breathing?*

Her gaze slid down to his bared feet and hair-smattered calves. It was such an unintentionally intimate thing that made her stomach give a self-doubting dive.

With a quavering breath, she stepped diffidently into the room, wishing that she could draw upon whatever nerve it was that had prompted her to concoct this ludicrous plan from the start.

Percy gave her a short bow and slipped past her into the hall, closing the door with an ominous *click.*

There was a muffled crunching sound before Mr. Notley

swallowed back the remainder of the drink in his hand, placing the emptied snifter upon a nearby table, and cleared his throat. "What brings you to my rooms, Miss Smith?"

In for a penny. After coming to the conclusion that, should her plans go awry, this could very well be her only way to withdraw from Jasper's arranged marriage for her, Juliana had come up with several propositions for Mr. Notley. All of which had fled her mind the moment she'd seen him in his robe.

Instead, she strode with a purpose that she didn't feel through his spacious master bedchamber—past the grand bed, table, tallboy, and wardrobe.

"Wha—"

With an internal pang of nervous anxiety, Juliana gripped the man's surprisingly broad shoulders, lifted up on her toes, and broke off his words with a kiss. Sparks seemed to tingle over her skin at the contact, and her heart hiccoughed.

His lips were soft but unmoving, his chest rising and falling with each quick breath. They stood thusly for several long, hard heartbeats. He didn't turn her away, but neither did he show signs of wishing to move further.

Perhaps he would refuse her. She ought to step away, leave him to his evening in solitude. He'd shown interest in an intimacy between them when they'd been in the conservatory, but perhaps that was just a moment of weakness. Mayhap she was not the type of woman that Mr. Notley enjoyed, or perhaps his interest had waned. He *had* fled the conservatory rather swiftly, and she hadn't even begun this encounter with conversation. She'd simply thrown herself at his person. Shame and embarrassment crashed through her. *What have I done?*

Her stomach in knots, she began to pull away. But he followed. His lips were no longer unmoving but seemingly stilted with hesitation and uncertainty. All at once, her feelings of humiliation fled, and her purpose and desire returned.

Juliana glided her palms over the thick muscles of his shoulders toward his neck, where she explored his hair, still damp from his bath. She traced her fingertips along the muscles of his neck and combed her fingers through his wavy blond locks. *So soft.*

His breath came in short, rapid bursts now, and Juliana exulted at his response. All prior thoughts fled from her mind as she focused solely on satisfying her need to touch him.

Heat radiated from his body, urging Juliana flush against him. While she'd enjoyed their kisses earlier, she wanted what came next, and didn't waste her time in getting it.

Opening her mouth to him, she let him inside while simultaneously rubbing her sensitive flesh against the hardness tenting his robe. A low growl emanated from his chest, harsh and predatory, and entirely thrilling. Lord above, the sharp zest of cinnamon coated her tongue and filled her nostrils. *Delicious.*

She fisted one hand in his hair and explored his back with the other. There was scarcely a scrap of fabric separating them, and that knowledge enflamed her even further.

His tongue flicked hers, probing and exploring as his hands pulled the pins from her hair. Heat spiralled through her body and curled her toes, her heart fluttering wildly and her skin coming alive with taut need.

Her kiss became urgent as her passions consumed her. She rocked her mound against the hard ridge of his erection in an effort to assuage the riot of feeling inside her.

A STRING of obscenities raced through Leo's mind. The woman had him wound so tightly he very much feared that he'd come off against the fabric of his robe. Hell, it had been too damned long. And her hair—*good God, her fucking hair!*

—was dark and full, and it bounced in ringlets over her shoulders as it was released.

At the moment, he didn't care a whit for his prior reservations; Miss Smith was in his arms, and she was glorious.

Seeking that rush of pleasure again, he slid one hand into her hair. The other squeezed her full, round arse and pressed her against his needy cock. He groaned again, rational thought all but entirely gone as he broke off their frantic kisses to trail his lips down her petal-soft neck.

The scent of flowers and lust radiated from her, driving him mad with want.

He rocked her hips against him once more, ready to lift her skirts and have her right where they bloody stood.

"Please," she moaned.

If his eyes had been open, they would have rolled backward at the arousing plea. Please, indeed. He wanted it, as well. But he had to ask. "Please what?" His voice was hoarse, scarcely recognizable to his own ears.

"Please," she repeated.

Please take me? Please touch me? His thoughts circled as he pulled her earlobe into his mouth for a gentle bite.

"I cannot return home like this," she burst out.

Leo paused, his eyes snapping open and his heart giving a hard punch to his ribs. Surely he'd misunderstood her. "I beg your pardon?"

Mimicking his previous motion, she trailed her lips along the side of his neck, and a shiver danced down his spine.

"If I return home with my maidenhead intact, I will be—" She broke off, scattering kisses along his collarbone. "Please, take me. I am yours to have."

As though a blast of frigid air from beyond his windows engulfed him, his ardour instantly cooled. With no small amount of regret, Leonard released Miss Smith and stepped backward, putting space between them.

God damn it, she looked appealing. Her lips and breasts were swollen with desire, her chest and neck flushed, and her hair fallen in dark curls about her shoulders. She looked entirely delectable, like a woman recently tupped. And entirely wrong for him.

Her brow crinkled. "Whatever is the matter?" she asked, breathless. "Will you not—"

Leo shook his head. "I cannot be the man to help you."

Percy's impertinent words rang through his mind. *"Fucking can sometimes just be fucking..."* But Percy was wrong. Leonard had been that man once, but he wouldn't be again, could not be careless about a woman and her future.

"But surely you don't mean that," she protested, her chest growing slightly pink.

"Indeed, I do, Miss Smith." He cleared his throat against the tight dryness there. "I cannot countenance your being injured by my actions. And I certainly cannot risk having someone angry with what I've done come back here to cause harm to my staff or to Lizzy. There is too much at stake, and I am unwilling to overlook the risks. I cannot—*will not*—be that man again."

She pulled her lips between her teeth and met his gaze. Her green-and-grey eyes glittered in the firelight and—God damn it to hell—watered around the edges. Shite, he'd hurt her. His gut clenched.

With a nod, Miss Smith turned and quietly slipped from the room.

An alarming discomfort prickled across his chest and down his arms to his fingertips. It was a distasteful sensation that he believed was linked to guilt...regret. He'd felt those emotions often enough, however, and this was different. Damnation, the woman had him in knots. He didn't care for it.

He retrieved his snifter and strode to the tantalus, pouring himself another three fingers of whisky.

FRIGID SNOWFLAKES BIT at Juliana's cheeks, neck, and ears as she rode hell-bent toward London. Well, she amended, it was the direction that the stable hand had told her was south, and she'd put her faith in his knowledge of the land.

Mr. Notley's stolen greatcoat flapped weakly in the wind, but it was warmer than she could have hoped. In the Wood-haven Hall stables, she'd *borrowed* some twine, and she'd knotted it about her waist, tightening the voluminous material around her. She'd also slipped a penknife into one of her deep pockets—along with the pistol and the rest of her meagre belongings—prepared to defend herself should it be required. Again.

Her heart gave a tight squeeze, and she urged her borrowed mount faster.

Mr. Notley's words echoed in her mind, like the ghost of mockery: *"There is too much at stake, and I am unwilling to overlook the risks. I cannot—will not—be that man again."*

What man was he unwilling to be? What had happened in his past? And why couldn't she dispel the feeling that she'd made a grave mistake? *You've been rejected, Juliana, precisely as Father predicted.*

The road wavered before her, and she blinked back the tears. It would not do to weep now. She would continue her journey to London, meet with Grace Huntsbury, and change the course of her life for the better.

She sniffled, her lungs burning with the cold. If her brother interfered, she would simply have to lie about her maidenhead to withdraw from the marriage that he'd arranged. And hope beyond hope that he would permit her to live in London as she desired.

Indeed, it was for the best that she'd left Woodhaven Hall. In fact, she ought to have left before she'd blundered, and certainly before Mr. Notley had grown curious about her carriage accident. The man had rejected her, and that was that.

It was her fault, of course; she'd approached the man and opened herself to rejection. *Never again*. She repeated the litany in her mind. Never would she allow herself to become so vulnerable, so open to hurt. She could only trust herself not to cause pain; being alone was best for both her sanity and her heart.

CHAPTER 10

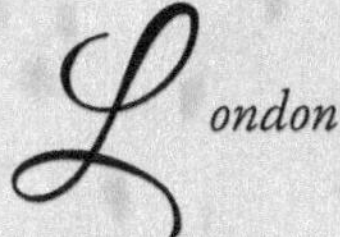

*L*ondon

THE SEA of pastel gowns and black tailcoats eddied and ebbed as Maria observed. Her thoughts wandered as she curiously watched a woman adjust her bodice when she thought no one was looking. It was both freeing and insulting that the wallflowers were invisible to the *haut ton*. At this ball, there were four of them; two of which were Maria and Heather.

She missed Juliana, who usually claimed a spot with them along the wall. Her friend, however, had recklessly fled home in the middle of a snowstorm.

London was veritably glacial during the little season, and most of society had remained at their estates. There were but a few of them in town with the Lords while parliament was in session.

"Look lively, Maria." Heather discreetly nudged Maria's arm with her glove-clad elbow. "Your man is here."

Maria's stomach swirled uneasily and her throat tightened

as she followed her friend's gaze. There he was at the entrance of the ballroom, scanning the small crowd with his half-blue, half-brown gaze. His black hair was dishevelled, and the bottom half of his handsome, angular face was shadowed with a hint of black beard.

"Lord above, why is he here?" Maria pinched her cheeks and fanned herself inelegantly with one hand. "He ought to be back in the country."

"For pity's sake, Maria, piece yourself together." Heather frowned at her.

She slanted a glare at her friend. "I ordinarily can, Heather. I was merely unprepared to encounter him this evening."

Heather clucked her tongue. "He's likely here in search of Juliana, not to continue his benign flirtation with you. Now, you recall that she requested our silence on the matter, yes?"

"Yes, of course," Maria replied hastily.

"Very good. He has spotted us. Don't fall in love with the bastard. I'll fetch us some refreshments."

"Don't leave me!" Maria hissed to Heather's retreating form.

Another quadrille began, and the dancers took their places. Her eyes widened, and a flash of panic ignited in her, the force of it wobbling her legs. Maria focused on the sea of colours in an attempt to distract her nerves.

"Miss Roberts," Jasper Sinclair, the Duke of Derby murmured, bowing shortly in front of her.

"Your Grace." Maria dipped in a curtsey, then clasped her trembling fingers behind her back.

He will ask you to dance, Maria, she reminded herself, *and you must refuse him. You must* always *refuse him.*

"Might I claim a waltz with you?" he asked brusquely.

Maria fought a frown. She realized that it had become a game for him—to request a dance even though he knew she would refuse him. But he could at least pretend to wish for one. "No thank you, Your Grace. I have an engagement elsewhere."

She moved to step past him, but he stopped her with a touch to her forearm and a helpless, pleading glance.

"Please, Miss Roberts. I *must* speak with you. Might you take a turn about the gardens with me?"

"Are you mad?" she asked in an incredulous whisper. "It is snowing, and I am in a gown that reveals all too much of my skin. I would freeze to death in a trice!"

His gaze lowered to her décolletage, and heat prickled behind her ears.

"Quite right," he murmured. He glanced around the ballroom and grunted in frustration. "What I have to say I don't wish to have overheard, but it seems as though everywhere I go, there are eyes following me."

Heather had been correct. The Duke was here to discuss Juliana's flight. Had she left *him* a letter, as well? If not, then Maria supposed it was not her place to interfere with their familial quarrel.

"I should think that you would be accustomed to that by now, Your Grace. Most of the young ladies in attendance are unmarried and looking for a husband; I'm certain that they're all waiting for you to seek a place on their dance card."

"But not you." His gaze was sharp on hers.

She clasped her hands tighter behind her back, steadily meeting his gaze and silently admiring his uniquely coloured eyes and the shape of his handsome features. "No, Your Grace. Not me."

The Duke shook his head. "I cannot elaborate on it now, Miss Roberts, so I beg that you and Miss Morgan would call on me at your earliest convenience. But the truth of it is... Juliana is in danger."

NOTTINGHAM

"*LEO!*" Percy shouted, jolting Leo awake.

He swung his arms wide, spilling the whisky that had been in his snifter, and sat up on the chaise with a curse. He groaned and slid a palm over the back of his neck, where an ache began. "Bloody hell, Percy. What time is it?"

"It is nearly half past the hour of midnight."

Leo stood with another groan as pain stretched through his back and hips. "You did well by waking me then, Percy. I'd much prefer to sleep in the comfort of my own bed."

"Leo, I have news."

For the first time since he'd awoken, Leo looked at his friend. Nothing was out of place, but there was an air of worry...of *fear* about him that had Leo instantly on alert. "What is it?"

"Before darkness fell this evening, the men I'd sent out found the carriage."

Hope threatened, but fear tamped it down. There was more, and from the way Percy's eyelids were angled upward, he was worried about it.

"It was not where Miss Smith had inferred that it would be," Percy continued. "In fact, the entire wreckage looked as though it had been dragged deeper into the forest and set afire."

Leo's eyebrows darted upward. "Set on— *What*?"

"There were several points at which a fire had been started, but the snow must have put it out a short time after. There was no sign of the horses or coachman, and even with the scorched wood and snow only brushed aside, the men could discern what appeared to be blood splattered upon the equipage. The men also said that—" He coughed to clear his throat, his complexion growing ashen. "The men said that the interior of the carriage was severely damaged, as though someone had attempted to claw themselves out. There were dents and—"

"I have the image, thank you, Percy," Leo said gruffly, his heart in his throat. Christ, he'd known that Miss Smith had been trapped within the carriage, but he'd not pictured it so vividly.

His man turned his grim gaze toward the door then back to Leo. "We very much fear that someone did this apurpose. That her accident was not, in fact, an accident. We know not the particulars, but it is possible to run someone off the road intentionally."

Leo gripped his hair and tugged against his scalp before he scratched at his beard, a curse on his lips.

"It gets worse, I'm afraid."

Leo growled. "How can it possibly get worse?"

"Someone is searching for Miss Smith."

All at once, Leo's lungs stopped working, and his heart all but halted its beating. "What do you mean?" he asked tightly.

"I had two men go into the local towns and make inquiries, as I'd wondered where Miss Smith's last stop might have been."

"*Get on with it, Percy!*"

"A man had been searching for a woman matching Miss Smith's description. I can assure you, Miss Smith's eyes are unlike many others in Nottingham; if she had been seen, that man would have her direction."

"Shite, goddamn, and bugger it all, Percy!" Leo rounded the chaise and began to pace. "We'd better warn her before she leaves at first light." He raked his hands through his hair. "I will, however, attempt to convince her to remain here, where I can keep her safe until we know more about what in the bloody hell is going on."

"But—"

"I admit, Percy, I'm in a quandary," Leo continued, not allowing his man to get a word in. But, damn it all, he needed to think this through! "What if there is some nefarious reason why Miss Smith has men after her? What if she deserves to be brought before a magistrate and sentenced for some wrongdoing?" The words rebelled on his tongue. "That does not feel right at all. But whatever it is, the woman deserves the chance to explain herself before I seek an audience with a man of the law." He stopped pacing and turned to face Percy. "I'd better wake her. We have much to discuss."

"But that is what I have been trying to say, Leo. Miss Smith rode out on a mount not two hours ago."

JULIANA'S TEETH chattered as a gust of wind and snow rushed past her. The horse had slowed to a walk, and the gentle rocking was making it rather difficult to keep her eyes open. She was relying entirely on her mount's sight, for she could scarcely see beyond the swirl of flakes to the milky blue layer of snow that coated the landscape. The moon, obscured as it was by thick clouds, was of little help.

Surely there must be an inn along this road somewhere—as long as they *were* on a road and not a field on someone's estate. She'd been riding for what felt like hours, and her mount wouldn't make it much farther without a proper rest. Come to it, neither would she. At the inn, she would take a room and resume her journey at first light.

She yawned, and blinked away the sleep and falling snow.

The horse snorted, and she patted its withers with a murmur of appreciation and encouragement.

The rhythm of her mount's steps abruptly altered, and through her sleep-addled mind, she heard an audible *click*. Juliana's neck prickled painfully, jolting her instantly alert.

Her mount spooked, side-stepping in agitation as she slowed to a stop.

A man strode out of the shadows toward her, his boots crunching ominously. The closer he came, the faster Juliana's pulse raced.

It's a ghost, her mind whispered, and for an impossible moment, she believed it. No, he wasn't a ghost. But how was he alive? How had he found her? And how could he possibly have known where she would be riding?

His face came into view, beautiful and horrifyingly evil all at once. His hair was as blond as the sun glinting off of wheat, his eyes as green as the trees, and his body finely sculpted. Even with the shroud of darkness around them, he veritably shone with his beauty.

"Stand and deliver, Juliana," he drawled, a pistol pointed at her and his eyes glinting with malevolence.

"But you're dead," she whispered hoarsely. "I killed you."

CHAPTER 11

Not for the first time in his life, Leonard was grateful for his long hair and beard. The wind that night was damned cold, but he had at least a modicum of protection against it.

The horses were tired, but he had hope. The prints that they followed were obscured by freshly fallen snow, but he could ascertain at a glance that Miss Smith hadn't run her horse for long, likely in an effort to conserve its energy. If he, Percy, and the carriage that followed behind kept their pace steady, they would intercept Miss Smith within the quarter hour. He hoped.

The skin behind his knees felt simultaneously numb and achy with nerves, and he had the urge to shake out his legs. His body was a confounding frenzy of emotions: confusion, frustration, concern, dread... In the past two hours, he'd had sensations of which he'd not known himself capable.

Percy rode his gelding alongside Leo and shouted over the audible crunch of horses' hooves in the snow and the carriage's rattling, "Her mount began dragging its hooves. And these marks are fresh."

Leo followed the man's gaze to the grooves in the snow, and nodded. "Not too much farther, surely."

THE HANDSOME, vile man laughed, his white teeth flashing behind the fog of his breath. "You shot me, certainly, but as you see I am still alive."

Despite the cold, a sweat borne of pure terror began to tickle between Juliana's breasts. She swallowed past the lump of fear in her throat. "How do you know my name?" The words came out slurred, her lips numb from the frigid air.

"Now is not the time to spoil that fun little surprise," he drawled. "Time to dismount."

She did as he demanded, her thoughts whirling. If she dismounted to her left, she would have a brief moment out of the man's view to retrieve her penknife. *Left, it is.* Landing hard, her legs wobbled, and she slipped her hand discreetly into the pocket of her stolen greatcoat.

Boots crunched. Her shoulders tensed.

The man rounded the horse, and her stomach twisted. He approached swiftly and without hesitation. His hand reached out and caught her face, squeezing hard. Juliana whimpered as his fingertips dug punishingly into her cheeks and jaw and pulled her to him.

"I have little patience," he growled. "I'm going to follow through with orders this time. I've been searching for you for far too long."

"Orders?" she asked with difficulty around his hold on her.

"*Orders.* I daresay you'll learn all about it."

She whimpered again as his grip tightened further. Her grasp stiffened on her penknife, still hidden in her pocket, and she pulled it open with her thumbnail. "How did you know where to find me this evening?"

His smile was brilliant. "A fortuitous phenomenon, as it happens."

Juliana glared at him, and he laughed, releasing her face to slap her mount's rear. The poor beast whinnied and turned, running back the way she had come.

Now! her conscience screamed.

The man's guard was down, his face turned to watch the horse run off. Wheeling her arm in an arc, she came down with the penknife in her fist, jabbing it into the muscle between his shoulder and neck.

He screamed, his mask of fury and agony swinging back toward her. His blood splattered her hand, her front, and disturbingly marred the snow around them.

In a haze of distraught panic, Juliana kneed the man squarely between the legs. *Bang!* His pistol discharged harmlessly into the fallen snow, the sound ricocheting in her ears. Juliana gave a startled yelp as the man cried out gutturally. A string of blasphemes and threats fell from his lips as he dropped to his knees. And Juliana ran.

"There, Leo!" Percy breathed.

Leo's gaze sharpened on the road ahead as a mare galloped fearfully toward them. His heart lurched.

"She has no rider," he noted grimly. "Have her put on a lead behind the carriage, and we will—"

Crack!

"Shite," Leo breathed, his stomach swooping with fear. "Was that—"

"A pistol being fired." Percy manoeuvred his mount toward the mare, leaned out, and caught her reins.

His skin taut with tension, Leonard urged his tired mount faster. He knew not what to expect, merely that he ought to help. Miss Smith was in danger, and he couldn't have her death on his conscience, as well.

They had been running for mere moments when a tall figure clad in black raced toward him. The figure squeaked and attempted to veer into the forest.

"Miss Smith!" he hollered.

She halted, turning to squint up at him in the darkness.

Leo dismounted and strode toward her. "I've a carriage. Come, I will walk you there."

"No," she said breathlessly. "He's coming! We must hurry before he regains his footing."

"*Who* is coming, Miss Smith?"

She shook her head, still gasping for air. "I do not know him."

"*Juliana*!" a voice roared, drawing out each syllable.

"Please," Miss Smith breathed. "*Run.*"

With a tight nod, Leo gripped his gelding's reins and ran on foot. If they'd had a longer distance, he might have considered riding with her on the horse, but not only were they only steps ahead of his party, but his mount was already exhausted and likely wouldn't survive the return trip if it had to bear the weight of two riders.

They didn't have to travel far before Percy came into view, followed by the team of bays and their coachman bundled in blankets.

"We must make haste," Leo muttered tersely to the men.

He led Miss Smith toward the carriage, the lanterns swinging eerily in the darkness as it rolled to a halt. A footman scurried to lower the steps and swung the door open.

"Thank you," Leo murmured before turning to face Miss Smith. "After y— Hellfire and damnation! You're injured!"

"Oh." She touched the tips of her fingers to her cheek. "Are bruises forming already?"

"*Bruises*? Damnation, I meant the *blood*." Crimson glistened in the lantern light, splattered across her forehead and hair, with a few stray droplets on her ear and jaw, and more, he suspected, on the front of his coat that she wore. He was aghast and furious that someone would do her harm.

Her lips twisted in distaste as she slid past him into the carriage. "It isn't mine."

That news both pleased and terrified him. Whose blood was it?

"Percy," Leo growled, turning toward his man. "Take a footman on my gelding and ride ahead. See what you can find."

His friend grinned. "Of course."

Leonard followed Miss Smith with another nod to the footman. The door closed, and they were safely ensconced in a bit of warmth. A low-burning lantern was lit within and foot warmers, woollen blankets, and furs had been stacked upon the seats in preparation for their journey. Miss Smith was already gathering material around herself and her foot warmer when he'd finished settling in across from her.

He rapped on the ceiling with his fist.

The woman's glittering gaze met his, and her lips curved in a small smile. "Thank you, Mr. Notley."

Despite the unanswered questions and the threat from whoever was still out there, Leo felt a moment of sheer, unbridled relief that Miss Smith was sitting before him, whole and alive.

"I do not accept your resignation," he grunted, pulling a set of furs over his lap.

Her lips thinned and her mouth opened, but it swiftly snapped shut. They jolted into motion, and her complexion paled.

"Miss Smith?"

She began to pant, and Leo cursed. The woman looked like she was going to faint.

"Juliana?"

Her eyes glazed.

Damnation. He set aside the curtains of one window and slid the sash, then repeated the same on the second window. The openings weren't large, but he hoped that the wind brought in enough fresh air for her not to feel trapped.

He reached across the carriage and clasped her chilled hand. "Juliana?" He waited, but she showed no signs of calming. "Oh, hell."

Crossing the carriage, he joined her on the front-facing seat and encircled her in his arms, both in an attempt to offer comfort and to quell the feeling of helplessness inside him. "We have men following on horseback, and my coachman is driving at a steady, manageable pace," he assured her. "You are safe with me."

THE COLD SWEAT that had formed between Juliana's breasts and along her spine increased as images from the carriage accident flashed horrifyingly through her mind. In her ears echoed the *crack* of wood...the horses' screams. Even the harsh, metallic scent of blood filled her nose.

Her face and hands began to tingle, and her gut churned as they slid in a turn.

Mr. Notley's arms tightened around her, offering security that she greedily soaked in.

Hold fast, Juliana, she reminded herself. This was not the same driver, and it was not the same night. Mr. Notley's men surrounded them, ready to lend their aid if anything unfortunate should occur. They were as safe as they could be while in flight from a madman whom she'd just injured.

A waft of cinnamon and coconut reached her senses before a set of soft, searching lips brushed across hers. It was scarcely a touch, but Juliana chased it, tilting her chin toward him.

Keeping just out of her reach, Mr. Notley peered into her eyes with an assessing gaze. "Are you well, Miss Smith?"

She cleared her throat and nodded once. "I believe so. Thank you."

Blinking, she registered where she was, and felt a moment of embarrassment.

His arms tightened around her once more, and his blue gaze warmed in the dim lantern light, his hair moving with the icy wind. "I will hold you for as long as you desire."

Juliana's stomach swooped. The man was an enigma. He'd not wished to engage in lovemaking with her earlier that evening, but he was willing to offer affection and emotional aid now. Not only was the *offer* of comfort from a man somewhat jarring, but receiving it was unprecedented. She was nonplussed.

"Th-thank you," she whispered, shivering as wind whirled past them through the opened windows. Gooseflesh spread over her skin, and her teeth chattered slightly.

His arms tightened again in response.

"If you are..." Mr. Notley cleared his throat. "...uncomfortable, Miss Smith, I would be glad to return to my—"

"No," she spoke over him, pressing deeper into the warmth of his neck. *Stay with me*, she wanted to say. *I need your comfort*. But she couldn't. It felt too deep, too *naked*, and certainly too dangerous to speak the words aloud.

She ought to have pushed him away, preserved her pride, and requested that he return to his seat. But she couldn't.

Despite her mortification over having her overture rejected, she relished the comfort and heat of his embrace.

The space between them grew silent, but heavy with what was left unsaid. Snow crunched beneath the carriage's wheels and the horses' hooves, the equipage rattling and sliding uneasily over every lump and through every turn. Shivers skittered down her spine, and Juliana pulled the collar of Mr. Notley's coat up further around her ears.

She knew what was to come. He was giving her time, now, to withstand the journey and to recover from her encounter. But Mr. Notley would demand honesty from her soon. She was just glad that she had but a few more moments before the truth came crashing down around her.

CHAPTER 12

ow-hanging branches tugged at his greatcoat as he manoeuvred his pilfered mount through the copse of trees. How had the bitch bested him once again? And with a goddamned penknife! While the bleeding had been staunched, his shoulder and arm had long since grown sticky from blood, and he itched to wash it off.

A low growl rumbled from his chest, puffing into swiftly dissipating steam as he turned his mount out of the trees and into an inn's courtyard. The upper floors were dark, but welcoming lights flickered in the foyer and taproom. His teeth chattered as a shiver wracked his frame, and he uttered a dark curse.

The bitch Juliana Sinclair was going to meet her end by his blade, by God, if it was the last sodding thing he did. He knew where she was, and he would be back. But first, he must see to bandaging his wound.

WITH EACH STEP toward Mr. Notley's library, Juliana felt closer to doom. After this, he would know what she'd done, and he would condemn her for it. But the sickening drop of her stomach and hard thump of her heart made no sense; she'd been about to leave his estate and his employment anyway—why should his ill opinion of her bother her so?

Kitty licked at her hand, pulling Juliana from her thoughts, and she scratched absently behind the dog's ear. At the very least, the dogs wouldn't think badly of her, and that ought to be something. She suppressed a cringe. Oh, but it wasn't! As absurd as it was, she craved Mr. Notley's approval.

Warm firelight flickered against the walls of bookshelves and cast haunting figures of dark, outstretched furniture along the large brocade rug. Their footfalls were scarcely audible over the rush of Juliana's pulse in her ears.

"Please have a seat," Mr. Notley said quietly, rounding his desk.

Juliana felt suddenly bereft without his large greatcoat enveloping her, having given it to a footman at the front entry. The hem of her skirts was damp and chilled, and her hair was half-fallen about her shoulders, windswept, and splattered in a man's blood. It left her feeling...*sullied*.

With trembling legs, she lowered herself into the proffered chair.

"Will you tell me, now, what happened?" he asked softly. "From the beginning, if you please."

Strangely, her stomach sank. She'd known that it was coming, and yet somehow, her heart had gone and hoped that it wouldn't. Would that he could simply pull her into his embrace once more, and they could—

"Miss Smith?" His voice was slightly more insistent this time.

She sighed internally, clasping her trembling fingers together in her lap and shifting her seat on the padded leather chair. No matter his rescue of her, and the closeness they'd experienced in the carriage, she had been foolishly hopeful and her heart had been broken. She must remember that. Whatever amity had been between them was over. She would still leave the estate, and Mr. Notley must keep his staff and his niece safely distanced from the dangers that evidently followed Juliana.

At that moment, she had no reason to withhold the truth from him. The blackguard—whoever he was—was not dead, and, in fact, posed a very real threat. She could, however, deny Mr. Notley the truth of her identity. What purpose would that serve but to cause scandal should the staff speak of it? And, if she were honest, she desperately wanted to hold on to something just for herself, for this man had manoeuvred his way too deeply under her skin, and it rankled.

"From the beginning," she repeated his words, swallowing past the thickness in her throat. "My father died just above one year ago, and the moment the requisite mourning period concluded, my brother arranged a marriage for me to a man who is aged nine-and-fifty, and would be sixty before the date of our wedding in the coming spring."

Mr. Notley cursed under his breath.

She continued on at a steady pace. "As you might presume, I refused the match. But my brother was unyielding. He took exception to my protestations and moved the wedding to the day of Saint Valentine.

"I felt...betrayed." Juliana licked at her lips and prepared the half-truth in her mind before the words tumbled from her lips. "I confided in an acquaintance of mine, and she offered shelter if I could but find my way to London. In a desperate attempt at freedom, I gathered as many of my family's jewels as I could carry and my years' worth of saved banknotes, and I fled after darkness fell."

A knuckle cracked as Mr. Notley clenched his fist on his chair's armrest.

"I rode to a nearby pub and requested a carriage and conveyance to London." Juliana's chin quivered, and her eyes prickled as memories flooded her. "The rest you already know, until..."

"Your escape from the carriage," he urged.

"Yes." She licked at her suddenly dry lips and wiped at her cheeks with the pads of her cool fingers. "I'd waited so long, tried so desperately to climb out. I cannot tell you the pure relief that I felt when the carriage door had finally been pried open. I'd thought that the man was there to help, that he was my rescuer. But—" she hesitated and licked at her lips once more—"h-he didn't wish to help."

Mr. Notley growled another curse.

"When he grabbed my h-hair, I realized..." Juliana cleared her throat, forcing herself to continue. "I'd thought that he was a highwayman, but he showed no interest in my pockets, despite my offering. He seemed r-rather more intent on hurting me."

Juliana wiped again at her damp cheeks and pulled her lips between her teeth, afraid of telling him what came next. Nerves fluttered hatefully in her abdomen, and she pressed a hand over them. He was silent and tense across from her, waiting to hear the rest.

"The man lost his footing while attempting to pull me from the equipage and, taking advantage of his distraction in a moment of terror, I slid my hand into my pocket to feel for the pistol that I'd secreted there. I'd not e-even known if it was loaded, but the thought—the *hope*—had been there.

"When the handsome blackguard..." She fidgeted, scraping her nails together and knotting her fingers in her lap as the hateful memory flooded her mind: the man throwing her to the ground, the fiery hatred in his gaze as he wrapped his hands around her throat... "When I was out, I used my brother's pistol to shoot the man that freed me."

Heat spread across Juliana's chest and bloomed hotter behind her eyes. It was a guilt that she'd carried with her since that night in the woods, and while she now ought to feel somehow unburdened, she felt the weight of it all the more.

The air between them was thick as more tears fell from her eyes.

"I'm sorry for your pain," he said softly, his voice scarcely audible over the crackle in the hearth.

"I'd thought that I'd killed him," she wept through a thick throat.

"But you didn't," he said with renewed force.

"I shot a man, Mr. Notley!" Her voice echoed off the shelves of books before the fire gave a crackle. "And this evening, I stabbed him in the shoulder with a pilfered penknife. No matter what he did to me, I'd never thought myself capable of such violence." She blinked away the last of her tears and swiped at her chin with the palm of her hand.

The muscle in Mr. Notley's jaw jumped. "You defended yourself, Miss Smith. No one would fault you. And, to be candid, he deserves a hell of a lot worse for what he did to you."

Her heart gave a sharp twist and her hands tightened in her lap. In another lifetime, perhaps, the man's actions would have incurred the wrath of the males in her family, encouraging them to call him out or have him put on trial. But *this* was her life, and her identity was currently *Miss Smith*, an unimportant governess in a difficult and dangerous circumstance. She was entirely at fault.

Mr. Notley leaned forward, placing his elbows on his desk. "It is vitally important, Miss Smith, that you tell me who he is. What is his name?"

Meeting his gaze, she grimaced apologetically. "I do not know his name...but somehow he knows mine."

Leo cursed under his breath. "What does he look like? Would you recognize him if you saw him again?"

"I would, yes. He is really rather...beautiful."

Something dangerous flashed in Mr. Notley's gaze as his lips raised in a silent snarl. "Describe him," he grunted, withdrawing a pen, ink, and a piece of parchment.

Juliana cleared her throat and waited until Mr. Notley's pen was poised and waiting before she spoke. "His hair is blond and wavy, his jaw strong, nose patrician. He has high cheekbones, and his eyes are a deep green." *And full of malice.*

She was silent for a moment before she shivered and described her encounter, starting with her pilfering a penknife from Mr. Notley's home and concluding with the kick to the bastard's cods and her flight down the road.

"He said that he was following through on orders?" Mr. Notley mused darkly, looking up from his notes to pin her with his sharp stare.

She nodded.

His lips tightened into a grim line. "Christ, Miss Smith, that cannot mean anything good." He leaned back in his chair and scratched at his beard. "I will speak with my man on the matter and come up with some solution. In the meantime, you are not to leave Woodhaven Hall."

Tick, tick, tick, tick...

The mantel clock in the library was excessively loud to Leo's ears, and he scowled at the irksome thing. He sat in his wingback chair by the warm embers of the fire, a brandy in his hand and worry in his heart.

He understood, now, why Miss Smith had come to him

wishing for a perfunctory deflowering, and while he might disagree with her methods, she deserved to have some semblance of control over her future. In fact, the notion was not quite so repellent now as it had been then...

The events leading up to that moment had felt forced from Miss Smith, pulling with them memories and emotions that she'd clearly wished to suppress. Damn, but they had stirred an unfamiliar primal need in him to find and destroy those who had wronged her. It was ludicrous. And hell if she wasn't in far deeper trouble than he'd thought. Not only was the villain searching for her, but she'd enraged him by foiling his original plan, whatever it had been.

Any intention to send her on her way was entirely dependent on what Percy and the other footman had found on the road. Was Miss Smith in further danger? Were he and Lizzy at risk having her at Woodhaven Hall? Or had the man been wounded enough to be captured?

Leo's skin tingled with nerves that he attempted to quell. There was no sense in worrying about something that had not yet occurred. He would await Percy's return to the estate before he considered their next course of action.

Tick, tick, tick...

"Damned clock," Leo grumbled before swallowing another gulp of brandy.

Boots' head lifted from his curled position at Leo's feet, and let out a soft bark.

"Leo?"

Leonard snapped his gaze to the library's opened doorway to see Percy striding in.

"What news?" Leo asked, standing.

Percy stopped an arm's length away, frustration and exhaustion marring his features. "We found a good spray of blood—even beneath the freshly fallen snow—and a large set of footprints retreating into the forest. We attempted to pursue the man, but he must have staunched the flow of his blood and found a way to cover his tracks, because the trail ran cold not far into the forest's entrance. We continued to search, but found nothing."

"Damn." Leo's gut sank. He wanted to know what was motivating the man to pursue Miss Smith.

There was also the trouble of this damned *feeling* he got when he was around her, as though his years of celibacy and punishment abruptly didn't matter, that he could lose himself in her stunning gaze and consuming floral scent.

He blinked away the bloody ill-timed thought and returned his focus to the matter at hand. "Thank you, Percy. Your work is appreciated, though I'm afraid that our night is not yet over."

Percy lifted one dark eyebrow in question.

As swiftly as possible, Leo launched into a retelling of Miss Smith's circumstance, concluding with her attacker's "orders." "It is entirely possible that the man saw my family's crest emblazoned on the carriage," he continued. "We must prepare for his imminent arrival."

LONDON

MARIA POISED her fist to knock at the town home's main entrance, but hesitated, twin prickles of fear tingling behind her ears.

"Don't lose your nerve, now, Maria," Heather said impatiently. "You woke me up before dawn to come down here; we'd dashed well better seek an audience with the man."

Chest flaring with heat, and the underside of her breasts feeling uncomfortably moist, Maria rapped on the door.

It was all of thirty seconds before a footman swung it open. "Oh!" He gave them a delayed bow. "So sorry. We'd not been expectin' visitors afore nine o' the clock. Do you have cards?"

"We've no calling cards," Maria said, suppressing a shiver. "But please inform His Grace that Miss Roberts and Miss Morgan are here."

The young man nodded, and closed the door on them.

Heather sniffed. "Well, I say."

A laugh bubbled up through Maria's chest.

They waited for several long moments before the door swung open once more and the harried-looking footman stepped aside. Juliana had not encountered this footman before. Mayhap he was new—he was certainly nervous enough to be.

"My apologies for making you wait. Please come in; His Grace will see you in his study."

Maria's knees wobbled as she crossed the threshold, following the young footman through the halls to an opened doorway.

"Miss Roberts and Miss Morgan," he announced to the room before retreating on nervously shifting feet.

Maria and Heather entered the candlelit study. She ought to have curtseyed, but the thought rebelled when it came to Jasper. She took a deep breath and smiled thinly, instead. The space was warm and smelled like parchment, leather, sandalwood shaving soap, and man.

The Duke of Derby stood behind his desk, his coat and cravat removed, his shirtsleeves rolled up to his elbows, and his collar opened far enough to reveal a smattering of dark chest hairs. Heaven above, he was like a man destined for the gallows, his hair mussed and his eyes creased with worry and hopelessness. He was also entirely lovely. Drat the man.

"Thank you for coming to speak with me. Please, have a seat." He gestured to the two chairs facing his desk.

Leather creaked as they all sat. Warm firelight flickered, and Maria took him in.

In the many years Maria had known Juliana and Jasper, she'd known them to have a comfortable, familial relationship. He had been charming and vain, but he'd never acted the villain. Never would Maria have thought him capable of attempting to marry Juliana off to a man of nearly sixty. *What* had Jasper been thinking?

Now, gone was the conceited and confident heir to a duke-dom, and here sat a duke with wild, finger-combed dark hair, shadowed circles around his too-beautiful eyes, and an air of panic. This man was changed, and it boded ill, indeed.

"You mentioned that this was a matter of some importance?" Heather prompted.

"I did, yes. Juliana is in danger." The duke retrieved some pieces of parchment from a drawer and slid them across the desk. "I've been receiving threats."

Both Maria and Heather scanned the letters, and Maria's heart and hope dropped further with each word.

"My God," she breathed. "But who would do this? Who would make such threats against you?"

"And what could possibly be their goal?" Heather added.

The duke grunted. "I imagine that they want me dead, and for Juliana to watch, just as the letters explain." He rubbed a hand over his face. "I do not know from whom they came, and the letters warn that if I bring this to the attention of the magistrate, more people will suffer."

Heather's nose scrunched. "Has this person—"

"Or *persons*," Maria cut across.

"Indeed." Heather simultaneously nodded and waved her fingers in the air. "Have they mentioned *why* they wish for your death, et cetera?"

"No." The duke's lips thinned, his skin growing increasingly ashen.

"What of the *how*?" Maria asked softly. "In one of these letters, did they describe how or where they intended to carry out these threats? Perhaps if we knew more about their intentions…" Her voice faded away at the duke's grim features.

"Again, no," he said gruffly. "And I'm afraid that I've only made things worse in my attempts to protect Juliana."

Maria sat forward. "I see. What can we do to help?"

CHAPTER 13

$\mathcal{N}$*ottingham*

Flames lapped and flickered around the logs in the hearth in Juliana's diminutive bedchamber. She stared unblinkingly at them, perched with legs tucked beneath her on the foot of her bed, waiting for her hair to dry while absently stroking Kitty's head perched on her thigh.

Morning sunlight shone through the room's small window, and she wished that it would leave her be for another few hours. Despite being dressed, Juliana was not ready for the day to begin; she'd scarcely gotten two hours of sleep on the carriage ride back to Woodhaven Hall, and not a wink since.

Unsettling memories whirled through her for the remainder of the night and all through her bath. Fear weighed heavily on her heart. Despite the pertinent truths having been revealed, the urge to flee Woodhaven Hall was overwhelming. But how could she do so while ensuring she not be stopped by that brigand once more? It was almost as though she required an armada of men surrounding her through the countryside for her to reach London safely.

A soft knock sounded at her door, and Kitty lifted her head, ears pointed toward the noise. Juliana called entrance, swiping her damp palms over her black frock.

"I'm sorry, sweeting, I'm not quite prepared for our lessons tod—" She turned, and scrambled from the bed, biting her lip. "Oh, it's you."

Mr. Notley closed her bedchamber door and strode silently forward. Heaven above, why would he close the door? Such things were simply not done. The room felt smaller with him inside, as though even his presence filled the air around them.

His gaze, the colour of the sky, roamed her face and lingered on her hair. The mass of thick, dark curls were beyond her control, hanging in damp ringlets around her head. She'd always been a little discomfited by others' curious stares when it came to her hair, most likely stemming from her father's constant criticism. *"Your unruly hair is coming out of its pins,"* the duke would say. *"You look like a tuppenny whore, and it disgusts me. Fix it."*

Despite years of attempting to steel her emotions, her heart gave a sharp pang before she could protect herself against it.

Well, her father was dead, and could take his opinions to the devil. Juliana was a grown woman and rather liked her hair. Because she looked nothing like her father, she imagined that it favoured her mother, which offered some comfort.

Mr. Notley cleared his throat and raked his fingers absently through his shoulder-length blond hair. "My apologies for intruding upon your morning, Miss Smith." His gaze slipped past her to the rumpled bedclothes and the greyhound still curled at the foot.

She gave him a small smile, the movement tugging achingly at the still-forming bruises on her cheeks. "It is quite all right, Mr. Notley."

The scent of cinnamon and coconut came off of him in hot waves, making her heart drum with desire as he neared. *Terrible timing, Juliana*, her mind rebuked. *He does not wish for intimacies between us. And neither should you, for pity's sake.* She ought to have been grateful that he'd refused her. Indeed. Grateful.

He slowly approached, and despite her inner quarrel, her pulse rushed and her knees wobbled. What she wouldn't give for another of his kisses. Her gaze slipped to his full, slightly pinkened lips, and she gripped the bed's post to steady herself. Heaven forbid she melt with want in front of a man who did not want her.

Inappropriate—and decidedly *unwanted*—desire notwithstanding, the man had entered her bedchamber without invitation and closed the door behind himself. What could he possibly want with her? "Is there something with which I might help you?"

He cleared his throat. "Preparations have begun to remove Elizabeth to a familial hunting box with several armed footmen and a small contingent of maids."

Guilt surged up her throat, and she swallowed it down, licking at her dry lips. "I must apologize, Mr. Notley, for this danger to you, Lizzy, and your staff. I'd not inten—"

"I know you did not."

Juliana nodded, her stomach knotting and her heart aching. "It is a wise course of action, I daresay. I shall miss her."

He eyed her shrewdly. "I imagine the feeling will be mutual."

The blue of his eyes seemed to darken as he considered her. "I must, however, ask you about the man's motive."

Juliana blinked, her brows turning downward as she frowned.

"Not the cad from last evening, but the person from whom the orders came," he clarified. "Do you know of any reason that someone would wish to cause you harm?"

A weary sigh escaped Juliana. She shook her head, her gaze locked on the lapel of Mr. Notley's coat.

In Derby, she'd lived a sheltered life, to be sure; the weather was often cold, but she had formed acquaintances with all of the local farmers and their daughters. During the season, Juliana attended every London social event, including Astley's, Covent Garden, and the opera. But being a wallflower, she had very rarely been noticed by anyone that wasn't a fortune hunter, and *those* men had been given a set-down directly they approached. She genuinely couldn't imagine it being any one of them. "I've wondered that, myself, and truthfully, I do not know. I've always gotten on with everyone at home. I believe I would need to ask that question to my brother, Jasper."

"I imagine that you would." His lips thinned, causing his whiskers to move like a wave. "I also wonder if it has something to do with *you*."

"What do you mean?" she asked breathlessly.

"What if the reason is both simpler and more *sinister*? You say that you'd visited a pub in order to find conveyance. When you arrived there, did you tell anyone your name? Mayhap the man intended as your betrothed found his way to you. Or perhaps your brother sent someone in search of you, and the man deviated from the plan."

Her heart dropped into her stomach. It had been the local pub in Derby, under her brother's thumb, of course. Everyone knew her name. Mr. Notley didn't know the truth of her identity—he couldn't know—but he could certainly be correct in his guesses.

She covered her face and groaned, her stomach twisting. "I didn't think—"

"Whoever he is, he must have followed you from that pub."

"That might explain the man who attacked me, but not his orders. And not *why*." Juliana chewed on her lips as she thought. She couldn't say it aloud, but it did, in fact, make sense if it was a pair of men who had planned some sort of abduction with the intent to ransom her to Jasper. Or, perhaps, someone owed Jasper money and was trying to exchange her for their debts. There were several plausible options, and each had everything to do with who she was. A shiver ran down her spine. Lord, but she was in a muddle.

Her bedchamber fell silent once more, the air heavy with unsaid words.

Juliana brushed her fingers nervously over the carved bedpost, her gaze locked on Mr. Notley's as their silence stretched.

The fire crackled, and the sound of their soft breathing filled the room. She was very aware of his presence, as though his body called to hers.

She wanted to kiss him, to apologize for thinking to use him, but also to shout and ask him why he'd spurned her. It left her feeling hot and cold, the fire both too warm and not warm enough. The odd combination of emotions made her flustered and confused, and all of it made her chest feel heavy.

His jaw tightened. "Despite our lack of understanding regarding this villain's motivation, we must continue on with our plans. Once Lizzy has safely vacated Woodhaven Hall, we will arrange for your transportation."

Pulling her bottom lip between her teeth, Juliana nodded. As much as she appreciated the protection he offered, more guilt suffused her. This was entirely her fault. She'd brought danger to his door that threatened not only him and his staff, but his loveable niece, as well. She'd not wished for any of this. "Thank you," she said, her voice just above a whisper.

"Before we disembark, I must say this: I'll not bring you to London. The answers and protection that you require will come from your brother, and as such, I will return you to him."

LEO EYED MISS Smith carefully as she stilled, her complexion growing slightly ashen and putting her fresh bruises in stark relief. The pulse at her throat began to flutter, and he had the absurd urge to flick his tongue over it.

Kitty yawned, stretched, and lowered herself to the floor, walking languidly to the corner of the room where she curled upon a folded blanket.

"I understand," Miss Smith replied softly.

"Good." He wished on her behalf that she could avoid her brother's matchmaking machinations, but Leo was not a member of her family, and she was certainly safer where she belonged. It made sense that she would be worried about the repercussions of her decisions—no matter how just—but it was, again, something from which he could not protect her.

He shifted his stance. "And where might your home be?"

A soft pink tongue darted out from between her bite-swollen lips as her gaze slid sideways. Leo's gut tightened. He'd wanted to kiss her the moment he'd entered her bedchamber, to tangle his fingers in her mass of curls and feel her body mould perfectly against his as he tasted her sweet mouth and explored the source of her scent. It was madness, naturally. He'd done his best to force his lascivious urges away, but the sight of that tongue sent his blood to thrumming once more.

"Derby," she said, cutting through his momentary haze of lust. "I-It's a small estate."

Fisting his hands, he dug his nails into his palms in an attempt to quiet the surge of hot blood through his veins. "Derby." He nodded once. "Very good."

The colour seemed to come back to Miss Smith's cheeks, and she sighed long and slow.

The urge to trail his fingertips along the soft skin of her jaw as he took those lips with his nearly overwhelmed him. Miss Smith was a dangerous woman, indeed. Years of well-deserved celibacy had passed without such intense temptation, but with *her*...his body simply fought valiantly to be with her. And he was tired of the internal battle.

"What are your intentions once you return home?" he asked, detesting the note of hopefulness that had crept into his voice. He was *not* hopeful, damn it. "Will you submit to your brother's desire to marr—"

"No," Miss Smith interjected. "While the task might require subterfuge, I have no intention of giving up my fight."

Another long moment of silence passed between them, in which Leo admired her. Not only did her beauty continue to stun him, but he found himself appreciating her intelligence, generosity of spirit, and, truthfully, countless other aspects of her personality even more.

Leo swallowed noisily, stepping closer, and admitted, "I felt something last night that I haven't felt in a very long time."

Gooseflesh spread across Miss Smith's skin, and her throat moved convulsively.

"Fear," he elaborated. "I've felt concern, worry, and trepidation, naturally, but *fear* I haven't felt in quite some time. I feel—" He broke off and traced the backs of his fingers along her eyebrows. "I feel a compulsion to help you. To be with you."

She searched his gaze, indecipherable emotions swimming in her eyes, and an answering jolt of awareness sizzled through him. A small smile tugged at the corner of her mouth, and

Leo's skin quivered with the need to embrace her. *Christ*, if he did not leave at that moment, he was liable to do something that he would very much regret.

You depraved sod, his inner thoughts chided. *You want to stay, you want* her, *and you would take every delight in having her, self-promises be damned.*

The heat of shame warmed him just beneath the collar. If he did not take his leave, he would take his refusal back, and take her. He would pull her into his arms and tumble her back upon the bed, and bury himself in—

Christ, he needed to stop this. He opened his mouth, but before he could speak, Miss Smith closed the space between them. Her breasts pushed against his chest, the soft globes brushing against him as she lifted on her toes, making his cods draw up tight, and pressed a kiss to his lips.

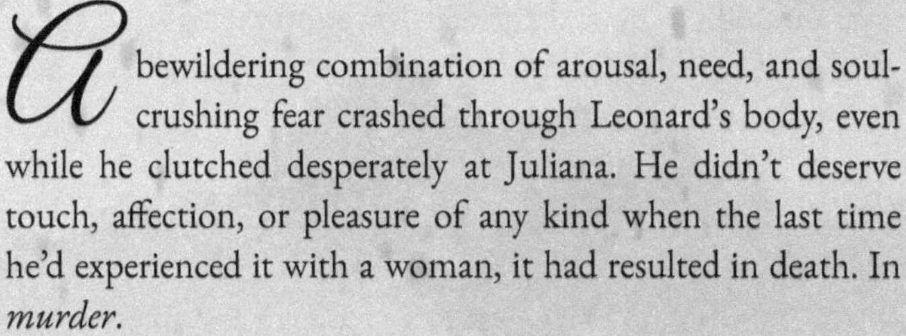

CHAPTER 14

A bewildering combination of arousal, need, and soul-crushing fear crashed through Leonard's body, even while he clutched desperately at Juliana. He didn't deserve touch, affection, or pleasure of any kind when the last time he'd experienced it with a woman, it had resulted in death. In *murder*.

What would happen once he'd been intimate with—had fucking despoiled—Juliana?

A helpless groan rumbled through his chest as his tongue found hers, hot and searching, and a jolt of pleasure travelled straight through his gut and filled his cock. Despite himself, his arms reflexively tightened around her, a groan vibrating through him.

"I want you," she whispered against his lips.

Whomp. Guilt hit him square in the chest, and another groan was pulled from his throat.

"And I you," he admitted, glancing ruefully down at the thick bulge of his erection pressing against his trousers. And he did want her. With an unparalleled need. But there was so much holding him back. "I desire you, Juliana. But I need to know that you—"

She shook her head. "I apologize for what I said. Losing my maidenhead was a goal only insofar as it might liberate me from my brother's control and from the marriage in which he thought to confine me. I oughtn't have intended to use you, and for that I am sincerely sorry."

Sliding her palms up his chest and over his shoulders, she hummed in what he understood to be appreciation. "You must know how attractive I find you. I am aware of the potential risks of intimacies between us, and I do not care. I want you to take me."

Eyes sliding closed, Leo swallowed back his moan. That *take me* undid him, and entirely unwound the tightly knotted hold on his reserve, his fear and guilt slipping easily to the back of his mind.

THE MUSCLE in Mr. Notley's jaw bulged, and for one humiliating moment, Juliana feared that she would be turned away. Again. She had very nearly begged the man to bed her, for heaven's sake!

With a deep growl, his eyes opened, heavy-lidded and hungry, before he took her lips once more.

Relief and desire flared to life within her, sparking in her lips and igniting a flame that swept over her skin. A shiver wracked her, and she gripped him closer. She wanted to feel all of him, and whether or not she would find her behaviour embarrassing later, Juliana would take this for precisely what it was: a moment of honesty. A moment when their passions told truths that their mouths dared not.

Finally, she gave in to her needs and ran her hands through his long, tawny hair. *Soft, thick, and stirring.* Their lips and tongues explored and tantalized while she touched to her heart's content. But soon, it wasn't enough. Her body clamoured for more: more lips, more touching, and more *friction*.

Mr. Notley's hands fisted in the fabric at her hips, and he rutted once against her. *Zing*. The jolt of pleasure that flared in her core threatened to buckle her knees. *Patience officially gone*.

Her fingers trembling with nervousness and desire, Juliana gripped Mr. Notley's lapels and shoved his coat back over his shoulders. Then, everything changed. His kiss grew deeper and increasingly fervent. His hands roamed her body, removing her fichu, loosening ties, undoing hooks, and fumbling with her stays.

Left in nothing but her chemise, she embraced the thrill that skittered up her spine. Nervousness and anticipation swarmed her. She'd never felt so...exposed. Mr. Notley's intense, admiring gaze made her feel rather powerful.

The smooth buttons of Mr. Notley's waistcoat slid easily through Juliana's fingers, the fabric slackening on his muscular frame as she unfastened each one. His coat, waistcoat, and cravat followed her stays to the floor, and for a moment, Juliana simply took him in. Half of his body was in shadow, but even so, she could see the duskiness of his nipples through the light lawn of his shirt. She took in the sight of his exposed neck, admiring the muscles that bunched just under his skin and the angles of his collarbones above a dusting of blond chest hair.

Her pulse throbbed, the rush of it in her ears drowning out the crackle of the fire and their harsh breathing as she tugged his shirt from his trousers.

Skin. So hot. His abdominal muscles quivered beneath her palms, and his breath hitched.

"Christ, your hands feel good on me," he said, his voice low and rough.

"You feel good to touch," she admitted in response.

With an impatient grunt, Mr. Notley released her to pull his shirt over his head. "Then, please, touch more of me."

A harsh gasp was pulled from her lungs, her gaze fixed on the large black markings on his shoulder and down his bicep. "What is that?" she asked.

The muscles in his jaw jumped, and his throat worked. "A tattoo."

Juliana blinked, reaching tentative fingers out to trace the dark curves. He flinched as she made contact, but did not pull away. His discomfort was evident in the sudden dulling of his irises and stiffness of his muscles, but Juliana desperately wanted to see more.

The design was intricate, in the shape of some sort of reptilia, with swirls, stripes, triangles, and spots, all pointed and at jutting angles to one another. She traced her fingertips along the artwork, and his muscles bunched.

"It's beautiful," she breathed. *And brings to mind the sort of designs one might see on a pirate.* She could not voice the thought, however, most particularly in the face of his discomfort. Lord, but it made him all the more intriguing.

He was silent for a moment as he observed her. "You would be the first to believe so."

Her brows creased, meeting his pained gaze, her palm resting fully over his warm, marked skin. "Surely not."

Something shifted in his eyes, and in a flurry of movement, they were both rendered nude. Shock rippled through her as she received a glorious view of his thick erection jutting from a nest of dark blond curls.

He was rather larger than she'd thought a man might be: thick and long, with blue veins wrapping around its girth and leading to the ruddy head. She wanted to ask if he was certain they'd fit together, but the heat in his gaze as he looked at her told her that he had no qualms about size.

"You're..." he said gutturally. "Hell, Juliana, you're the most beautiful woman I've ever seen."

She smiled brilliantly at him, and in one smooth motion, he wrapped his arms about her, lifted her, and carefully deposited her on the narrow bed. Leaning on one elbow, he covered her body with his, taking her lips in another hungry, earth-quaking kiss.

Their movements were driven by need: swift and urgent. As overwhelming as it was, their joining felt instinctual, *right*. The tingle of cinnamon lingered on her tongue as they kissed, and her lungs filled with the unique scent of him.

Using his free hand, Mr. Notley sought and found the most sensitive parts of her body: the curve of her elbow, the underside of her breasts, the dip of her waist... And he teased them with lazy swirls of his fingers before following the movement with his lips and tongue. It was entirely delicious torment. Her skin puckered with gooseflesh, and her muscles quivered in delight.

Juliana moaned helplessly, her body on fire and writhing beneath him. He ground his erection deliciously against her thigh, and she slid her palms down his back, desperate to feel him beneath her fingers.

He found one of her nipples with his tongue before sucking it into his mouth, and Juliana arched off the bed with a gasp as tingles of sensation travelled over her skin. "Mr. Notley!" She clutched at his hair to draw him closer.

"Leo," he returned, turning his attention to her other breast. "Your nipples are the colour of chocolate milk—and taste just as sweet."

Another gasp escaped her as he gently scraped his teeth over the sensitive nub. Her abdomen twitched at the contact, and molten heat gathered at her centre. She wanted more, wanted *everything* that he was willing to give.

With a grunt, he nudged her legs apart with his hand and she willingly moved, opening herself to him.

"Please," Juliana breathed.

"Please, what?" Leo's hand slid up one thigh, causing a wave of gooseflesh to spread over her skin once more.

"Touch me."

He groaned, taking her lips with his as he thrust against her thigh once more.

To her great relief, Leo complied, dipping his fingers between her labium and caressing her there. Her body came alive with sensations, all tingling awareness and pooling desire that sped her pulse.

Helpless in the face of her lust and unable to stop herself, she thrust her hips in time with his ministrations, silently urging him on. Leo delved deeper inside with one finger, and Juliana moaned into his mouth. She clutched at his back, pulling him closer, needing more and *more* of his delicious caresses.

He stroked her in earnest now, finding the little nub that sent sparks of pleasure bursting through her. Dipping and swirling and dipping and swirling, he continued for what felt like so long, but not nearly long enough.

"Leo," she breathed, arching into his touch.

"*Christ*," he muttered before swallowing her cries with his mouth.

She panted against his lips, tangling her tongue with his while she squirmed against him. One of her hands found its way to his hair, and fisted. The movement of her hips became helplessly frantic, following the delicious touch of his hand, reaching, *needing* to find release. She needed more, *more...*

Her back arched, tense against his chest as she gripped him, and like a torrent of fireworks shot into the sky, she burst. Light fanned out behind her eyelids, and her skin burned with pleasure, pulse after pleasurable pulse rushing through her.

With a murmured curse, Leo settled himself between her legs, and Juliana sighed, a bright, euphoric sensation making her feel languid while her pulse throbbed throughout her body.

Leo poised himself on his elbows above her, his chest and stomach teasing her with the gentle rasp of his hair.

His gaze sought hers, searching. Sensing his unspoken question, Juliana wrapped her legs about his smooth, muscular hips and cupped his head in her hands. "I want you, Leo."

He groaned, and his eyes slid briefly closed. "I'm afraid that I will not last long, love."

Not knowing how to respond, she tilted her hips upward and brushed her lips across his. Leo's eyes glazed, and in that moment, she felt a probe at her entrance. He began the slow slide inside, stretching her. The intrusion was tight, to be sure, but not at all unpleasing.

A vein on Leo's forehead bulged, and his skin grew red with strain. His hair, fallen over his shoulders, was lit from behind by the fire in the hearth, lending him a crown of orange light.

"My God, you're—" He broke off with a grunt as he thrust himself deeper.

He moved heart-wrenchingly slow, but was soon fully sheathed.

The woman that her brother had engaged to teach Juliana the duties of a wife in the marital bed had mentioned that upon her first coupling, the tear to her maidenhead would possibly hurt, or, at the very least, sting. But what Juliana felt was *full* and stretched—certainly not pain.

"Are you...well?" Leo asked breathlessly, a sweat breaking out across his forehead.

"Yes." Juliana nodded, clasping his shoulders, the muscles bunched with his exertions. "It is merely tight."

He groaned again. "*So tight.* I'm sorry, I can't—"

Pumping his hips, he moved inside her, creating a delicious friction that caused the heat to return to her core. She gasped and lifted her hips, eager for more.

Leo moved faster, thrusting erratically until that coil of tension within her built to an unbearable level. But the explosion was frustratingly just out of her reach. So between his thrusts, she slid one hand between them to swirl her fingers around the pleasure nub. Then, that delicious firework burst inside her again, hard and wonderful, wrenching a cry from deep within her chest.

Withdrawing his member to the tip, Leo swiftly penetrated her once more, and jerked. His teeth bared and the vein on his forehead pulsed in time with his member as he spilled his seed inside her.

At length, he withdrew completely and slumped to the bed beside her, his breath coming heavily. Juliana's eyes drooped, and her energy waned. She turned to her side and put a hand to his chest, feeling the pounding of his heart. *I did that.* A smile tugged at the corner of her mouth at that exhilarating pride. Her gaze slid to his flagging member. He really was an impressive man.

"If you keep looking at me like that, Juliana, I'll have no choice but to take you again," Leo murmured, a grin on his lips.

His arm came about her shoulders and pulled her to his chest, and she settled comfortably against his warmth.

They lay thusly for several long moments, and Juliana closed her eyes. She'd done it, then. She'd given away her virtue in order to escape her brother and an arranged marriage. *Well,* she amended, she hadn't made love to Leo for that reason, but the result was the same. And so was the question of her future.

What did she do, now? And how would Jasper handle the news of her loss of virtue?

He would be furious, she was certain, and would very likely find a dreadful punishment for her. Juliana would take banishment, service in a convent, or whatever her brother might decide, over a forced marriage to a man doddering on the edge of the grave. She would *not* give her body to a man that had paid for her. No matter how it was described, it felt far too much like whoring for Juliana's comfort. With luck, however, she would not have to. She would meet with Grace Huntsbury and accept her position in London before her brother was the wiser for it.

Jasper would hold no power over Juliana any longer.

Leo's embrace tightened, and an abrupt wave of panic crashed through her. He made her feel warm and cared for, and an alarming bubble of joy—*elation*—threatened to fight its way free of the box that she'd carefully constructed around her heart. It was precisely what she'd *not* wanted to have happen. She could hardly make love to Leo and not feel some sort of connection, but she was not meant to develop deep feelings for the man.

Her lips thinned, and she clenched her jaw as her emotions warred within her. People were inherently untrustworthy and would break her heart at the first opportunity. Leo was no different. She'd best remember that.

CHAPTER 15

A sense of warmth and calm settled around Leo as he held Juliana in his arms. The soft ringlets of Juliana's hair, the arch of her eyebrows—and the glorious feel of her pale, naked breasts pressed to his ribs—gave him an undeserved yet overwhelming feeling of pride. He was not a vain man, but just the memory of the way her eyes had widened with appreciation when she'd first gazed upon him had his pulse speeding again.

He'd come quickly, just as he'd thought he would, but he'd given Juliana pleasure, as well, and that was a damned fine thing. The utter euphoria of those minutes would be branded on his memory for years to come. *It must*, his conscience reminded him, for he could not allow it to happen again.

Minutes passed, and with the glow of release gradually fading, the lightness in his chest was slowly replaced by a growing sense of apprehension. Juliana had not given him any assurances that she would withhold his identity from her brother when she revealed the truth of her virginity, but that was not what frightened him. Leo *welcomed* exposure. He deserved whatever punishment the man deemed fitting, most particularly because Leo knew that despite his assertions, it would prove a struggle to keep his hands—and eager cock— from Juliana during their six-hour journey to Derby.

But then there was Elizabeth. Any ill attention to *his* name would transfer to her.

Damnation, he'd cocked it up. He'd sworn to himself, and to his brother's memory, that he would remain celibate, and yet here he was with a freshly deflowered woman in his arms and the scent of sex permeating the air.

Juliana stroked her fingers along his side, blissfully unaware of the silent battle being waged in his heart. Goose- flesh spread over his skin, and he bit back a curse. Damn, but he'd missed being touched thusly.

The door burst open. "Good morning, Miss Smith. I understand that we're preparing your belongings for travel this —" The maid broke off on a gasp.

Leo smoothly pulled the coverlet over the both of them as the startled maid covered her eyes with one hand.

"My apologies, your lordship!" the maid squeaked before awkwardly clomping from the room.

A sense of doom settled on his heart. That was it. Leo's gut churned, and he closed his eyes on a silent oath. The fragile glass house that he'd built around himself would come crashing down.

Juliana's pulse drummed in her ears. *Lordship?* Her gaze darted to Leo's face. His eyes were closed, his face a mask of resignation. A dreadful prickling began in her hands and at the back of her neck, and her skin felt cold all over.

How could he be a lord? In all the time that she'd spent in his home, she'd not heard a single servant address him by his title or as "my lord"—until that very moment. Not even little

Lizzy had mentioned a title in their tea service rehearsals. And if he *did* have a title, why in heaven's name would he not use it?

"Juliana, I—"

"Who are you?" she asked in a hoarse whisper, pulling away from his embrace and putting as much distance between them as the bed would allow.

His eyes squeezed tightly shut, his complexion growing pallid. "I am the Marquess of Livingston."

Juliana frowned. "The Marquess of—" Her eyebrows snapped up, and in an effort to sit up, she lost her balance and toppled from the bed.

Thunk. Pain shot through her hip and back, and she hissed a breath.

The Marquess cursed and scrambled from the bed, offering his hands to her. "Juliana! Are you all right?"

No, she was not. His was the name that had darkened newspapers, gossip columns—even fashion magazines, for pity's sake!—for nearly seven months. *The Murderous Marquess*, they'd named him, the label often accompanied by piratical vernacular, most likely in reference to his large tattoo. She did not know precisely what had occurred, but she knew that the true murderer had come forward and the Marquess had been acquitted only days before his scheduled hanging. Good heavens, and here he was!

Ignoring his proffered hands, she crawled to her chemise and slipped it over her head.

"Juliana," he said gutturally.

She sat upon the floor, her back against the bed and her knees drawn up to her chest, and wrapped her arms about her legs. Being furious with the man for withholding the truth of his identity would make her a hypocrite. Though truthfully, Juliana wasn't certain that was what she felt. Shock, certainly, bemusement, naturally...but also pain.

Covering her chest with one hand, she recognized the ache there. Yes, she was hurting. Due not, perhaps, to what he'd kept from her, but to the simple affirmation that she oughtn't trust anyone. And that she'd clearly begun to trust Leo.

Neither of them had been honest and, her feelings notwithstanding, she couldn't blame the man for withholding the truth of his title.

She blinked back into the moment and looked at him.

The floor grew too cold, so Juliana stood, her hands twisted in the thin fabric of her chemise. Her core throbbed twice, vividly reminding her of what she'd just done with this man. With Leo, the acquitted Murderous Marquess.

His hair was mussed and his skin pallid. He must know that she recognized his name—for surely all of England recognized it. It had only been two years since he was released, after all.

He cleared his throat and scratched at his short blond beard. "You know, then."

Unsure what to say, Juliana nodded.

Indeed, what *could* she say? Did he keep his title a secret only from her, or did he try to hide from it, himself? Very likely, the circumstance of his crude misnomer caused him heartache, and—oh, Lord! That must be Elizabeth's father: the brother that Leo had been accused of murdering. It would certainly explain the uncle and niece's strained relationship before Juliana had arrived.

She locked gazes with the man before swiftly turning away to retrieve her discarded stays and frock from the floor.

Whatever his reasons, and no matter her feelings of hurt, she must move forward. Certainly, she hadn't hoped that a romance might bloom from their acquaintance. She'd had no brief imaginings of her raising Elizabeth and keeping his home. Indeed not. Juliana had enjoyed a very satisfying tryst with the man and would not allow her feelings to be engaged any further on the matter.

For pity's sake, he still did not know her name. That nagging guilt bit at her once more, but she stifled her wince, tying the knot in her front-lacing stays and lifting her frock over her head. It was for the best that she had not shared her true name, for the maid's intrusion would have ruined her otherwise. Juliana cared naught for her own reputation, of course, but she did wish for her brother to make a happy union one day, his ill treatment of her notwithstanding. And her good friends, Maria and Heather, might incur the *haut ton*'s wrath merely by associating with Juliana. That, she could not abide.

She finished fastening her frock and became aware of Leo's movement behind her. He'd donned his trousers and was slipping a foot into one boot, his bared back rippling and bunching with his movements. It was entirely captivating.

"I-I..." She cleared her throat and licked at her suddenly dried lips. "I ought to bid Miss Elizabeth farewell."

He returned her gaze, his blue eyes dark with anguish. "Juliana, I—"

A hard knock sounded at the door, cutting off Leo's words. Before Juliana could call entrance, the door swung inward and Percy marched in.

"Miss Smi— Oh." His dark gaze darted from Juliana to Leo, then landed on the bed. His jaw jumped, and he closed the door before facing them both once more. "The estate has been compromised."

"What do you mean?" Juliana asked, nervousness buzzing suddenly in her abdomen.

The man's lips thinned. "Several of our horses have been lamed, three stable hands injured, and the carriages have been destroyed."

"Has the bastard been apprehended?" Leo came forward, his face tight with dread.

Percy shook his head once. "No. He continues to evade our men and has hidden himself somewhere on the property."

"*Elizabeth*," Juliana breathed.

"I will take Miss Elizabeth and armed footmen on the curricle and accompanying mounts," Percy added. "You both will have to ride."

WITH A SOFT *CLUNK*, the door closed behind them. Leonard caught Percy's narrowed eyes in the dim light of the corridor, and his guilt swelled.

"I know what you will say," Leo grumbled. "You believe that I ought to do right by her."

"I am not your conscience. And I believe I told you that sex mi—"

"*Tsst!* Percy, for Christ's sake, lower your voice," Leo hissed. He bit at his bottom lip as they strode to his bedchamber.

Percy's lips thinned. "Mayhap you ought to have locked the door."

"I hadn't entered her bedchamber with the thought of—" Leo growled. "Confound it, man, you know why I am no good for the woman."

Percy remained silent as they entered Leo's bedchamber and found his saddlebags. The silence between them as they hurriedly packed was almost worse than any recrimination.

Leo's guilt built, weighing on his soul and crushing the wind from his chest.

"I will take Miss Elizabeth north," Percy said into the silence.

"To the hunting box in Scotland?" Leo clarified.

Percy inclined his head.

"Very good. I will write to you once the danger has passed so that you might bring Lizzy home."

His friend gave a mock salute. "Good luck, sir."

LONDON

MARIA ROBERTS PACED her familial town house's parlour, awaiting a response to a summons. She'd already received a reply from Heather stating that she could not attend due to prior obligations with her cousins—the odious hate mongers who treated her like a servant. Now, Maria waited on the Duke of Derby.

When last they'd met, he'd told her that there was nothing she could do to help, aside from keeping him informed of any correspondence that she received from Juliana. Well, she'd not precisely kept to their bargain. Juliana hadn't written to her or to Heather since she'd told them of her intention to take a position in London, but it was Maria's habit to pore over the newspaper, and rather more so after Juliana's silence. And that morning, she'd noticed something abnormal.

The front door opened, and Maria hurried into the foyer. There he stood, extending his coat, hat, and gloves to her butler. Lord, but her breath was all but sucked from her body as she took him in. He moved with the grace and ease of a large, predatory cat; it made her wonder if his muscles would bunch and stretch beneath his skin as she'd seen on the animals at the menagerie.

He turned to face her, and she remembered her tongue. "Welcome to my home. Thank you for coming, Your Grace."

She dipped in a curtsey, and he offered her a shallow bow. "Please, join me in the parlour."

The butler lifted nary a brow at the exchange before continuing in his duties as Maria led the duke away.

The fire was built up in the parlour, lending the air a warmth that, at the moment, Maria found too stifling.

"Do have a seat." She gestured toward the sitting area. "The tea in the pot is fresh."

He ignored the offer. "What news have you?"

The shadow of his beard was slightly darker than it had been when she'd last seen him, and that small outward sign of his discomfiture and worry made apprehension prickle behind her ears and the underside of her breasts grow damp. She retrieved the newspaper from beside the tea service and made certain that it was folded to the correct page.

"Have you read the newspaper this morning, Your Grace?"

He lifted one shoulder. "I glanced at it over coffee. Does it say something about Juliana?"

"No, but—"

"Then you have nothing of import to say to me, Miss Roberts." He clicked his heels and nodded, then began toward the door.

Embers of anger lit in Maria's soul, and she scowled at the man's retreating back. "I've found that newspapers are a useful tool, Your Grace, in piecing together a story when ordinarily a story mightn't be uncovered. Separate occurrences mightn't appear to connect but, placed in the correct order and viewed from the correct perspective, a link is found." He halted but didn't turn, so she continued. "By dismissing my theory, you grant me your nonverbal permission to do with this information what I will. And I assure you, I shall be vocal and ruthless."

"Enough, curse you, woman." The duke turned, his thick, dark brows angled low and fierce over his glittering blue-and-brown eyes. "Do you make a habit of piecing stories together from newspapers, Miss Roberts?"

She shrugged one shoulder. "It is merely a hobby, Your Grace. I find the human condition fascinating, no matter how profane or unrefined we are as a species." She smiled humourlessly at him. "Now allow me to show you what I've found."

NOTTINGHAM

COLD WIND BIT at Juliana's cheeks as she listened to the footman's instructions, and she burrowed deeper into the lapels of another of Leo's coats that she'd borrowed.

"It must be packed just so," the footman said, tilting the pistol so that she might observe.

Juliana nodded. "Am I to carry these items on my person?"

"It would be prudent, ma'am."

"Thank you." She accepted the loaded pistol, sachets of powder and shot, and the odd ramming stick, and put them in the deep pockets of Leo's coat.

The gelding that was to be her mount nudged at her shoulder with his nose, and Juliana turned to offer him an affectionate pat. The saddlebag with her meagre belongings was already fastened to him, and even with the little added weight, she knew that their hard ride would be a struggle for the beastie.

"You oughtn't be in the open." Leo's gruff voice came from behind her, his footfalls crunching on the snow and gravel of the drive as he came near.

Juliana's stomach gave a flip at the sight of him. He wore the same clothing as when he'd left her bedchamber, but for his coat, now green, and his greatcoat flowing overtop of it. It somehow made the blue of his eyes brighter.

Sensing his urgency, Juliana heaved herself onto the gelding and settled herself in the saddle. He was right; knowing that the cad who had attacked her was on the property ought to have been enough for her to remain indoors while the footman gave her the demonstration. But she'd not thought...

"Keep close, Juliana," Leo called from his mount. His gaze held hers for several quick moments, but even in that short time, she saw hesitation, worry, and resignation flicker over his features.

She nodded, and opened her mouth to respond, but before a sound could escape, he'd urged his mount into a gallop. A pang of...longing?—Lord, she hoped not—went through her as she nudged her gelding after him.

The snow had stopped sometime in the night, but upon the road remained a thick, lumpy layer of blinding white. The sun shone through the clouds but provided very little warmth against the biting winter chill.

Juliana's pulse thrummed in her ears, fear keeping her close to Leo's mount. The horses huffed out their breaths, each exhalation puffing past.

Despite her knowledge that her attacker was injured, Juliana was exceedingly aware that he was in pursuit. The hair on the back of her neck remained on end, and the tingle of nerves that ricocheted through her body told her that he was not far behind. She simply did not know how to react. Would he detour through the forest and appear before them? Or would he be torturously patient and attack when they were forced to water and rest the horses? Not knowing was painful.

Hours passed in which there was no sign of a pursuer. The sky had once more grown dark, threatening additional snowfall.

A shiver travelled down Juliana's back, the force of it rattling her teeth. They'd run and walked their horses intermittently, resting only briefly throughout the day. The muscles along her spine and down each of her limbs trembled and ached. Her sex throbbed in time with her heart, each of her mount's movements causing an extra jolt of pain where she'd joined with Leo mere hours before. And her bottom... heavens, but each cheek had grown numb from pain.

Their mounts must fare just as ill. The poor beasties.

Leo turned slightly in his saddle, calling to her over his shoulder. "We must soon rest. Perhaps—" His eyes widened, and the blood drained swiftly from his face. "*Juliana!*"

Bang!

Even with that slight warning, Juliana was unprepared for her gelding's instant fear and the responding gallop of her own pulse. The poor horse's eyes grew wild as it matched the swifter pace of Leo's mount.

Bang!

Juliana screamed in both shock and fear as the ball flew past her.

Leo cursed long and loud. "Into the forest!"

Cold sweat tickled the space between her breasts, and her numb legs fought for purchase in the sidesaddle as she jostled with the gelding's movements. They were forced to slow their pace as they navigated the darkness between the trees. It afforded them some protection, but surely their pursuer would catch up.

Her stomach was knotted, and tingles of unease travelled down her gloved hands. Perhaps this was *her* chance. It was madness, of course, but her life of late had been madness, and dying now was not to be borne. She knew that Leo carried a blade, but that would not aid them in their current predicament.

Guiding her mount over a fallen tree with one hand on the

reins, Juliana reached into her pocket and withdrew the loaded pistol.

Branches cracked behind her, and she swung around, her stomach a raging storm of dread and her palms damp with sweat. He was too far away for her to get an accurate shot—not that she was particularly skilled with the weapon from the start—but she must make the attempt.

The twist of her body was awkward, but she put it from her mind as she lifted the pistol to aim. Her arm bounced with the gelding's movement, and she gritted her teeth in frustration. She could not reload the pistol while mounted, and she was unsure how many loaded pistols their pursuer had stashed upon his person. She *must* make this shot count.

Forcing her breath to slow, Juliana sighted down her arm at the upper half of the dark shape that followed them, and squeezed the trigger.

CHAPTER 16

*B**ang!* A high-pitched scream slammed Leonard in the chest. With a flash of terror riding him, he pulled on the reins and turned his mount around.

"Juliana," he breathed.

His throat closed as he saw her gelding stomping anxiously, the beast's nostrils flaring and his eyes wide with fear. And Juliana was nowhere to be seen.

Dropping to the forest's floor, Leo ran the few steps to her horse, his gaze darting beyond in search of their pursuer. But he was gone. *Or hiding.*

Juliana sat upon a pile of white snow, her face pained as Leo approached.

"Juliana," he whispered hoarsely, his throat still tight and his muscles tense as he took her in. "What happened? Where are you hurt?"

"Did I hit him?" Her voice was small and quavering. Teeth glinting in a flinch, she slipped her spent pistol into a coat pocket.

Leonard chanced a glance around them into the dark,

snow-blanketed forest. "I'm afraid I don't know the answer to that. Neither the bastard, nor his horse, are within my sight."

He returned his attention to Juliana, crouching at her side and sliding his hands over her head, neck, and shoulders. "Tell me if you hurt anywhere."

"I hurt everywhere," she said with a grimace. "But the snow and moss cushioned my fall. I will have bruises, to be sure, but I don't believe I have any broken bones."

Leo's lips thinned. "We must see you someplace warm. Come." He aided her slowly to her feet.

More than he cared to admit, Leonard wanted to keep Juliana in his arms, to ride with her safely in his embrace. But neither mount could withstand the weight of both of them after their long journey.

As carefully as he could, he returned her to her sidesaddle. Not knowing where she was injured made his insides knot, but in order to assess her, he must see her safely indoors. Lord knew where their pursuer had gone, but Leo couldn't take the risk of a surprise attack.

"Are you well enough to ride, Juliana?" he asked softly.

She nodded with a grimace. "I believe so, yes."

Her complexion was wan, and her lips tight. She was clearly suffering, but he could do nothing for her now, most particularly in their perilous environment. With only a slight hesitation—and a great desire to see her away from potential harm—Leo gave her knee a gentle squeeze and returned to his own gelding.

His attention divided between Juliana following along behind him and his suspicions of every shape or shadow that they passed, Leo walked his mount further into the darkness. At some point during their flight in the forest, night had fallen, though he didn't expect it was very late into the eve.

Gradually, the copse of trees grew less dense, until they

were riding in an open field. The wind grew steadily colder, and Leo's thighs and back burned with overuse.

He no longer knew in which direction the road lay; he only knew that he must find a safe dwelling. With every trot his mount took, Leo scanned their surroundings in search of light.

As the next hour wore on, the fear in his heart mingled sickeningly with the churning guilt in his gut. He'd used Juliana ill. The best that he could hope for would be to see her safely into her brother's protection, and bid her farewell. Lord knew that spending more time in the company of the Murderous Marquess was the very last thing that she needed, particularly when he evidently could not keep her safe. He'd failed abysmally.

They crested a hill, and Leo scanned the landscape, his sunken spirits already expecting the worst. But then, he spotted it.

"There!" he said, looking at Juliana over his shoulder as he gestured toward a grand estate in the distance.

She shook her head with a cringe of pain, her complexion growing increasingly ashen. "No. That is a home, Leo. Why d—"

"I'm certain they will offer help if we—"

"No," she said more firmly, her eyes wide and pleading. "We can return to the road and ride to the nearest inn. Surely there is one not far. I do not wish to importune this—"

"Juliana," Leonard said gravely. "You have been injured. Our horses require food, water, and rest, and we are both chilled to the bone. I will do whatever it takes to find you safely situated this evening." *And maybe then I will prove to us both that I can provide protection.*

Damn Leo and his gallantry, Juliana thought bitterly.

Her gaze slipped past him to the grand estate beyond. It was the very last place she wished to be. She wouldn't—*couldn't*—take Leo there.

Biting at her frigid bottom lip, Juliana thought quickly. If he insisted on this location, then perhaps she could control the circumstance. "The family's knowledge of our presence could put them in danger from our pursuer. It would be best if they maintained their innocence in truth if questioned." She bit once more at her bottom lip, hating that she was capitulating. "I would suggest that we conceal ourselves in the stables. In a building that large, I imagine that there are empty stalls and an abundance of sustenance and supplies."

As a matter of fact, she knew precisely where a bag of apples hung, delivered daily from the trees in the neighbouring estate's small conservatory. It would not be enough to fully satisfy their hunger, but they would not starve, and that would have to be enough.

She shifted tenderly on the saddle, her legs long since gone numb and her bottom and back screaming in pain.

Leo looked grim, his blond brows drawn down in a frown. "I do not care for—"

Juliana lunged for the proverbial kill. "Look at us, Leo. Do you truly believe that they will allow us admittance? I, a woman in dirty, rumpled, ill-fitting attire, and...*you*? How would you introduce yourself? You know full well that neither of us would inspire their pity. We would be fortunate if they did not summon the magistrate directly."

That stopped him, and Juliana hid a grimace at the harshness of what she'd done. *Falsehood after falsehood. For shame, Juliana*, her conscience whispered.

It was the first time that she'd mentioned the impact of his title since she'd learned of it that morning. It felt wrong to abuse his feelings in such a way.

"The stables," she prompted again.

His lips pursed, causing his beard to bunch. "Very well."

They walked their mounts down the gentle slope in silence. The estate was blissfully still, with only a few windows of flickering light in the main building.

Reaching the stables, they dismounted—or rather *attempted* to. Juliana's muscles had long since seized, which had her toppling to the snow-covered earth at her mount's feet with a hard *oof*. Leo moved stiffly to her side, silently helping her to her feet. Her body cried out in fresh waves of pain, but she managed to stand. The bitter movement was both awful and reviving.

Together, they snuck their horses in through the—wonderfully silent—rear doors. The scent of horseflesh, leather, and hay filled her senses, and Juliana nearly wept with homesickness.

"Here," she whispered, limping her way through the darkness to some unused stalls.

Fresh hay crunched beneath them, and despite her gelding's exhaustion, he gave an excited shake of his head.

Once they'd situated their geldings in stalls next to one another, Leo began to unfasten one saddle. "I will brush them down," he whispered. "Do you think that you could find food and water for them?"

Of course she could. Juliana nodded and left him with the horses.

The walk to the buckets, feed, and water trough was a familiar one, even in the nearly pitch darkness and with her throbbing ankle slowing her progress. Out of habit, her gaze lifted to the fifth stall on her right, and a curious nose poked through the opened upper half of the door. *Mona*. The grey nose was swiftly followed by a white, speckled face and an excited whinny. The girl would probably know Juliana's silhouette and scent anywhere.

Her stomach jumped, and she limped to Mona's stall. "There, girl," she whispered, giving the mare a rub on her neck. "I've missed you, as well, but we mustn't alert the stable hands."

Mona nudged Juliana's back with her chin, pulling her against the door and forcing her head against the mare's neck. Juliana held back the hiss and groan of pain that threatened to escape. She wrapped her arms around her friend, enjoying the familiar scent.

They stood thusly for several long moments before she was forced to bribe Mona with an apple so that she might leave her to complete her task. Juliana's body ached something fierce as she silently busied herself retrieving buckets and filling them with what she required. All the while, her mind drifted back to her new problem.

How was she to be rid of Leo, now? Leo thought that he was meant to return her to Jasper, but how was Juliana to convince him to leave her without revealing her identity?

As odd as it was, she did not wish to spoil Leo's opinion of her. She wanted him to remember her just as he had imagined her: as a governess of uninspired birth running from an ill-fated marriage. It was idiocy, she knew, to have such desires, but it could not be helped. The man made her feel such conflicting emotions—the last of which she had not truly considered since their flight from his estate. And yet...no matter how many times her heart hurt around him, she still anticipated every moment of closeness. It was nonsensical.

With a grunt, she deposited the buckets of water on hooks in each stall then left to retrieve the feed, her muscles protesting.

Much as she disliked the notion of inspiring worry—or anger—in Leo, Juliana did not believe that she had any other recourse. Indeed, only one option was plausible: in the middle of the night, she must leave him.

LEONARD'S BODY burned with every movement. He'd finished cleaning and brushing down the horses and had joined Juliana in a stall across the stable from their mounts. She'd removed her borrowed greatcoat and laid it upon the floor, padded beneath only with lumpy stacks of hay.

He would not have a sound sleep, that was for certain. With the aches in his body, however, he was simply grateful to be neither on his feet nor on his rear for a few hours.

Silence descended upon them as they shared the apples and water that Juliana had gathered. He wanted to return to their easy conversation, to share theories about where their pursuer had gone, to discuss their plans for the morning, or—*hell*—even to apologize for what had occurred between them. But nothing came.

Indeed, his tongue felt swollen, far too large for his mouth.

Surely they were not far from Derby. If they reached her home by early or mid-morn, he could return to his estate before supper and send a note on to Percy to inform him of the day's events. He would not wish for Lizzy to return home until at least four-and-twenty hours had passed without incident, of course, but he could tell them that Juliana had been returned to her family.

A nagging feeling pulled at his gut, and he shook it off. He would leave her behind without looking back; it was what was best for them both. At the moment, however, with his thirst and hunger satiated, his concern for Juliana took over.

"I must check your injuries," he said, finally breaking their silence.

Juliana winced, pulling her legs beneath her where she sat. "I do not believe that it is necessary."

Leo's lips thinned. She could at least *pretend* to not find his touch so unappealing. "You fell from a horse, Juliana," he said, as though she required reminding. "And you've only just begun to heal from your previous injuries. Please, allow me to assess you."

He hadn't much experience with doctoring, but he and his brother had found themselves in a number of scrapes as lads, and he'd been forced to learn some skills in bandaging.

The recollection of his brother dug the dagger of pain deeper into his sternum, and he scowled, his words coming out harsher than he'd intended. "If you will not allow me to help you, I will be forced to seek aid from the landowner, to the devil with the consequences. I don't give a damn what they think of me; they will sure as hell help you."

He hadn't liked Juliana's assessment of what the family would think of her. In fact, his internal acknowledgement that she was wearing a maid's uniform that was clearly not meant for her was entirely discomfiting. She had been his governess, paid for her services, but upon reflection, he realized that he'd treated her ill by not providing her with something suitable to wear. He'd given her clothes previously worn by his other staff, but they were too short, and far too snug around her breasts and hips.

"Very well," Juliana said, pulling Leo back from his thoughts.

Damn, but it was going to be a long night.

CHAPTER 17

$\mathcal{J}$uliana bit back her groans and gasps as Leo gave her a perfunctory examination. She hated that it was necessary, but with the constant pain throbbing through her, she found it difficult to judge the severity of her own injuries.

Leo made a *tsk* sound with his tongue. "I have no way of knowing how badly you've bruised without seeing your skin." His voice was soft and close in the darkness. "How does your ankle feel?"

Her aches notwithstanding, she rolled her foot around, testing her movement. She grimaced as a small twinge shot up her calf. "I've twisted it but, given the night to rest, it should be well enough to travel."

I, however, will not be travelling with you, her conscience whispered. Guilt gnawed at her stomach once more.

Leo nodded, apparently satisfied with her response, and an unsettling silence descended over them. She missed the easiness of their previous conversations. But that was before...

There was a part of her mind—and a small, secret part of

her heart—that wanted to flame her fears and mistrust, to rage at the Murderous Marquess for deceiving her.

Her gaze slid sideways, watching as Leo chewed the meat of another apple. His long blond hair was rumpled and wind-blown, his shortly-shorn beard bunching with each movement of his strong jaw. And, even through the darkness, she could see the slight glisten of apple juice on his bottom lip.

Despite the many reasons why she should regret their tryst, Juliana did not. Discovering his withheld truth had hurt, certainly, but she must face the very bald fact that she was lying, as well, and had no grounds to punish him. And, of course, there was the delicious fact that bedding him had been achingly wonderful.

A yawn caught her by surprise, and she realized how weary she was. The piles of hay would be uncomfortable, but at the moment, she didn't particularly care. With a soft groan, she reclined and closed her eyes.

"I'm sorry, Juliana." Leo's whisper cut through the silence.

Her eyes snapped open, and she gazed at his shadowy, stricken features.

"I wish that..." He chewed on his bottom lip, lapsing into silence.

What do you wish?

He sighed, and his breath fogged in the air before he shook his head. "I apologize, Juliana. I abused your tru—"

"No," she interjected, her stomach giving an awful, nauseating flip. "Please, Leo. You do not need to apologize." And, *Lord*, she couldn't stomach hearing his regrets about their intimacies.

His pale blue eyes were stormy in the gloom, but he nodded once more and unfastened his cravat. Juliana's gaze followed his movements, the gentle *snick* of the material sounding loud to her ears.

"I don't care to sleep in my cravat," he explained.

An odd, noncommittal noise escaped her as she greedily took in the exposed skin of his neck. The man was too delicious by half.

The edge of his inked skin peeked out from behind his shirt's collar, and Juliana spoke entirely without thinking. "Where did you get your tattoo?"

"On a small island in the Dutch East Indies. We spent days there, during which the rest of the crew had one done."

"The rumours are true?" she breathed in astonishment. "You were a pirate?"

He nodded once, settling down beside her. "I was. Both Percy and I."

Her heart stuttered, her curiosity suitably roused. She gazed at him through the shadows. "How did you come to be a pirate?"

The hay rustled as he shifted his position. "I was young, on a ship bound for Spain, and we were overtaken by pirates. I tried to fight, but I could scarcely hold a sodding sword. So I hid while the rest of the crew were murdered. The pirate captain found me while his crew were pilfering goods, and took pity on me. I was small, fast, and quick at learning, so he had me working the top—where the ship's rigging and sails are."

"You poor thing." Sorrow for young Leonard tightened her chest.

He yawned. "Eventually, Percy and I managed an escape and found ourselves on an English naval ship. We sailed for a short time before coming ashore." His lips pulled in a half smile. "But that is the tale of my tattoo."

She returned his grin before they fell once more into silence.

Juliana ached, not only on her body, where there would undeniably be bruises, but also in her heart. She did not want this to be the last time that she saw Leo.

To the devil with prudence. Juliana curled into Leo's heat, resting her head in the crook of his shoulder and sighing as his arms encircled her. Her heart told her to stay. Indeed, that was precisely why she was determined to go.

A COLD DRAFT of air encompassed Leo, and he shivered. He nestled further into his bed, then cringed at the ache in his back.

Snick.

Leo's eyes popped open at the discrete sound. *Juliana. Where is Juliana?* The stall was still pitch dark, but it was clear that she was gone. Had she left to use a chamber pot?

The clomp of a horse's hoof made him sit up.

The words "good boy" were scarcely audible, but unmistakable.

Swift suspicion and anger filled him, and he scowled at the stall's door. Was Juliana leaving without him? His heart gave a hard, painful *thump,* and he swallowed past the abrupt thickness in his throat. His eyes narrowed. *The devil she would.*

"S-stop!" The fearful, trembling voice of a young man pierced the air, driving Leo to his feet. "Don't m-move!"

Leo scrambled for his boots and coat.

There was a whispered "For pity's sake!" from Juliana, and a shuffle of feet.

"Lady Juliana!" the young man squeaked.

Leo stilled. *Lady...*

"*Hsst!*" Juliana shushed him. "Do keep your voice down, George. I do not wish to alert the house to my presence."

The battered organ in Leo's chest beat a hard, painful tattoo against his ribs. Juliana was a lady. *Juliana is a sodding lady!* The thought repeated itself in his mind, over and over again until he felt dizzy from the overwhelming emotion twisting his insides: anger at her deceit, guilt for having deflowered a virginal lady, fear of the inevitable exposure harming Elizabeth, fury that Juliana had led him into temptation by his cods, and the god-awful fucking agony at the knowledge that she'd intended to abandon him.

A familiar, hated stinging began behind his eyes, and he snarled. He wouldn't cry, for Christ's sake.

"… And where is Jasper?" Juliana whispered.

"The duke is in London, searching for *you*, Lady Juliana."

"Shh! Please, George, do keep your voice down," she hissed. "And thank you. I intend to ride after him directly."

"His Grace expressed concern over your safety; surely you can write to him and await his return?"

A grim silence fell between them while Leonard's heart ricocheted in his chest. *Duke. Devil take me, her brother is a bloody duke!* With a tug on his coat sleeves and a cursory finger-comb of his hair, he reached for the stall door's latch. And paused. Something did not feel—*no*, did not *smell*—right.

He lifted his nose in the air and inhaled deeply. *Smoke!*

Twisting his gaze upward, he saw it: the first, wispy tendrils of smoke curling along the stables' ceiling.

"*Fire!*" he roared, bursting from the stall.

LONDON

"FIRST JUST BEFORE DAWN, and now after dusk. You have me committing all sorts of punishable offences, Maria," Heather muttered at Maria's elbow, her breath a cloud of fog.

Maria clucked her tongue. "You know damned well that this was your idea just as much as mine."

"And a smart mouth on you. What an indignity to be in your presence. Why, I'd thought you a proper lady." She nudged Maria in the ribs with a wicked grin on her lips.

"You try my patience." Maria narrowed her eyes at her friend, but affection filled her heart.

"Which is why you love me," Heather replied curtly. "Now knock, will you? I'm freezing."

Bracing herself against her own emotions, Maria lifted her fist and rapped her gloved knuckles against the Duke of Derby's front door. The absence of a door knocker was a clear statement for the public to remain away, but they had rather urgent business with the infuriating man.

"Do not let him cow you, Maria," Heather reminded her. "We must stand strong. This is for Juliana."

The door swung inward, and the same young footman who'd greeted them previously peered out.

"Oh, it's you. Come in, then." He stepped aside and helped them with their cloaks, gloves, and bonnets before showing them to the nearby drawing room. "I will see if His Grace is in to accept callers."

The young man strode away, leaving Heather and Maria in the room alone.

"He really ought to have learned if the duke would accept us before removing our cloaks," Heather grumbled.

Maria grinned at her. "The man will hear us if we have to barge into his private rooms to make it so."

"Oh, yes." Heather winked suggestively. "That must have been your plan from the start. Come at an odd hour of the night, wearing a shimmering ball gown, and appear in the duke's—"

"For pity's sake, Heather, hold your tongue."

Anger was what she felt for the man at present, not esteem or desire. He might be as beautiful as any fantasy, but he was shirking his duty and she would let him know it.

"Miss Roberts. Miss Morgan." The Duke of Derby emerged just inside the drawing room door. He appeared drawn, his complexion pallid, his jaw unshaven, and his coat hurriedly donned. "To what do I owe this pleasure?" He didn't appear pleased to see them at all, in fact.

Well, neither are we, Maria reminded herself, soothing the unwarranted pang in her abdomen.

She stepped forward, her movements sharp. "When last we met, I'd shared with you the newspaper clippings and detailed the possible connections between the carriage accident in Nottingham and the string of thefts and animal attacks on the outskirts of London. You assured me that if I allowed you and your men to take care of the matter without my 'interference,' Juliana would be safely returned home. I—"

"And she will." His face darkened with ducal anger and outrage.

Maria stiffened her spine and stood her ground. "I do not see evidence of that, Your Grace."

"Do not go looking for evidence!" he barked.

Her chin notched downward slightly. "Whyever not? If it helps my friend, I will do everything in my power to aid her."

Heather's hand slipped into the crook of Maria's elbow. "*We* will do everything in our power to aid her."

Sending a silent note of thanks to her friend, Maria drew strength from their harmonious concord and sent the man a stern look down the length of her nose.

"Something odd is occurring with these threatening letters, Your Grace, and I intend to secure my friend's safety. Whatever it is that you and your 'men' are attempting, you are, I'm afraid to say, failing at it. It is time to allow some women to have a go."

"You will not *have a go*," he seethed. "You will leave this well enough alone! It is not your affair."

"Neither are you behaving as though it is *yours*, Your Grace."

"That is *enough*!" he bellowed, his face reddened. "Despite your low opinion of me, I *am* searching for my sister. This is a dangerous business, and I'll not have two interfering harpies ruin my sister's chance of being found."

Interfering harpies, indeed. "Very well, Your Grace," Maria clipped out. "We shall not bother you any further."

With a flounce of their skirts, Maria and Heather entered the foyer and donned their cloaks, bonnets, and gloves. The air was still and heavy, the argument hanging around them like a dark cloud. Maria sniffed. The man was obstinate, but Juliana did not have to suffer because of his stupidity.

The air outside was crisp and cool, and it hit Maria like a slap to the face. Arms linked, she and Heather strode quickly down the dark road and around the corner toward the hack they'd hired to wait for them.

"You do not truly intend to leave the duke to this search alone, do you?" Heather asked.

Maria turned to gaze sharply at her friend. "I'm shocked that you even have to ask. Of course not! The man is blinded by arrogance, and clearly has no notion of the power a woman can wield."

"And you intend to show him." Heather smirked into the darkness.

"Damned right, I do."

DREAD, fully formed and intense, surged behind Juliana's breastbone. *Fire.* Her father's stables were ablaze in one low corner, the fire spreading rapidly along the outside of the building, despite the damp wood.

Shock held her feet still as chaos erupted. Leo rushed past her to open the next stall, hurriedly leading the horse out.

"Bring them to the rear paddock," George called over his shoulder.

Those words broke Juliana from her shock, and she blindly raced to the next occupied stall, her aching muscles and throbbing ankle notwithstanding. The horse inside was wild-eyed and frightened by the commotion and the smell of smoke.

"Alert the house," Leo called to George. "We require as much help as can be offered."

George bowed quickly, as though he were accustomed to taking orders from Leo, and fled the stables.

Juliana's racing pulse drummed in her ears, but it couldn't drown out the whinny of the terrified horses. Her stomach clenched, she sped to the next stall and swung the door wide, then did the same with the next door, and the next. She and Leo worked together until all of the occupied stalls had been emptied.

Shouts came from beyond the stable's walls as the household staff called out and began what Juliana knew was their plan for such emergencies.

Tears pricked and blurred Juliana's vision as she spotted a wild-eyed mare at the rear of her opened stall. *Mona*. The space between them was filled with thickening smoke, and the horse's fear was palpable.

Juliana slowly approached. "Come here, my sweet. We must get you to safety." A cough caught her by surprise.

The flames in the far corner of the stables lapped up the walls toward the hayloft. Once the hay caught fire, the interior of the stables would be engulfed.

CHAPTER 18

Water sizzled as it reached the fire. Leo turned, handing the empty bucket into awaiting hands before accepting a full one and splashing it upon the flames. *Tssss!* His back burned with each movement, ached with every breath, and his skin felt scorched by the heat of the fire. But he continued on.

He'd guided the cattle from the stables then united with the servants in putting out the blaze. Only minutes had passed, but they'd felt like hours.

Tsss! Another bucket of water. Men and women surrounded him in organized rows, passing buckets to be filled at the water pump and a nearby pond, and others threw handfuls of snow. With each splash of water, the flames grew less intense. If it had not been for the time of year, the dampness of the wood, and the deep snow that covered the ground and the stables' roof, Leo was certain that it would have caught aflame entirely.

Despite the focus on his task, Leo kept stealing glances toward the others in search of a familiar swath of pale skin and curling brown hair. He had lost sight of her while they were releasing the horses from their stalls, and worry for her safety began to gnaw at him.

Tssss!

The sizzle of water on flames was swiftly followed by a muffled, terrified whinny. *Juliana*. His heart squeezed and his throat all but entirely closed around the scorching smoke. With only one thought on his mind, Leo abandoned his post, leaving the footman behind him to toss the next pail of water, and ran toward the stables' entrance.

He dragged an empty bucket as he ran, scooping up a mound of wet snow. He skidded through the large doors only to jump back as a horse and rider dashed out. A plume of smoke billowed out behind her and dissipated as she brought the beast toward the gathered horses.

Relief hit Leo hard before he recalled himself. Content with knowing that the confounding woman was safe, he returned to the front line of the fire and tossed the snow upon the low flames.

IN THE EXCITEMENT of the predawn hours, Juliana's aches and pains had fled to the back of her mind, but now that the fire had been put out and the horses had been found warm, temporary homes on neighbouring estates, she felt every ounce of the weariness and pain in her body.

And, with one glance at the banked fury in Leo's eyes as they were ushered into her familial home, Juliana knew that they had a difficult discussion ahead of them. It had been impossible to withhold her true name, particularly once the fire began, and at that moment, she wasn't certain how she felt about it.

She was apprehensive, to be sure, but an undercurrent of

relief flowed through her. She was finally free of the deception that had held her truth prisoner.

Their steps echoed on the marble foyer, and the servants' voices rang out as her housekeeper issued demands for hot baths and fresh clothes.

"I do not intend to stay, Mrs. Blyth," Juliana said, slowing her steps.

The housekeeper frowned, her grey eyebrows puckered with worry and determination. "His Grace has been searching for you, my lady. I would be remiss if I did not keep you safe at home while we await his return."

"Our home is not safe while I am in it!" Juliana gripped the older woman's hand in hers and squeezed it. "Do you not see? The fire did not merely start—it was *started*. I must go to Jasper in London."

And she would leave directly, whether or not the staff approved. She could not risk their lives. Instead, she would gratefully take her bath, refill her saddlebags, secure provisions, and be on her way.

The skin on the back of her neck prickled, and she slid a glance toward Leo. His blue eyes were stormy and intent, his cheeks smudged with soot, and his long hair rumpled from sleep and activity. The sight made her knees tremble.

"Surely you require a chaperone, my lady." Mrs. Blyth's curious gaze followed Juliana's.

"I cannot risk a chaperone being lost or frozen on my account, Mrs. Blyth. Mr. Notley rescued me after a carriage accident and jeopardized his own wellbeing to aid me on my journey. I owe him the debt of my life, and I trust him to keep me safe." *That is,* if *he joins me on the journey,* she reminded herself. She'd intended to continue on her own to London, whether he wished to join her or not. As much as she craved his company, she could not endanger Leo any more than she could her familial staff.

The woman's cheeks pinkened. "Pardon my impertinence, my lady, but while I appreciate all he has done to help us, he is ill-equipped to be a chaperone."

With as much confidence as she could muster, Juliana stiffened her spine and straightened her shoulders. "I require baths for myself and Mr. Notley, a satchel of provisions, and our mounts readied. I would like Mona, if you please, and Mr. Notley will borrow Dash. We leave directly."

Lips thinned, the housekeeper curtseyed. "At once, my lady." She turned sharply and left the grand space, clearly displeased with Juliana's decision.

Silence descended, and Juliana could feel Leo's gaze on her.

"I'll show you to the peach bedchamber," Juliana said, starting toward the staircase on the left side of the foyer. "It will afford you some privacy while you bathe and change. I imagine that you will wish to be on your way back to Nottingham as soon as may be."

They reached the landing, and Leo gripped her elbow, halting her in her tracks.

"I'll not abandon you, Lady Juliana," he said gruffly.

She flinched at the courtesy title on his lips. "You are not required to sacrifice yourself on my behalf, *Lord Livingston*. I —and I alone—will go to London."

LEO'S BROW TURNED THUNDEROUS, and his chest ached with... *Christ*, was it disappointment or pain? He feared it was both.

"Think you so little of my character that I would leave you to fight not only the elements, but a murderous blackguard on your own?" He did not trust for one moment that her intention was to see her brother upon arriving in London. The woman had something else in mind, but what, he could not fathom.

Her eyebrows lifted. "Do you believe me incapable of protecting myself, sir?"

"Hardly," Leo scoffed. "The man is mad to continue his pursuit of you, most particularly after you continue to best him."

The frown left her face and her shoulders lowered slightly, the praise deflating her anger.

"You will, however, require a travel companion," he urged. "If unaccompanied, you would suffer the inconvenience of unwanted attention. And I can easily secure rooms, meals, and conveyance with nary a second glance."

As furious as he was with her, he could not abandon her to the harsh elements or her determined attacker. Tolerable or not, he would keep her safe.

She chewed on her bottom lip, drawing his gaze. *Damnation*. He'd kissed those lips. And she, the daughter of a duke! God, but he'd blundered, following his cock instead of his head. *A duke's daughter, for Christ's sake!*

Gossip from nearly seven years ago sprang to mind: the Duke of Derby's harridan daughter sitting firmly on the shelf only two seasons after her come-out. The rags had written that she was unmarriageable, and entirely unappealing to the opposite sex due to her height.

Leo's gaze sharpened on the beauty before him. The *ton* must be mad. Juliana was fire, passion, determination, and bravery...and a little bit of fear. She was a goddamned Aphrodite.

"Very well," she said softly, breaking through his thoughts. "But make haste. Lord knows how close our pursuer is after the fire he set, and I hate to think on what he would do to my brother's estate or the staff if we linger."

Leo nodded, for lack of a better response, and followed Juliana to his temporary bedchamber, where she left him.

The space was bright and cheerful, contradicting the emotions that roiled within him. Juliana was correct: their pursuer could be anywhere; it would behove them to keep alert. Complacency would be their downfall.

Footmen entered with his bath and water, leaving him to bathe in peace. His wash was perfunctory, despite his desperate desire to lie back and give his sore muscles the opportunity to soak in the water's heat.

Once dry, he donned the smoke-scented travel wear he'd stored in his saddlebags and retrieved after the fire had been put out. Determination to accompany Juliana to London—and the undeniable feelings that she stirred within him—aside, Leo was incensed over her deception. She'd learned *his* true identity, the dishonesty for which he'd felt horrible, and yet even after they'd come to a place in which he'd thought they could be honest, she'd withheld the truth.

Striding to the dressing table, Leo used a comb on his damp hair and beard, his gaze snapping upward at his reflected movements. The man gazing back at him through the mirror was one he recognized: a man filled with anger, his skin flushed with guilt, and his mane of hair a disguise. He grimaced, one corner of his lip lifting up to show the tip of his white canine tooth.

For nearly three years he'd hidden behind the unkempt mask, hating the appearance of himself in the mirror and wishing to God that he'd perished in his brother's stead. If he intended to be the man that *Lady* Juliana required for her journey, however, he ought to shed the guise of an animal and once more become a man. He must look the part.

Without a second thought, Leo searched the dressing table's drawer, withdrew a pair of shears, and began to cut. He made quick work of his hair, using his fingers to judge length and keeping it short. Maintaining his focus and momentum, Leo set aside the shears, readied the implements, and began to shave.

There he was. With each pass of the blade, memories flooded his mind: his days as a carefree young man, the time he'd dedicated to building his reputation as a rogue and a reprobate... It was all there in each strip of clean, pale skin that he exposed.

The base of his spine grew damp with an anxious sweat, and his gut churned mournfully. He'd hidden his face for far too long, accepting the gift of being nondescript, even to himself. It was time that he owned his life for what it was: rife with mistakes, but *his*. And if he was to return to London, he'd damned well do so with his head held high—even if it was the very last thing he wanted to do.

He met his own gaze in the mirror, and he flinched. *This* man was still angry, but resigned.

A knock sounded at the door, and he called entrance as he wiped the last of the cream from his neck and jaw.

"Leo?" Juliana's soft voice called as the door crept open.

"I am ready to depart," he confirmed, anticipating her question.

He finished tying his cravat as he strode to the door, and was struck dumb. It was the first time that he'd seen her in a dress that was uniquely *her* and not something ill-fitting or coated in stains. She'd chosen a pale-green walking dress with a slate-coloured sash that sat just below her bosom and had matching embroidery along the décolletage, at the wrists of the long sleeves, and around the bottom hem. The frock as a whole were the exact colours of her eyes.

Christ, but the dress fit her impeccably: long and full. And he took in the sight of her, so tall, so beautiful. His heart gave several hard thumps as his gaze roamed over the delicate line of her neck, the smooth skin of her chest, and her damp, upswept curls held tightly in place by pins. *How did her maids do that so quickly?* She was simply amazing.

Her lips worked as her gaze scanned his face. "Leo, you—"

"Have you a spare pistol, powder, and shot that I might borrow?" he asked hoarsely. "It would be wise for us both to be prepared for another attack."

Worry crossed her features before she nodded. "Follow me to my brother's study."

With a nod, he followed, saddlebags in hand. The woman had him twisted in knots.

"The dress suits you," he muttered as they walked.

"Thank you." Juliana inclined her head, averting her gaze from his. "I will borrow one of Jasper's greatcoats to don over my redingote."

She'd need it both for warmth and for protection from *him*, he imagined. Bitterness roiled in his gut, and he bit back a curse. She was far above him, and deserved so much more than he was capable of giving. But, damn it, he would see her safely returned to her brother if it bloody well killed him.

HELL AND BLAST. The bitch had survived the fire. And the house had been awoken before she'd fled the stables, giving him no opportunity to strike.

He kicked at a cluster of snow, but the fluffy spray was anything but satisfying. He wanted the woman dead. She and her brother held everything in their grasp. They had taken everything from him, and he would see to it that those wrongs were righted.

He needed a new plan. Juliana was home now; would she remain, or would she travel to London to her brother?

He glared through the moonlight toward the glowing

windows of her home, his body all but numb to the cold while a fiery, passionate hatred burned from within.

If she should remain, he would find his way indoors and kill the bitch in her sleep. A slow smile stole over his lips. If, however, she chose to journey to London to her brother, he would take any opening to strike.

MISTY SNOWFLAKES DUSTED Juliana's eyelashes and slowly melted on the frigid, exposed skin of her face. Dusk threatened, brightening the sky beyond the snow clouds to a brilliant mixture of pink and orange.

The day had passed in relative silence, the only words between her and Leo being clipped discussions on stops to rest. Her body had gone far past aches, pains, and numbness and into an odd immersive vibration.

But neither the breathtakingly beautiful sunset nor the punishing ride from Derby toward London was the cause of the pang in her heart or the frequent misting of her eyes.

Her gaze slid sideways to the man riding beside her, and her chest squeezed. His cloak and turned-up collar obscured her view of him, but the change was still apparent. Hair shorn and clean-shaven, the man inspired both an ache at the loss of his stunning hair and a keen longing to run her fingers through his locks and her lips over his skin. She could have wept with the want burning through her.

"Whoa!" Leo hollered over the thundering of their horses' hooves.

Juliana slowed her mount to match his new pace and gazed at him expectantly.

He notched his chin forward. "An inn sits just beyond this copse of trees. We will procure a room for the night and take the mail coach on the morrow."

Alarm prickled behind her breastbone. "If we stop, my pursuer will find us, and I cannot in good conscience risk the safety of the innocent passengers aboard the mail coach." She shook her head. "There must be another option."

She'd been expecting the reappearance of her pursuer all day, reflexively—and frequently—feeling for the weight of her brother's pistol in her pocket.

"We will be safer surrounded by people at the inn, and we both require rest," he replied pragmatically. "Our method of conveyance can be discussed on the morrow, but I insist that we stop for the night."

In an act of betrayal, her spine chose that moment to creak, the sound echoing in her head. And her muscles soon joined the rebellion, abruptly panging and twitching with the need to dismount.

With a sigh, Juliana conceded. They would both undoubtedly come to regret the decision, but she could not turn down the prospect of a bath, some food, and a few stolen moments of rest. If, of course, her body would allow her such a luxury with the temptation of Leo so near. Lord, but she wanted to rub herself all over his day's growth of stubble.

"Very well," she agreed. "A night at the inn." But she would damned well be prepared for their inevitable visitor.

CHAPTER 19

"At once, sir." The innkeeper inclined his head and scurried toward the main stairwell down the inn's dark corridor.

"The baths have been requested and will arrive after our meal. According to the innkeeper, we have the good fortune of arriving this night." Leo said, closing the door to the bedchamber. "The cook prepared partridges, white soup, gooseberry cheese, and Bath buns, with pudding and trifle for dessert."

"Oh, I do love a trifle." Juliana hummed as she paced before the blazing hearth.

Leo strode forward, closer to where she walked, the heat only beginning to thaw his chilled body. He scratched at his chin and grimaced at the gentle abrasion. Hell, but not having his familiar facial hair was a damned nuisance.

The air between them was stilted, *forced*, but he didn't know how to change it.

Putting his hands outward, he leaned into the warmth of the fire while Juliana's pacing swirled the air against his back. The inn was by no means a comfortable establishment, with peeling, greying paint, fogged windows, a lumpy bed, and an acrid aroma that he was unwilling to contemplate. But it provided shelter and a modicum of safety for the moment, and he would be damned grateful for that.

Juliana made another pass at his back, and the faintest hint of her unique floral scent reached his nose. He bit back a curse at the sudden rush of blood in his ears and the stirring of his cock. Even after her lies, he still wanted her. *Damnation.*

He ought to put some distance between them, go to the taproom, and leave Juliana to her meal and her bath...but he couldn't bring himself to leave her side. And, damn it, he wanted to be there with her, wanted to discuss the monumental impact that the revelation of her identity had on his emotions and what they were doing together.

He opened his mouth to speak just as Juliana halted in her pacing and spun to face him. The little gasp on her lips drew his gaze, where it fixed.

Her bottom lip was slightly pinkened, as though she had worried it in thought. The contrast against the darker pink hue of her cheeks sent his heart to racing. An intense want— no, *need*—to kiss her burned through him, and every rational thought fled his mind.

With great strength of will, Leo held himself back and refused to allow his feet to move that last step toward her. Because he might bend her over the back of the dilapidated armchair by the hearth and find his pleasure in her sweet heat. But he was no animal, and she was a sodding duke's daughter.

He cleared his throat. "I—"

The air whooshed from his lungs as Juliana swept forward and pulled him against her chest. In a moment of combined panic and arousal, his body remained still, while his cock eagerly swelled.

Fingertips roamed his jaw and found purchase in his hair as she rocked against him.

"Oh, Christ," he moaned against her lips before finally letting go and kissing her with every ounce of the desire roaring through him.

Zing. A jolt of pleasure tightened his ballocks and sizzled up his spine as Juliana overwhelmed his body with sensation. Her nails abraded his scalp, her teeth and tongue tangled with his, her breasts pressed against his chest, and her *mons* rocked against his erection.

Leo breathed her in, the scent of flowers and desire driving him nigh into madness. With clear intent, he walked her backward toward the bed. Keeping one arm around her, and trailing his tongue in a thin line along her jaw, Leo drew down the bedclothes.

"Please let me taste you," he begged, nibbling at her collarbone.

"Taste me?" she asked, her voice high and husky.

He guided her backward, hovering over her as she half splayed upon the bed. "Do you trust me to ensure your pleasure?"

As though she were temptation incarnate, she wrapped her legs about his hips and nudged his length once more. *Bloody hell*, but the heat from her was heady, even through the tedious layers of clothing.

"Yes," she breathed.

Oh, what that little word did, tightening his gut and causing warmth to spread across his chest and back. He would show her this bliss.

Ignoring the sharp pang of protest in his back and legs, he slid to his knees on the oft-trodden rug, his heart thundering. With purpose, he glided his palms up her legs, slowly exposing them to the air. Bruises marred her beautiful calves, thighs, and her delectable, taut arse, and he pressed tender kisses over each of them in turn.

Gripping each thigh, he carefully draped her knees over his biceps and curved his hands toward her apex.

"L-Leo," she stuttered. "What are you—"

"Trust me," he murmured.

His fingers found her labia, exploring playfully, before opening them for his view. At one time, he was practised in the art of delighting women in the bedroom, even to the point of tedium, but in that moment, finesse was gone and in its place was raw carnality. Never had he experienced such naked trust from a woman.

A grin on his lips and fervour driving him, he lavished attention on her swollen bundle of nerves. He drew her pearl into his mouth with a tender pull and flip of his tongue, then returned his focus to the sensational cluster that he knew would delight her, and flicked it back and forth.

Juliana's gasps and little breathy sighs filled his ears. Her hands found his hair and her hips began to rock.

Leo groaned, his neck flushing as his cock throbbed. Good God, he might very well come untouched. He'd not done that since his youth, but Juliana's keening, clear arousal, and *shite*, her musky scent and taste were driving him to distraction.

He redoubled his efforts, swirling his tongue and rolling her pearl between his lips.

Her breath hitched between short gasps as she rocked faster against him.

"Leo, I—*oh!*"

With her back arching off the bed and her fists tightening in his hair, she shattered, crying out his name and trembling beneath him.

Leo found himself thrusting against nothing but the trousers that confined him, desperate for friction and relief.

Juliana gripped his shoulders, pulling him up and over her. Wiping his mouth with the back of his hand, he lay atop her and groaned.

"Please...Juliana," he grunted hoarsely.

She arched into him with a contented sigh. "You may have me however you wish."

"*Yes.*" Lifting himself away from her, he flipped her onto her stomach and lifted her skirts.

WITH HER FRONT pressed to the lumpy mattress, her bottom lifted high, and her toes pressing against the floor, Juliana felt rather vulnerable. But she'd had the same moment of nervousness when Leo had knelt before her, and he'd given her an abundance of pleasure, so she would trust him once more.

There was a rustle of fabric before something nudged at her entrance. Her flesh was swollen, still throbbing in time with her heart, and slick enough for him to slide in.

He groaned, pressing his lips to the back of her neck.

"My God, Juliana. You feel—" He broke off on a moan as he thrust.

And he was right; that position, that *angle* touched a spot inside her that rekindled the flame of her desires. She grew hotter with each of his drives, a flush spreading over her skin and making her want to squirm.

"Leo, that's so—" Her breath caught as he bit lightly on her ear.

"I know."

To her surprise, her pulse sped and her muscles clenched, the heat spreading over her, tingling down her legs and out her fingertips.

"I'm going to—" she breathed bemusedly, clutching the bedclothes beneath her. "Oh, Leo, I'm going to—"

Sensation rushed through her as the paroxysm of pleasure hit, tingling throughout her body and glowing with light behind her eyelids.

"Fuck! *Yes*!" Leo stilled, one hand gripping her hip and the other covering hers as he bellowed his release.

They lay thusly for several long moments, breathing heavily, until Leo rolled to his back beside her with a grunt. His features were soft with gratification, yet drawn and tired. And so dearly handsome.

She reached out a hand to run her fingers through his hair once more, still unused to the short, blunt ends where he'd cut it. His jaw was defined, and bristly with his day's growth. It was familiar and yet so foreign to her.

He turned his head toward her, his blue-grey eyes full of some unreadable emotion. Worried? Or, perhaps resigned?

"Marry me, Juliana?"

Heart hiccoughing, Juliana blinked at him. *Marry* him! At one time—even mere months ago—she might have been elated at the sudden proposal, but this...*this* was not a part of her plan. Difficult as it was, however, she couldn't deny the feelings he inspired in her. Her body veritably vibrated with awareness when he was near. She consistently had the urge to touch him, to kiss him. And, despite their quarrels, she rather liked the man.

To her astonishment, she was tempted to accept. He was a man accustomed to living outside of the *ton*'s expectations. If she could confide her plans and anticipate a response in the positive, she would gladly take the protection of his name... and the regular comfort of his body.

She blinked again, refocusing her thoughts. *But that look in his eyes.* He didn't wish to be married, did he? *Oh, Lord.* Disappointment trickled down her spine like a bucket of frigid water. The man had proposed out of a sense of duty. Now that he knew of her true identity, he felt obligated to offer his hand, for God knew he hadn't intended to marry after their *first* coupling.

With a dejected flick of her wrist, Juliana righted her skirts and sat up, all feelings of delight after their intimacy gone in the face of his *duty*.

"I thank you for your generous offer, Leo," she replied brusquely, "but I do not intend to marry."

CHAPTER 20

*H*ead still reeling from the sensational bedding, Leo forced himself to pay attention to Juliana's facial expressions. Shock widened her slate-and-green eyes as she scanned his face, taking him in as though searching for the feeling behind his words.

To his great astonishment, hope blossomed in his chest. Did he *want* to marry Juliana? The question had slipped out, but in that moment, he'd realized the protection that their matrimonial state could provide her—most particularly if their coupling resulted in pregnancy.

Now that he had a moment to consider his impetuous proposal, however, he rather liked the idea. He enjoyed her company and knew that he would never tire of bedding her.

She righted her skirts and sat up. "I thank you for your generous offer, Leo, but I do not intend to marry."

Pain jolted through his chest and he rose, as well, returning his softening cock to his breeches. "Might I ask *why* I am rejected?"

"Do not insult my intelligence. I am aware that you asked out of a sense of duty." She stood and paced to the washbasin.

"It was an impulse," he admitted. "But I do not regret it. I believe that you and I would be a good match."

She performed a perfunctory wash and spun to face him. "Be truthful: you do not wish to sire a bastard."

"Of course I do not wish to sire a bastard!" He raked his hands through his hair, cursing himself again for the whim of cutting it. "I must express my regret at not taking precautions while bedding you, but..." His voice trailed away, his lips thinning.

Hurt flared on her face, and an answering ache knotted in his chest. He was not a good match for *anyone*, so why should her rejection cut so deeply?

He remained there for several heartbeats, hating the pain tingling through him. Hell, he'd gotten himself too deep. He needed to put some distance between them.

"I'm going to the taproom," he ground out. "If you require me, I shall be there. If not, I will return later."

Not waiting for her to respond, Leo turned on his heel, gathered his coat, and stalked out the door. Retreating was cowardly, but Juliana likely desired solitude just as much as he. Being in her presence forced him to *feel* things that he simply wished not to. And, *Christ*, the room still smelled of sex.

The taproom was one floor below, humming with the low buzz of conversation. Very few tables were occupied, and Leo took one against the wall nearest a blazing hearth, suppressing a groan of pain as he sat.

Their ride had been long, cold, and punishing, and whatever energy surge had fuelled his sex had now fled. He was exhausted.

The taproom maid caught his eye across the room, and he inclined his head, signalling that he wanted to order.

Within minutes, Leo was swallowing down a mouthful of ale. He replaced his tankard on the roughened tabletop and wiped absently at the foam on his upper lip, inwardly groaning. It had been years since he'd partaken, and yet despite the familiar warmth in his abdomen, the drink did nothing to dull the ache in his chest.

Juliana had rejected him. Marriage wasn't something that he should want. He ought to have been pleased at the course their passions had taken: he was able to satisfy his lust for the woman but was not forced into matrimony as a result. And yet...he felt distinctly ill about it.

He took another swig of his ale and coughed.

For some ungodly reason, a part of Leonard had actually *wanted* her to agree to his proposal. *That was hardly a proposal, old man*, his inner voice rebuked. He supposed that he could have made some sort of declaration, but he did not think that Juliana would require such things—most particularly after what they'd done. And it felt dishonest to flout poetry or some such nonsense when he wasn't that sort of man.

Sighing, he ran his fingertip over the tankard's handle, taking note of every dent and chip. Whatever the reasoning or method of his proposal, it had been a monumental blunder. He wished that Percy were there to tell him what a fool he was and set him back on the path of logic. For right at that moment, Leo wished only to return to his rented room and fall asleep with Juliana in his arms.

HAIR DRYING in a mass of unruly curls down her back, Juliana sat at the room's small table and loaded her pistol. The tray containing her meal had been pushed aside to allow her space, the food sitting heavily in her anxious stomach. After the inn's staff had brought up the bath, Juliana had made haste with her washing and donned a frock rather than a night rail. Lord knew she would likely require a swift escape, and that was most expedient.

Leo's indignation at her refusal rankled. She had every right to refuse him, and she would not be cowed by the fear of impregnation. The topic was a firm reminder, however, that she must take care from then on, for with her current aspirations, she could not afford to get with child. But whatever might happen, she would find a way to live this dream.

Indeed, once she'd heard Grace Huntsbury's proposition, Juliana knew it was the right course for her. No matter what was occurring in her life now, she knew where she belonged. It was for that reason that when she reached London, she was not going directly to Jasper. She would secure her future by completing her rendezvous with Grace. Only then would she demand answers from her brother.

Snick. She loaded the shot and patted it down with the ramming stick that had been given to her. There was a far more critical concern at hand than her disappointment over a proposal. Leo thought them safe to rest, but *he* had not witnessed the cold determination in their pursuer's beautiful eyes. Such a man would not stop after the fire. He was still following them; of that she was certain. Therefore, she must be prepared.

Muscles aching, Juliana replaced the shot and powder in her greatcoat's pocket where it draped over her chair, and strode with the pistol to the rumpled bed. She didn't wish to sleep when the threat of danger hovered over her head, but the better course of action was to rest as much as possible before their next encounter. And, of course, she was exhausted.

She gingerly placed the pistol on the table at her bedside, and slipped between the bedclothes. It was a lumpy affair that pressed uncomfortably into the bruises on her hip and thigh, but it was better than the cold ground.

Turning the gas lamp low, she reached out to keep one

hand on the pistol and closed her eyes. The flickering fire of the hearth and the low-burning lamp wavered beyond her eyelids, creating soothing silhouettes.

A slight dampness formed behind her knees, the only outward sign of her nerves. She ought to feel frightened, even terrified, but all she could muster was trepidation. Perhaps it was due to her conflict with Leo, or mayhap it was because she had previously faced her pursuer and prevailed, but she felt rather calmer than she could have imagined.

She took a deep breath and settled further into the mattress.

Creak.

Juliana's eyes snapped open.

Creak.

Her hand tightened around the pistol, and she slowly turned her gaze toward the noise. A hulking figure crouched in her window, sliding the sash open to allow his bulk through.

That's not Leo.

Gritting her molars, Juliana held back her shout, waiting for the right moment. He moved slowly, as though in pain, until he finally breached the room.

Nerves tingled up her legs before knotting heavily in her stomach. Once he aimed his weapon at her, the upper hand would be his. She could not allow that.

All at once, she sat up, swinging her arm to cock and aim the pistol at the large shadow. She turned up the lamp with her free hand, and light flared through the room, revealing her pursuer's handsome, drawn features. There were dark circles under his eyes and a short growth of beard on the bottom half of his face, but those couldn't disguise his pallid complexion. The man was clearly exhausted and hadn't allowed himself to heal from his injuries.

Juliana bared her teeth at the approaching figure. "Why have you been following me?"

He laughed cruelly, the sound echoing hollowly off the thin walls. "I'm shocked, Juliana, that your brother didn't warn you of our plans."

Her heart tripped over as pain slammed into her chest, but she did her best to mask it. Jasper had known about the threat? And he'd never told her. It was yet another stain upon her relationship with the dastardly Duke of Derby.

"Just a moment," she said, forcing strength into her voice that she didn't feel. "You said *our* plans."

A derisive laugh rasped from his chest. "Of course you must have questions." He snapped open his pocket watch and examined it.

In that moment, Juliana truly looked at the man. Though travel-worn and dirt-smudged, he was dressed in a finely tailored suit of indeterminate colour. He had blond tousled hair, blue eyes that sparked with malice, a broad jaw, and hard lines around his mouth and forehead that spoke of pain and many long days out of doors.

How did he know Jasper?

He closed the pocket watch with a *click* and slipped it into his waistcoat.

The man's wicked smile deepened. "Truth be known, it isn't necessary to kill you, Juliana, and I hadn't intended to. But then you shot me...and stabbed me, and since then I've thought of little but the many ways in which you could die. Oh, what fun we shall have."

"*Fun*? Sir, you forget yourself. It is I who is pointing the pistol at *you*."

He barked a laugh. "Do you not recognize me, dear cousin?"

Juliana stilled, the air in her lungs frozen, her heart slamming against her back. *Cousin.* "No," she whispered. No, he couldn't be. The spark of recognition grew to a blaze as memories of long ago filled her mind's eye. The boy she remembered had been vile. Aberrant and dreadful, he had taken pleasure in and boasted about harming animals on their estate when they were children. On several occasions, he'd attempted to show her the results of what he'd done.

He spread his arms to the sides, a wide, hateful smirk on his lips. "*Yes.*"

Slowly, the puzzle pieces of childhood memories fell into place, and her gut lurched. "Miles." Miles Sinclair, the younger of her two cousins and the more physically destructive of the two. His older brother was always the architect behind their plots—he preferred emotional torture—but Miles was most often the perpetrator of violent acts, always eager to destroy, and to watch as something suffered. But she hadn't seen them since that day long ago... "Where is Francis?"

Miles withdrew the watch from his pocket once more, glanced at it with a satisfied sigh, and returned it to his pocket. "The Duke of Derby has run out of time."

Juliana took a quavering breath. "Miles, where is Francis?"

"He followed your miscreant of a brother to London," the man spat. "It is too late to beg for mercy, Juliana, and even if it weren't, you are not the Sinclair that had a time limit."

"I'll not beg you for anything." She filtered quickly through her memories for something that might dissuade the man from his path And she caught on her cousins' deceased sister, Jean. The poor young woman had perished in 1802. "You don't have to do this. Jean would not have wanted her brothers to become murderers—"

Miles' nostrils flared, his eyes blazing with vehemence. "Don't you *dare* speak her name!"

Her stomach wobbled. *Drat.* That had only served to incense him.

"You will answer my questions, or I shall shoot." She swallowed, focusing on keeping the quaver from her voice.

He jutted his chin in a mulish gesture, his gaze feral. "You have only one shot. What if you miss? What will you have to defend yourself?" He grinned. "Your fate is sealed, and, if you'll recall, I enjoy watching things suffer."

Narrowing her eyes at him, she refused to give in to his machinations. He wanted to see her squirm, but she couldn't give him the satisfaction.

"Why? Why are you chasing me, and what do you want with Jasper?"

The man's mien was disturbingly clear, as though he thought the answer were obvious. "To kill him, of course."

CHAPTER 21

*L*eonard stared into the bottom of his empty tankard for Lord knew how long. He'd nursed the one drink for at least an hour and had no desire for another. In fact, the first sat ill in his stomach. He'd eaten, mulling over his regrets, hurt, and anger over Juliana's deception and rejection.

Marriage was evidently not something for which Juliana pined. He ought to have realized that after learning that she'd fled her home to escape one. And, of course, after their discussion in his library.

Despite how much his body craved hers, he'd best learn to do without. She was correct: he did not wish to sire a bastard, and he could safely presume that she didn't, either.

The din in the taproom had risen as the ale flowed, and Leo recognized that his time there had come to an end. He required a washing and sleep before he and Juliana set out once more on the morrow.

Suppressing a groan at the pain and stiffness in his body as he stood, Leo made his way out of the taproom and up the flight of stairs. He reached for the rented room's latch, and swung the door wide.

Leo froze and cursed as he took in the scene. The room was awash with lamplight, and Juliana had her pistol trained on a man standing menacingly by the opened window.

Her gaze swung his way at his entrance, and the intruder took that opportunity to lash out with a kick, knocking the weapon from Juliana's hand.

Bang!

The pistol landed, spent, on the floor, the acrid scent of gunpowder filling the small space and breaking Leo from his momentary stillness.

"Juliana!" He rushed to her side, dimly aware of the intruder's flight through the window.

"He's absconding!" Juliana shouted.

She tossed the bedclothes aside and tumbled from the bed. Leo reached her side just as she leaned out the window, the lose spirals of her hair waving with the breeze.

"Attempt to attack me again, and your life will be forfeit," Juliana shouted. "You shall never catch me unprepared!"

Leo peered over her shoulder at the man scaling the bottom of the inn's wall. He hopped to the ground and offered them a mock salute.

"I shall see you soon, cousin!"

Leo reared back, retreating into the room as Juliana straightened. *Cousin!*

She turned to face him, her expression grim, and he knew instantly that it was the truth.

Disappointment slammed into his chest and made his breath catch thickly in his throat.

"Cousin," he said flatly. "You knew who your pursuer was from the first, and yet you allowed me to believe differently." He shook his head and cut off her protest. "You've deceived me yet again." Of course she had. How could he be so gullible?

Juliana's beautiful green-slate eyes turned beseeching. "*No. That is not—*"

"*No*," he spat self-deprecatingly, his stomach roiling. "You had me fooled this entire journey, and I blindly went along." Anger curled along his nerves, swiftly replacing his self-reproach. "You make a habit of lying as though it comes as naturally to you as breathing air, *my lady*."

Sadness and righteous pain battled for control of Juliana's emotions. She wanted to fight Leo, to tell him that she'd genuinely not recognized Miles and had every intention of being honest with him. But her fight was gone. Weariness settled in her bones. She longed for sleep. She longed to finally begin her new position in London and put this entire journey behind her.

With a sigh, she retrieved the spent pistol and sat carefully at the table with the fresh shot and gunpowder, prepared to reload the weapon.

"Why did you accompany me after you learned my true name? You evidently have no regard for me or my fraudulent ways; I see no reason for you to be here."

Leo blinked, frowning. "I have already told you why."

Again with his sense of *duty*, his wish to see her safely into her brother's care. She resisted the urge to scoff. It had never been about *her*, or any desire to spend time in her company. Indeed, it was foolhardy to imagine that he could come to develop a *tendre* for her.

Her movements became stiff as she worked. "Perhaps it would be best for you to return home to Miss Notley. I am sure that Mr. Percy is ready to resume his regular duties, and you must be eager to be away." She kept her gaze carefully focused on her task. "I absolve you of your duties and relieve you of any notion of heroism."

There was an unyielding silence for several beats of her

heart, the thudding an erratic rhythm as she waited for him to leave. Surely he would; his distaste of her character was clear.

"Despite my past," he began judiciously, "I am a man of my word. I will not leave you to journey alone."

Lips trembling and throat tight with sadness, Juliana couldn't utter a response, so she simply dipped her head in a nod.

Thump-thump.

Her head came up as Leo spun toward the bedchamber door. It burst open to reveal the innkeeper and several large stable hands.

"You two need to leave," the innkeeper announced, glancing warily between them. "We've 'ad complaints, and there'll be no guns firin' on these premises."

"Of course, sir." Leo stepped forward and the man flinched. "We will gather our things and be on our way. Please see our mounts saddled."

The innkeeper twisted his lips and narrowed his eyes, but nodded before departing.

LONDON

WITH A DISCREET GLANCE over her shoulder, Maria Roberts closed the door of her unmarked—and entirely unremarkable—personal hack and knocked a knuckle against its side before hurrying down the muddy path of St. James' Park toward her home. Her movements were routine but entirely condemnable. But only her two best friends knew of her secret, and rather than reproaching her for it, they rather appreciated her clandestine life.

Unfortunately, her secrets would not aid in finding Juliana.

She hurried her steps along the thoroughfare and turned onto her street, feeling a sense of home wash over her as she spotted the familiar front steps.

Days ago, Maria had put out an ad in the fashion magazines and gossip rags, requesting information about a woman matching Juliana's description. Unfortunately, her plan had gone awry.

A carriage rolled by, the horses clopping on the cobblestone. The wind was biting, and she eagerly darted up the front steps of her home and entered the opened door.

"My goodness," Maria breathed, her lips gone slightly numb with cold. "I am pleased to be indoors."

Her familial butler bowed shallowly and accepted her outerwear, a swift frown creasing his brow as he took in the state of her walking shoes and petticoats. "A guest awaits you in the parlour, miss, and this arrived while you were out."

Maria gasped, and accepted the note, tearing it open. Whoever awaited her could be patient another minute if this was what she hoped.

The direction was written in an unsteady and unfamiliar hand. Anticipation spiked. She scanned the first paragraph, and hope filled her. *Juliana*.

"Thank you." She smiled at the butler and turned toward the stairs. She could not very well entertain callers dressed as she was.

The aging man cleared his throat behind her. "I beg your pardon, miss, but your guest was quite insistent that you see him directly upon your return."

Juliana nodded and redirected to the parlour. The scent of sandalwood touched her senses before she'd reached the door, and she inwardly groaned. She knew what he'd come to say, and she wished that she could avoid it. Instead, she drew her shoulders back, stiffened her spine, and entered with confidence.

Jasper Sinclair, the Duke of Derby, halted his pacing by the hearth to scowl menacingly at her. She could feel his displeasure from across the room, but she continued toward him, her stomach wobbling.

"How *dare* you?" he snarled. "I specifically said to leave matters well enough alone, and you—"

"I've found her," Maria cut over him.

He blinked. "You've... *What*?"

Maria stopped within arm's reach and waved the parchment in her hand. "I've received a response from the advertisement."

"*And*? What does it say, damn it?"

Maria read. "*Dear sir or madam. I am not at liberty to interfere, but I believe that I have seen your missing person.*" Maria lifted an eyebrow at Jasper before returning to the letter. "This missive describes Juliana precisely, down to the colour of her eyes. It goes on to say that she was found nigh starved and covered in blood by the lord of the estate after a carriage accident."

Jasper cursed and resumed his pacing, and Maria flipped the parchment over.

"She was abed, sick with the fever for days before she became a governess to the lord's niece." Maria skimmed ahead, her stomach knotting as the servant hinted at debauchery. *I would not write of such things*, the letter continued, *if you had not expressed such concern in your advertisement.* "It is concluded with a warning that someone dangerous was in pursuit of Juliana when she left."

The duke's mien turned mulish. "What are you withholding?"

Maria huffed. "Nothing of import, Your Grace. Our attentions would be best served elsewhere. Juliana is alive but in danger. We must—"

"*We* mustn't do anything, Maria. I will search for her. Does the missive say in which direction she went?"

"I'm afraid not. But I shall inquire—"

"*No.*"

"But I—"

He sliced a hand through the air. "It is far too dangerous. I'll not have *your* life on my conscience, as well."

Maria bit at her lips, her mind working. Jasper did not know of what she was capable and, therefore, could not trust her discretion and stealth. She, however, knew herself. She would simply have to find a way to aid in the search without riding uselessly about the countryside and speaking to innkeepers.

CHAPTER 22

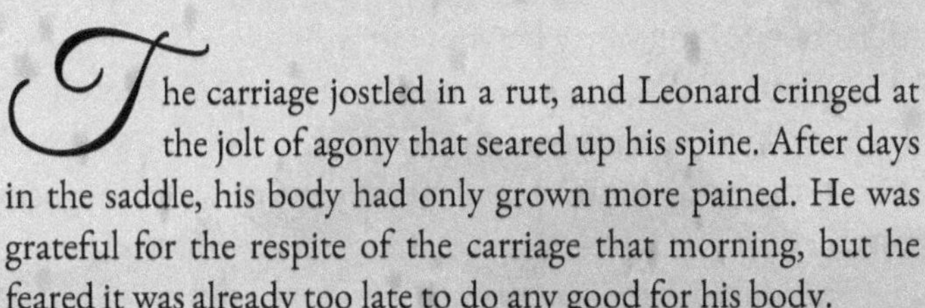

The carriage jostled in a rut, and Leonard cringed at the jolt of agony that seared up his spine. After days in the saddle, his body had only grown more pained. He was grateful for the respite of the carriage that morning, but he feared it was already too late to do any good for his body.

At night, they behaved as virtual strangers, eating their meals in the public rooms and renting separate rooms in which to wash and sleep. The loneliness fisting in his chest made him feel oddly hollow. He despised being so...exposed in the public eye, and now with Juliana's silence, he felt even more isolated than he did at his estate.

He rolled his cinnamon drop over his tongue and tucked it into his cheek, savouring the sweet spiciness. The air in the carriage was cool, though not as crisp as the air out of doors. Snow coated the ground in a bleak curtain turned a hazy grey in the predawn hours. The trees dripped as the snow melted and fell. It was cold enough for the snow to remain, but nothing fresh had fallen in the past three-and-sixty hours.

Juliana shifted in her seat across from him, a yawn tightening her features. The silence between them was deafening.

They'd agreed to hire a carriage, but the driver had wished to return home before luncheon, forcing them to depart in the middle of the night.

He glanced once more at the passing darkness, disappointment heavy behind his ribs.

"We are nearing London," he said into the quiet. "Perhaps four hours more before you are returned to your brother."

"This silence between us has gone on long enough." Her voice was brittle, and her complexion pallid in the darkness. "Whether because of our evasive riding or some other fate, Miles has not approached us again on our journey. I am grateful for the respite, but we cannot become complacent. He might see you as a target, as well, and no matter what you think of me, I still worry for your safety."

"Worry not." Leo cleared his throat and scratched idly at his bare chin. "I have summoned Percy to London. I will await him at my house in town, and we will return to Nottingham together."

She pulled her lips between her teeth and worried the flesh. "Very good, then." She paused, tracing her fingers along the hem of her brother's greatcoat. "I am sincerely sorry, Leo. For all of this. I need you to know that I truly did not identify Miles. He was a rather lanky child when I knew him, whose ears and square jaw had seemed over-large for his small frame. He grew into his features, to be sure...and I did not recognize him."

Small lines of worry formed between her brows, and Leonard's lungs deflated. Truthfully, the past days had rather subdued his anger into a melancholy. He wished that he could have reclaimed the easy camaraderie between them.

He inclined his head. "Thank you."

She returned his nod with one of her own, a small smile curving the edge of her mouth.

They rounded a corner, the carriage wheels sliding in the

snow, and Juliana's spine stiffened, her hands clutched together tightly in her lap. They hit a rut, the carriage jostling. Her eyes squeezed shut and her breath came in rapid, uneven huffs.

Leo cursed, and crossed the carriage to situate himself next to her on the seat, spreading his furs over the both of them. Distraction, Percy had said, was what she required.

Reaching into his inner waistcoat pocket, he withdrew his spectacles and put them on with one hand.

She gave him a tight, tremulous smile. "You brought a book with you?"

"I did. Haven't had many an opportunity to read it until now. In fact, it was in my saddlebags until we agreed to take this carriage. How do you feel"—he pulled a book from his coat pocket and glanced at the inside title page, tilting it to catch the light of the driver's carriage lamp—"about *Travels into Several Remote Nations of the World. In Four Parts. By Lemuel Gulliver, First a Surgeon, and then a Captain of Several Ships* by Jonathan Swift?"

Her smile grew incrementally. *Gulliver's Travels*! Papa detested those tales, but I made my governess read them to me in secret."

"Settle in, then," he urged. "I shall read to you."

Juliana peered up at him in bemusement, and he offered her a tentative smile. It was a gesture of peace that would, with luck, simultaneously ease Juliana's fears and quell the torrent of despondency within him.

Clearing his throat, he read. "My father had a small estate in Nottinghamshire..."

THE LENGTHS to which Maria would go to speak with the dratted Duke of Derby would astound most anyone.

When she'd learned that he had gone for an early morning ride at Rotten Row, she'd re-mounted her mare and had ridden after him. Her familial staff was accustomed to her clandestine flights from home, but at the moment, she wished that she'd considered wearing a darker riding habit. She was far too visible in the predawn light.

The wind was brisk, but what she needed to say was important, and worth the cold-rouged cheeks.

She galloped through Hyde Park, only slowing as she neared Rotten Row. As promised, a rider approached in the distance.

Maria's knees tingled, and she frowned at them. Her body's reaction to the duke's nearness was entirely irksome.

She opened her mouth to call out to Jasper, but his bellow cut her off.

Heart in her throat, she watched in horror as the horse's saddle came undone and he was thrown with it from the horse, landing with a hard *whomph*.

Maria dismounted and ran the short distance to him.

"Your Grace!"

He groaned, sitting up.

"Do be careful," she said, kneeling at his side. "Have you broken anything?"

Without prompting, Maria put her hands to his arms and neck, feeling for anything out of place.

"No," he said, his voice rumbling. "The bruising will be a sight, I'm certain, but no broken bones." He put a hand to his forehead. "What the devil happened to my saddle?"

"I shall examine it." The overwhelming relief that he had not killed himself made her voice high and breathy as she left to inspect the saddle several feet away.

The leather was pleasantly warm beneath her gloved fingers, but she didn't take the time to ruminate on the fact that the duke's very fine bottom had moments before been resting on its surface. Instead, she turned her attention to the straps and buckles.

Her stuttered breath clouded before her face. *Oh, hell.*

"Your Grace." She looked at him over her shoulder as he stood. "These straps have been severed."

Crack!

The Duke hollered in pain once more, clapping a hand over his left bicep. "Christ, I think I've been shot!"

His wild gaze flew up to meet hers. "*Run*, Maria! Get back to your horse!"

Crack!

He flinched, cursing again. "*Go!*" he called to her as he mounted his gelding bare-backed.

Feet moving as though of their own accord, Maria ran to her frightened mare, and leapt. Her inelegant sprawl upon the beast's back was both painful and unwise, but she hadn't a choice. She shifted her position until she'd hooked her leg over the pommel and was situated sidesaddle. Then, they broke into a gallop.

She did not wait to see if the duke followed; she simply rode. Her pulse thrummed in her ears, her stomach whirled, and her cheeks burned from the cold, but she kept going.

Grosvenor Square came into view, and Maria veered toward the duke's home. A footman came out and accepted the reins from her mount, and only after she'd lowered to the ground did she look back to see the duke.

With a grimace, he dismounted and led the way inside.

Warmth enveloped her as they entered the building.

"Hot water in my study, if you will," Jasper grunted at the butler.

"Of course, Your Grace," the butler bowed. "I—*oh! Your Grace!* You are bleeding!"

"Yes, it seems I was grazed by a bullet."

The butler gestured frantically for the footmen, demanding a doctor be summoned.

The duke ushered Maria into his study while the servants fluttered nervously, and while the cleaning and bandaging of his wound were important, she had sought him out for a reason.

"I received another letter about Juliana," she said without preamble.

His gaze turned sharp. "And?"

"It was from an innkeeper's wife located just outside of Leicester. She said that Juliana and a tall, fair-haired man had rented a room—"

"*Together?*"

Maria nodded. "She informed me that there had been gunfire, and her husband had no choice but to force them to leave."

The duke cursed under his breath and stalked to the hearth and back. "That is a more recent account than I've had."

"You've heard from them?" Maria's eyebrows lifted, and her chin rubbed aggravatingly against the ribbon of her bonnet. With a huff of frustration, she untied it and tossed it to a nearby chair.

His gaze scanned her face before he sighed in resignation. "I had a letter from my estate. The details in the letter were ambiguous, but Juliana and a man named Mr. Notley had been in the stables when it was set ablaze. They were able to relocate all of the horses and the fire was extinguished, but they'd left swiftly thereafter."

"They left?"

"They're on their way here, apparently." He gestured at himself with his uninjured arm. "I couldn't sleep for worrying over her safety. According to the date, they ought to already be in London proper. I went for a ride to clear my head of worry. It didn't bloody well work."

"And it seems that someone wished it to be your last ride."

"THIS CANNOT BE THE CORRECT ADDRESS," Leo grumbled, his eyes narrowing suspiciously on Juliana.

Her stomach flopped over as she nodded in the affirmative. "It is the direction that I gave the driver."

She reached for the door's handle, but his gentle fingertips on her wrist stopped her forward momentum. Gooseflesh spread over her skin and a shiver threatened. Lord, what the man's touch did to her.

The journey had been a struggle. She ached all over, and their silence before today had been strained and discomfiting. But in the carriage, they'd seemed to come to an unspoken accord. And goodness, but she'd missed him.

He notched his chin out the window to the nondescript house. It was attached to its neighbours and faced the grand entrance to the Royal Opera House. "This is Bow Street, Juliana. I have little doubt that your brother—the *duke*—lives in Mayfair. Mayhap even Grosvenor Square."

He was absolutely correct, of course. But she could not relent.

"I am aware of the street, I assure you. This is where I belong. Now if you please, allow me to exit."

His eyes were wary, but he withdrew his hand and preceded her from the carriage. With a puff of foggy breath, he turned and aided her descent.

The air was crisp, and the hint of rouge to Leo's cheeks somehow brightened the blue of his irises. She wanted to give him a proper farewell, to kiss him one last time before the carriage clattered away with him inside, but she was not his to kiss.

"Thank you," she said. "Our challenges notwithstanding, I enjoyed my time with you." *I will miss you.*

Leo reached a hand toward her, but with a glance around them swiftly pulled it back. His gaze turned sad, almost imploring. The sight sent a responding ache through her chest.

The silence between them stretched on, and the twinge in her heart spread. It tingled down her arms and quivered in her stomach. Her breaths felt heavy, her shoulders slumping of their own accord. She ought to be pleased that she'd finally reached her destination, but she was having the devil of a time leaving the man who had made her feel so very much.

"I do not wish for you to go," he said, his voice nearly inaudible over the trundling of a nearby hack and the horse's hooves.

But she'd heard it. Hadn't she? Oh goodness, what if it was merely her curst hopeful heart? And dash it, she shouldn't be hopeful! The man had broken her heart and wanted her only out of a sense of duty. While he was a fine man in many regards, Juliana deserved to be loved by a man she called her own. *Forming close attachments is dangerous, and will only hurt you in the end.*

He cleared his throat. "I would like to help you, if I can."

Help. Her stomach sank. Was that another obligation that he felt?

All at once, their unfinished argument at the inn ran through her mind: his dutiful proposal, his desire not to sire a bastard on her, and the pain she'd felt when he'd fled to the taproom. She'd wanted him to *want* her, just as she now wanted him to help because he could not countenance leaving her.

"You would?"

"As I mentioned, Percy will be in town soon, and two men aiding you and your brother in defence against Miles would be invaluable."

Her chest—and the hope within it—deflated. "I thank you for your kind offer, but I cannot bear the responsibility of your life being put in further danger. It is too great a risk."

"I believe that is for me to decide."

She shook her head. "Miles is not alone. His brother Francis is apparently already here in London, keeping Jasper under close observation." Her shoulders lifted with her sigh. "It would be prudent for you to return home with Percy. Remain safe."

His face twisted in a flinch, which he attempted to cover with a short bow. "As you wish."

Without another word, he retrieved her saddlebags and brought them to the door. "Be careful, Juliana."

Dipping in a curtsey, she turned and rapped on the door with shaking fingers.

CHAPTER 23

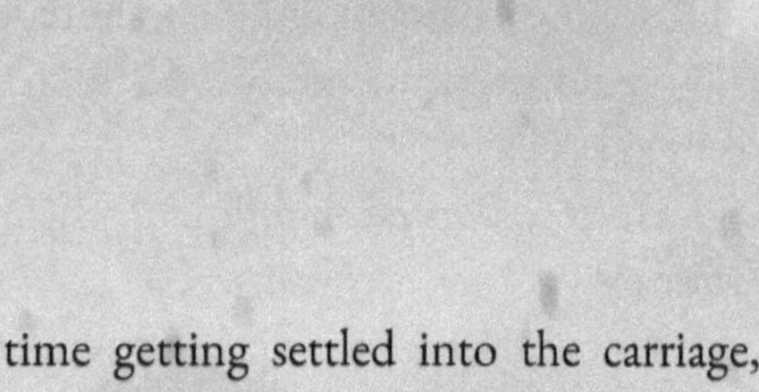

Leo took his time getting settled into the carriage, ensuring that Juliana made it safely into the building before he rode away. The young woman at the door seemed genuinely pleased to see her, so he supposed that she was in the correct place.

The door shut with finality, and Leo rapped on the carriage's ceiling.

Juliana mightn't wish for him to interfere, but it was inevitable. He couldn't leave London without first knowing that she was safe from her cousin, couldn't live with himself if he had another death on his conscience.

The carriage stopped in front of his house, and he alighted, saddlebag slung over one shoulder. He paid the driver and found his way inside, the building cold and filled with linen-covered furniture and art. If it hadn't been entailed, he would have sold it three years hence, but now he was grateful for the shelter.

If he was to find the Duke of Derby's home, he'd best make himself presentable. He'd never had to fend for himself, but he managed to fill a pitcher at the water pump in the garden, and he used a cloth to wash himself in the kitchens. The frigid water stole his breath, but he was soon clean and wearing a change of attire.

It had been years since Leo had frequented a club or pub on St. James' Street, but if he was to learn the duke's direction, it was a promising place to begin his search.

Misty rain hung in the air and crept beneath his coat, where it seeped into his aching bones. He was grateful for the respite of a hack, and finally the warmth of the club.

"Name, sir," the doorman inquired.

Leo hesitated. It was the first time since his incarceration that he'd been forced to give his name and title, and it rankled.

"Leonard Notley, the Marquess of Livingston."

The man checked a book, then nodded him through with a lifted brow.

The club was well-appointed, the furnishings costly, and the green-and-burgundy carpet and wall hangings lavish. There were but a few men seated quietly in the main parlour, so Leo strode to the rear rooms, where the dining tables were set and a bar was located near the far wall.

Despite his discomfort, Leo crossed the room. Juliana required his assistance, whether she desired it or not. And, damn it, he knew that she had been withholding something from him. There hadn't even been footmen to retrieve her saddlebags, and the door hadn't opened when she'd approached the front step. Nor was there a butler in residence. There was certainly something not right about where she'd gone.

"Good day, your lordship," the barkeep nodded.

"Good day," Leo replied brusquely, sliding some coins on the counter between them. "Do you happen to know the direction of the Duke of Derby?"

A man rose from his seat at a dining table nearby, his eyes

flashing with hostile suspicion. "Why would you care to know?"

Leo turned to face the vaguely familiar gentleman with a nod. "I have urgent business with him."

"Going to share your drink with him, too, Livingston?" the man sneered.

Despite himself, he could feel the faint hint of a blush rise up his neck. And he hadn't the beard to conceal the bloody thing.

"O-of course not," he stammered.

Christ, he felt too hot. Men at the surrounding tables turned to watch the exchange, and the feeling of exposure expanded in his chest. They knew who he was, what had happened to his brother...

Beads of perspiration formed on his back and began to tickle the fine hairs on his spine as they dripped toward his trousers.

"Don't give the marquess anything to drink," the man said to the barkeep. "He might decide to poison someone."

Horror rooted Leo to the spot as memories of that ghastly day raged through his mind. His brother's expression of gruesome shock, the gut-wrenching pain of losing the man that Leo had always looked up to, and the hollowness that had come once he'd accepted his inevitable death by hanging.

"Is that what you're planning to do with the duke?" the gentleman continue with a sneer. "Poison him?"

Shame prickled over Leo's skin, and his fingers began to tremble. He would never be able to clear his name. To the *ton*, he would always be known as the man who murdered his brother. Of course Juliana had rejected him; it made all too much sense to him, now. Leo was not capable of giving Lady Juliana the life that she deserved.

That familiar ill, hollow feeling settled into his chest, spreading like icy river water through his body, until he was covered in a sheen of cold perspiration and miserable acceptance.

It had been too soon to return to London. Hell, *forever* would be too soon.

He cleared his throat and mumbled his excuses before flee-ing. Like the bloody coward he was. The gaze of every man in the club burned into his back as though they were extin-guishing their cigars on his bared skin.

MIDDAY LIGHT SHONE through the tall windows of the diminutive drawing room situated just off the foyer, and Juliana soaked up the warmth. Rain pattered against the glass, the sound soothing her rattled nerves.

Would she ever see Leo again? The question repeated itself in her mind, taunting her with all of the things she ought to have said to him before they'd parted. The moment she'd turned away from him to walk to the door, she could feel his gaze boring into her back as though he'd stroked it with his hands. She despaired at the intimate feeling.

I'll not be an obligation, she asserted. No matter how much weight had settled on her chest at rejecting him, at leaving his side, Juliana knew that living in a marriage of unre-quited love would be—

She stilled, her eyes growing wide. *Love.*

No, it couldn't be. She would not allow herself to feel love for the man. The emotion would not serve her well when he returned to Nottingham and she began her work in London. It would be best for her to focus her attention on the new changes to her life. And yet her pulse drummed in her ears.

Forcibly turning her thoughts away from the matters of her foolish heart, she took in the room.

One of the few rooms on the main floor of the building,

the drawing room was to be used as their space for conducting business. To one side stood two wide desks, behind which towered a wall of bookshelves. The remainder of the space was filled with cream-and-green upholstered chairs and chaises, with white-painted wood tables. It was an attractive sitting room, bright and inviting—ideal for both recruitment and for discussions with potential patrons.

Tingles of anticipation raced up the backs of her legs.

"Oh, Juliana! I'm so pleased that you're here." Grace Huntsbury glided into the room, her face wreathed in smiles and her arms outstretched.

Juliana stood from the settee and swept her friend into a tight embrace.

"Tell me, how fared your journey?" Grace led her back to the settee, where they sat.

Careful to omit the very sordid aspects of her misadventure, Juliana told her friend all that had occurred. Tea had been brought while she spoke, and Grace served. It had been far too long since Juliana had enjoyed such a luxury that it nearly brought tears to her eyes. Of course, it was also, perhaps, that her heart was slowly breaking.

"I sense that there is more to this tale," Grace said frankly after she'd concluded, her shrewd gaze scanning Juliana's features. "However, I believe that we might be able to help you."

A smile tugged at Juliana's lips, hope finally blossoming. "And that is precisely why I came to you first." She took a sip of her tea then edged toward her friend. "Tell me, how have preparations come along? Do we have many women?"

"We've had a promising number of preliminary interviews, but not one woman has yet completed her first task."

"And my friends, Maria and Heather?"

Grace's grin grew. "I'd rather thought that we could interview them together."

"Splendid."

"Now." Grace's tone grew sober. "Are *you* prepared for your first task?"

PULLING his coat tightly around himself, Leonard tramped across Grosvenor Square. He had guessed that the duke was a resident nearby and, as gauche as it was, Leo knocked on several doors, requesting direction, until someone at last capitulated.

Those few patrons who passed him on the rainy walk eyed him with open curiosity. The numbness in his heart provided him with protection from their stares, and his purpose kept his feet moving. He must warn the duke before further danger befell Juliana, and the man needed to know that it followed him, as well.

Striding with determination, Leo came to a halt before the red door of a grand building and rapped on its surface with his numb knuckles. Several long moments passed before a man of middling years opened the door.

"The duke is not in," the man said bluntly.

Leo stepped closer. "My name is Leonard Notley. I have urgent business with His Grace."

"His Grace has said that I'm not to admit anyone—"

"I come bearing news of Lady Juliana."

The door swung abruptly inward, swirling the mixture of cool and warm air around him.

"Do come in, sir."

The butler took Leo's wet outer garments and led him through the surprisingly modest foyer and down a corridor into what appeared to be a sitting room.

"Please do make yourself comfortable." He bowed. "I shall inform His Grace of your presence directly upon his return."

With a nod of thanks, Leo took to an under-stuffed armchair and waited in silence. The room was blissfully warm and, despite himself, his eyelids began to droop.

Leo jolted upright with a start, and blinked. Christ, had he fallen asleep?

Heavy footfalls and loud voices echoed from the foyer, growing muffled as the man strode down the carpet runner of the corridor.

Leo stood just before the door swung inward and admitted a tall, dark-haired man with eyes... *Damnation*. His eyes were the same unique mixture of colours as Juliana's.

"Who the devil are you, and what news have you of my sister?" the duke barked.

"My name is Leonard Notley—"

"The man who travelled with her!" The duke's skin reddened. "What in the bloody hell were you doing alone with her without a chaperone? And where is she, now?"

Leo opened his mouth to reply, but a familiar lilting voice from the doorway halted him.

"I'm right here, brother." Juliana swept into the room wearing a serviceable grey walking dress that lovingly accentuated her curves and height.

The air rushed from Leo's lungs before he could gather himself under control.

"*Juliana*," the duke breathed, rushing to envelop her in his arms.

The two stood in their embrace, murmuring relieved greetings into each other's shoulders, and all at once, Leo felt out of place.

After several long moments, she stiffened, her jaw hardening as she pulled away. "I'm here with a purpose, Jasper."

It was then that Leo noticed the travelling writing box that she carried in one hand. *What—*

Striding to the settee, Juliana perched on its edge and

withdrew the writing implements before snapping the lid shut once more and using it as a portable desk. She cleared her throat. "We have business to discuss."

"*Business*," the duke spat.

Juliana nodded, but there was a hint of wariness in her gaze.

"I must ask you some questions, brother."

"What are you doing, Juliana?" The duke scowled at her.

She took in a deep breath and drew her shoulders back, her gaze defiant. "I've taken a runner position on Bow Street."

CHAPTER 24

"*The hell you have!*" Jasper roared. "You are no more capable of enforcing the laws of the lands and handling the citizens of London than I am of sprouting wings and flying to the moon."

"I'll not be required to handle the citizens of London." The nerves in Juliana's abdomen intensified. "I gave my word some time ago, and I fully intend to follow through with my promise. It is what I want, Jasper."

"What does the job entail?" Leo's question cut across Jasper's outraged blustering.

Her chest tightened as she turned her gaze on him. Leo appeared ill: pale and despondent. Had something untoward occurred since they had seen each other that morning? Or, perhaps, had *she* caused his change in demeanour? Another wave of despair washed over her, and she gritted her teeth against it.

"It doesn't bloody matter what it entails," Jasper growled. "She will resign her post and wed Viscount Rivers directly. I'll not stand for this, Juliana!"

"I shall be a Bow Street runner among other women. We will—"

"Bah!" Jasper scoffed. "What could you possibly do that the men cannot? Surely you would not count yourselves among the horse patrol?"

Juliana drew herself up in affront. "Indeed not. Women are capable of plenty, I assure you. But our focus will be on women in need of aid, or those who do not trust the work of the men."

Jasper's "What a foolish notion!" came at the same time as Leo's "Capital idea."

"Who *is* this man to you?" Jasper's scowl deepened as he turned his narrowed gaze on Leo. "And why do you presume to interfere?"

"This is Leonard Not—"

"I know his bloody name, Juliana!" Jasper hissed. "Why is he here with you?"

Leo cleared his throat. "I came to warn you, Your Grace. Lady Juliana and I encountered a man named Miles Sinclair on our journey to London, and knew him to be in town and intent on doing harm to both of you."

"Notley..." Jasper's eyes narrowed further as he thought. "Sodding hell, you're the Marquess of Livingston!"

The distress in Leo's stormy blue eyes tugged at Juliana's heart.

"*This* is the man you travelled with?" Jasper glared accusingly at Juliana. "The former pirate notorious for his philandering and accused of murdering his brother?"

Leo paled further, his shade positively alarming.

"Yes, he is," Juliana nodded, her spine stiff. "He offered shelter and the healing hand of a doctor when I required aid, and he gallantly provided protection on my journey from Nottingham to London."

Her brother's jaw worked, the muscles bulging as he took in her words. Fury radiated from his every pore.

"I've completed my objective," Leo said softly. "Juliana is safe, and you're aware of the threat. I will take my leave of you now."

Jasper put out a hand to halt Leo's movement. "You'll go nowhere until you've done right by my sister. As much as I despise the thought of her being associated with your reputation, you impugn her honour by not offering your hand."

"I have already offered it." Leo's voice had grown hoarse, his lips thinned. "She refused me."

"You did *what*?" Jasper whirled on her. "You cannot refuse to marry everyone, Juliana! And you most certainly cannot become a runner for sodding Bow Street. You'll marry the viscount, and I'll not hear another word on the matter."

The argument that she was no longer in possession of her maidenhead was on the fringes of her lips, but she refused to throw what she and Leo had shared into the light. And certainly not as a weapon against her brother. It would be turned around on Leo, and that, she could not abide.

It was rather strange that even though her feelings about Leo were conflicted, just one glimpse of his uncertainty and discomfort, and Juliana was possessed of an intense urge to comfort and soothe him.

"Your Grace." Leo sketched a short bow then strode toward Juliana, his gaze haunted. "I wish you good fortune and joy."

She opened her mouth to reply, but before she could utter a sound, he gave another swift bow and left on a cloud of shaving soap and cinnamon. Intense longing pulled at Juliana's chest as she watched him walk away. Would he turn if she called out to him? Very likely. But she must force the urge aside. Only after she had completed the task of interviewing her brother would she permit herself the time to seek Leo out and discuss her bewildering feelings of loss and betrayal.

Lord, but she could not make sense of it all. It bore considering, but not now. *Later*, she promised herself.

Settling the portable writing desk on her lap and dipping her pen in the ink, she gazed determinedly at her brother. "How long have you known about the threat against us?"

Jasper paled, and his eyes narrowed. "Why must you insist on defying me?"

Indignation speared Juliana's chest even while nerves twisted inside her. Her fingertips found the decorative side of the inkpot on her lap desk, and she traced the leafed pattern.

"You flee the estate," Jasper continued, pacing before her, "abandoning the marriage that I had arranged to protect you. You travel alone with a man whom you do not know, and whose reputation is abhorrent." He placed his hands upon his hips. "Only to take a position as a sodding runner—all while damaging our family name!" He stopped his pacing and spun to face her, his features heated with distaste and disappointment. "How in the bloody hell *could* you?"

That look hurt far more than Juliana wished to admit. She steeled herself against the pain and focused once more on her task. In her position, she would undoubtedly encounter difficult individuals. This was a test, after all, and who better to test her than someone with whom she shared history?

"Your pardon, brother, but how in the hell could *you*? You have the title and dominance, but you withheld information from me; you drove me to flee our home! Leo saved me."

Jasper's eyes flashed with irate suspicion at the use of Leo's given name, but she powered on.

"Now." She calmed her voice and took a deep breath. "How long have you known about Francis and Miles' desire for the dukedom? What are their habits? Do you know of any hobbies or societal interests? What drives them, aside from the death of Jean and their desire for wealth and status?"

"*I'll not encourage this*!" Jasper burst out, his red face a mask of fury. "Think you that I have not considered these questions? That I have not discussed them with my own men? That I am not searching for them myself? You believe me a simpleton, Juliana? Do you believe that I am merely sitting back and awaiting their attacks like a bumbling—"

"Of course not!" She set aside the writing desk and stood to face her brother. "I trust that you—"

"*Trust*," he spat. "You do not trust a soul, so fearful that everyone is the same as our father. You could not even trust *me* in my decision to arrange your marriage."

She gritted her teeth, her chest tight with fresh pain. "The viscount is an old man, Jasper!"

"And ill!" he returned on a shout. "The man has mere months left to live—and estates throughout England, Scotland, and France; an arsenal of staff; a title; and wealth to keep you happy for years to come. I selected him for you precisely because he would protect you and not emotionally imprison you. I was trying to give you your bloody freedom!"

Like a wave of tiny pin prickles, Juliana could feel the blood drain from her face as she stared in shock at her brother. Could it be true? Had he actually considered her feelings before arranging her marriage? The hurt and indignation on his features told her that he had, indeed. But why hadn't he told her? Would she have listened?

Shame washed over her. She'd been wrong, so very wrong about everything.

All this time, she'd thought that Jasper had betrayed her, had tried to force her into a lasting marriage with a doddering old fool. And while she'd had reason to believe that, it hadn't been true. What if she had remained at his side and discussed her circumstance with him? Would she still have absconded as she had? *Indeed*. She'd made the right decision in reaching out to Grace, but the way she'd left home had been wrong.

What impact would her actions now have on Jasper? He was a duke, so any gossip or cruelty would pass swiftly and the *haut ton* would soon forget everything. But what of his heart? Would *he* recover from *her* betrayal?

Dismay spread from her core out to her limbs.

Did she know *anything* based on fact, or had she assumed everything for years? And what of Leo and her new position on Bow Street? Had she made assumptions that led her there, as well? Had Leo actually proposed because he felt duty-bound to protect her reputation and not sire a bastard?

A sickening wobble filled her stomach, sending a ripple of anxiousness through her limbs. Her fingers trembled as she brushed a stray ringlet off her forehead, and she swiftly clasped her hands in the folds of her skirts.

Oh, Lord. She'd failed herself, she'd failed Leo, and she had inexorably failed her test. She knew nothing more about her cousins than when she'd entered, and likely never would...but she certainly knew more about herself.

The heat of shame and recrimination began in her calves and worked its way up her legs, spreading and causing a tingling numbness to follow swiftly in its wake. *I've failed.*

With her interpretation of the world around her so compromised, would it be wise for her to continue in her pursuit of employment on Bow Street? Her heart squeezed even at the notion. Not becoming a runner was not to be borne. She needed that sense of purpose. But would she be fair and just? *Yes*, her heart whispered. But somehow, she felt that she needed to prove that, even to herself.

The heat and numbness found their way to her chest and prickled down her arms and into her fingertips.

"I...I am profoundly sorry, brother. Please excuse me."

Juliana retrieved the portable writing table and strode woodenly toward the door.

"Where are you going?" Jasper asked, coming to her side.

Where *was* she going? She didn't know. She just needed to get out, to clear her mind and think this through without Jasper's scrutiny.

"To the gardens," she lied. She needed to go further than that.

He nodded, his mien still stormy. "Bring a guard with you. Miles and Francis will stop at nothing." He placed a gentle palm to his left arm with a grimace. "I cannot countenance their succeeding in their task. But I have not yet concluded with you; I expect to see you in my study directly upon your return."

"Of course." Without another word, Juliana fled, numbly donning her cloak and bonnet as she dashed out the door and into the drizzling rain, offering a small smile to the footman who had darted out beside her. She'd done well enough on her journey not only to London, but also from Bow Street to Grosvenor Square, and she was never without her pistol. But she couldn't trust her own reactions at the moment.

Her feet guided her away from Grosvenor Square, while her thoughts continued turning in a jumbled mess. Her trembling hands fisted at her sides. She wanted to shout, to scream out in frustration, but gnashed her teeth together, instead. Of all of the possible outcomes of her journey, she'd not imagined that she would have made it to the end only to fail in her very first task.

The past, however, could not be changed. She had made many mistakes, but she must now look forward. What could she do? What was her next course of action?

A solid tug of longing filled her chest, and she abruptly wished that she were back at Leo's estate in Nottingham, playing by the warmth of a blazing hearth with Elizabeth.

She'd known then what was required of her, and she'd received affection and appreciation in return.

How *did* Lizzy fare? Was she frightened by her flight from her home? Did Percy read to her in the evening as she enjoyed?

Her footfalls—and those of the footman—clicked on the cobblestones, the sound scarcely audible over the *clip-clop* of horses' hooves, the rumble of carriage wheels through puddles, and the steady hum of voices and activity in the rain around her. But she couldn't focus on any of it.

She huffed a sigh, her breath clouding the air and dispersing quickly as she walked through it.

Mayhap she could write a letter for Lizzy. Bringing it to Leo would give Juliana the opportunity to speak privately with him. What she would say to him, she didn't know, but she hadn't a choice; her heart needed to be near him again.

Her next step did not reach the ground. With nary a sound but for a swift intake of breath, she was gripped around the waist and pulled bodily into the nearby close.

CHAPTER 25

$\mathcal{M}$aria tugged her cloak nervously closed as they approached Grosvenor Square. Her stomach fluttered, and her knees tingled in an irksome manner.

Heather scoffed. "For pity's sake. Tell the duke you love him and be done with it."

"*Heather*!" Maria hissed. "I don't—"

"If you'll not be honest with me, at least be honest with yourself. You are undeniably infatuated."

"I'll not have this discussion now. Our friend is missing!"

"Quite right," Heather capitulated.

They continued in silence, rounding the corner onto the desired street.

"And," Maria continued quietly, breaking their silence, "you know why I cannot pursue him."

"*Pish*. If he loves you in return, he will accept *all* of you."

Maria rolled her eyes despite the curst flutter in her chest. "He doesn't love me, Heather; we infuriate each other. And if he did, there is undoubtedly too much for him to accept."

"Infuriate, desire… I do not see much of a difference."

A growl sounded from deep in Maria's throat. "I regret

showing you that dratted book, Heather. You've become positively indecent. Now, hush."

She raised her hand, poised to knock on the duke's door, when it swung inward. A waft of warm air rushed past her, and she shivered.

"Maria! Er—Miss Roberts, Miss Morgan." The duke bowed his head. "I was just on my way to find Juliana."

"As we have been for—"

"She just left," the duke clarified, scowling at Maria.

"She was *here*?" Heather's eyebrows arched high.

His gaze narrowed. "You did not expect her to come home at first, did you? You both knew about her intentions to become a Bow Street runner."

Maria chewed on her bottom lip before she responded. "She did not wish for you to worry—"

He bared his teeth in a snarl. "I must find her. She left only moments ago with a footman. Both of you get into my carriage; we are going to Bow Street."

THE DOOR CLOSED with an ominous *thunk* that echoed in the empty foyer. With a shiver, Leonard strode toward his study, keeping his gloves and cloak on. He passed two rooms and idly glanced inside. White sheets draped the furniture like short, misshapen ghosts.

Before that day, it had been more than three years since he'd stepped foot in that building, and longer since he'd kept it staffed, so it oughtn't have been a shock how damned cold it was inside.

Thump.

Leo's spine straightened, his ears trained toward the closed door to the parlour.

A low rumble of a voice set the hairs on the back of Leo's neck to standing on edge. Someone was in his house.

As soundlessly as he could, he crept toward the door. And it burst open.

"Uncle Leo!" The trilling voice of Elizabeth split the air as she ran toward him, her arms out wide.

Relief washed over him, and he dropped to one knee. She barrelled into him in a mass of stickiness and crumbs. Leo pressed his nose into her hair and inhaled the scent of sweet soap and sugar.

"I missed you, Uncle Leo."

"I've missed you, as well, Lizzy."

He glanced over her head at Percy standing in the parlour's doorway, and narrowed his eyes at the man. "What brings you both to London?" *Why did you bring Elizabeth to town?* his gaze asked.

"Your letter!" Lizzy pulled back and stuck one hand in the sleeve of his coat, her fingers playing with the hair on his wrist.

Leo glanced once more at Percy. The man knew very well that he had been directed to bring Elizabeth to the estate before continuing on to London alone.

"May we please have tea?" Elizabeth asked, her hands clasped pleadingly beneath her chin.

Heart clenching, Leo nodded. "Come along, then."

He led the way to the cold kitchens and set to arranging materials in the hearth for the fire. Leo had been forced to care for himself on several occasions, and while he knew what to do, he was hardly adept at it. Most particularly when his mind was consumed with both the mystery of Lizzy's presence in London and the bewildering grief he felt at losing Juliana.

Percy's heavy footfalls came to a stop at his side, and Leo looked up at him, his eyebrows raised.

What is she doing here? his eyes asked.

Percy responded with a jut of his chin and a single-shoulder shrug. *I hadn't a choice*, the gesture said.

Leo narrowed his eyes. *We'll discuss this in detail later.*

With a nod, Percy gathered the pot and sought out the tins containing tea and sugar, with which he'd travelled. Leo trod to the water pump outside to rinse and fill a bucket of water, and together he and Percy prepared tea.

Clunk-clunk, clunk-clunk… Elizabeth absently swung her feet, knocking the kitchen chair's legs. Leo was tempted to comment, but the girl was likely trying to remain warm, and—

"Where is Miss Smith?" Lizzy asked sweetly, adding sugar to her steaming cup.

Leo shook his head, sitting across from her at the table. "Her name is Lady Juliana Sinclair. She's the daughter of a duke."

The little sprite's eyes grew wide as saucers, and her blonde ringlets bounced in her exuberance. "*Truly*, Uncle Leo?"

"Truly."

"What was she doing in Nottingham?" Percy asked, pouring his own cup of black tea and sitting next to Lizzy.

"It is rather a curious tale. She—"

"I want to see her again. I miss her," Lizzy interrupted.

His chest gave a sharp twist. "I miss her, as well."

Elizabeth traced the pad of her index finger along the floral design of her teacup, around the rim of the saucer, and down to the hard-edged surface of the table. "Do you love her, Uncle Leo?"

Hot tea burned over Leo's tongue and down his lips and chin as he spluttered into his teacup.

Love. Denial of the word immediately sprang to his lips, but his mouth wouldn't cooperate. He couldn't love Juliana. Could he? The word determinedly rolled around in his mind, teasing him with impossibilities.

The woman was fiercely independent, caring, thoughtful,

imaginative, intelligent, and damned strong. She was unique...
and someone that he would be honoured to have at his side,
both in his home and in caring for Elizabeth. A rapid fluttering filled his chest and stomach as the realization crashed
through him. He blinked. "Holy hell, maybe I *am* in love with
Juliana."

It would certainly explain his recent despondency and the
strength of his urge to return to her side. She'd refused his
hand, but that was of little matter. Whether or not she was his
wife, he wanted to be at her side.

His chair's legs scraped on the wood floor as he stood.
"Please excuse me."

Juliana's cry was muffled behind a damp palm. A cold
chill swept over her as she was pulled deeper into the close—
the narrow alleyway dark and instantly colder than the air
beyond.

She knew who had grabbed her, and she could not allow
him to best her.

Feet scrabbling for purchase on the uneven cobblestone
ground, she attempted to use her unbalance to her advantage
and pull the bastard down. Miles grunted and held her tighter
while she struggled.

A flash of crimson caught Juliana's gaze, and for a
moment, her heart all but stopped. There, slumped at the
close's entrance was her footman, blood cascading down his
uniform. Her heart squeezed painfully and a sob caught in her
throat.

"I'll best you, Juliana, if it is the very last thing that I do,"
Miles hissed in her ear.

No. She could not allow that.

With a burst of strength, she twisted in his arms, forcing

his grip to loosen. For a fraction of a heartbeat, uncertainty forced itself in alongside her determination and panic. Despite his injuries, her cousin was larger and stronger than she.

In that moment of uncertainty, Miles gripped a fistful of her hair through her bonnet and yanked her head back with a snarl. "Fighting will not help you, cousin."

"Perhaps not," she breathed, "but I shall try." With one great arch, Juliana lifted her writing box over her shoulder.

It gave a sickening *crunch* as it connected with Miles' forehead. He cursed long and loud, and loosened his grip just enough. Juliana made to step away when Miles' fist shot out in a wild swing, his knuckles glancing off of her cheekbone.

An explosion of pain and stars burst through her head, and she stumbled back. Giving herself a quick mental shake, she followed her instincts and hastened away.

The *clomp-clomp* of her faltering footsteps echoed off the stone walls of the close, the sound loud to her ears. She reached the opening of the close, the day's sudden light chasing away the rain and the chill that had settled into her bones. Ignoring the curious stares of onlookers, she forced herself into a run.

How had she been so foolish as to allow Miles to find her? She'd been too distracted. She ought to have remained aware of her surroundings, for pity's sake. Most particularly when she knew that she was at risk. *Fool, Juliana.* Neither had she been successful in receiving answers from Jasper!

Body burning with exertion, Juliana threw her hand up to hail a hackney. She sighed in relief as one clattered to a stop in front of her. With a quick shouted direction, she ascended the step and closed the door, slumping breathlessly against the squabs.

Her footman's visage flashed in her mind's eye and she cursed silently, a tremor of fear travelling down her limbs.

It would appear that her stratagem required adjustment.

This could not go on; she could not live in fear, wondering when Miles or Francis would finally succeed in taking her life —and Jasper's. Something must be done.

A seed of a thought planted itself in her mind, gradually germinating into a fully formed idea.

Soon, they rolled to a stop before the Bow Street offices, and she flipped the driver a coin before darting up the front steps.

The door swung inward. She passed a bemused Grace and halted just inside, her eyes wide with shock.

Jasper turned at her entrance and cursed soundly.

"Juliana!" Maria and Heather swept forward to embrace her.

"What happened?" Leo's low voice cut through the moment, drawing her gaze over her friends' shoulders.

Leo was there. Despite their abrupt parting, he'd come back to her. Her heart gave a hard *thump*, her pleasure at seeing him palpable.

He came to her side, and reached toward her cheek, his gaze raking her from head to foot and back again. Despite the concern and anger in his gaze, heat followed his perusal, warming her just beneath her skin.

"Miles found me," Juliana replied.

"Where is your footman guard?" Jasper demanded.

Juliana shook her head, and regretted the action immediately. "I do not know. I was grabbed, and he disappeared. Mayhap Miles got to him, first."

Chaos erupted in the small foyer as everyone spoke at once, Jasper's face crimson in the height of his outrage. The volume spiked, and Juliana's aching head protested.

Juliana lifted her arms with a cringe and announced, "I have a plan."

CHAPTER 26

Retreating voices faded down the corridor as Juliana's friends and family began preparations for their plan, but Leo couldn't bring himself to leave her side.

The woman he'd fallen in love with was about to place herself in danger, and he could not let her go until he'd had his chance to speak. His abdomen gave a slight wobble, and he cleared his throat in an attempt to alleviate the discomfort.

"Juliana," he said, joining her at the window, where she stood gazing at the gardens.

"Thank you for coming, Leo." She turned to face him.

"I oughtn't have left as I did. My pride was wounded, but that is not an excuse for my behaviour."

Heat from her palm permeated his coat sleeve and seeped into his very soul. "I've come to learn that I am swift to assume the worst regarding the intentions of men."

Leonard nodded, his gut now entirely in knots. But she ought to know the truth. "Elizabeth's mother perished in childbirth," he began.

Juliana's palm stilled, but she nodded encouragingly.

"It was two years later, after the required period of

mourning that I forced my brother, Walter, to host a dinner party." Leo blinked back the burn that prickled his eyes, and continued. "I was so cavalier and sodding selfish that I'd tupped one of his maids a fortnight before. My apathy infuriated her, and during the house party she sought her revenge on me.

"Walter was miserable throughout the night." Leo sniffed and cleared the lump from his throat. "And instead of leaving the man to mourn, I forced him into a salutation—even giving him my untouched drink."

Juliana made a soft sound of dismay, and Leo groaned.

"It was poisoned." He turned to face her. "It remains my greatest mistake. And until my blunder at the inn, I'd thought it would be the only error that would ever occupy my thoughts."

"Leo... I'm so sorry."

He shook his head. "We both have faced challenges in our pasts. Let us not allow those to cloud our futures any longer." She nodded, and he continued. "I need you to know that I believe in you. This scheme might seem daunting, but you are strong, capable, and admirably independent. You can both outwit the bastards and launch your new position as a runner. You belong on Bow Street, Juliana."

Her eyes swam with unshed tears, and she pulled Leo in for a kiss.

Warmth swirled in his chest. Her lips moved over his, her tongue teasing and arousing.

"Wish me good fortune," Juliana whispered.

A maid entered, requesting Juliana's presence elsewhere, and Leo was forced to let her go, much to his chagrin.

The next hour rushed by in a flurry of activity as cloaks were donned and weapons were obtained and loaded. Leo had hoped for another opportunity to speak privately with Juliana, to tell her how he felt. Sadly, that moment never came.

Seemingly before he was truly aware of it, he was crouched inside a small gazebo, the setting sun at his back and his gaze on Juliana, sitting on a bench alone in the gardens. Long seconds passed into minutes as they waited, silently observing Juliana reading by the slowly dimming light. It was a fool plan, a reckless plan...but it was their only plan. And as he'd said to Juliana, he trusted her.

What, however, if Miles spotted her over the garden wall and decided to shoot her from a distance? That would not only foil their intent to overtake him, but it could also forfeit Juliana's very life!

The heaviness that had threatened to crush him all afternoon settled ever heavier upon his chest and shoulders. He wanted to sit with her. If he were next to her, he could shield her if Miles made an appearance.

"I'll do it," came a whisper from a short distance behind him.

Leo turned, making eye contact with Jasper through the trellis. He'd heard it, too.

"You've failed before, Miles," a new voice said. "I should—"

"No, damn it!" Miles hissed. "The bitch has crawled under my skin. I'll get her."

"Do it quickly. We want the duke, as well, and I'll not miss my next shot."

There was a shuffle of feet, and Leo followed the sound with the tilt of his head.

"For Jean."

Crack!

Leo's heart jumped to his throat, and his stomach sank to his toes. *Christ. Juliana!*

As another shot fired, she squeaked and sprawled beneath the bench upon which she'd been sitting.

Damnation. They couldn't move until the brothers were

within the walls of the gardens and close enough to Juliana that Leo, Jasper, and the others nearby could surround the bastards. If they kept firing from afar, the plan would never come to fruition.

"I need to reload," Miles growled.

"There isn't time! She'll flee."

The men scrambled over the garden's wall and made a run toward Juliana. And Leo's heart squeezed.

Their time was nigh.

EARS TRAINED ON HER COUSINS' movement, Juliana maintained her position on the ground. Dirt and sharp rocks dug into her front, and the stone bench caught at her green cloak. The air grew increasingly chilled as the sun retreated, and she fought the shivers that threatened to wrack her frame.

Her body still ached fiercely from her days of riding, but she would withstand any amount of temporary pain as long as her cousins were caught.

Much as she despised the thought of using her pilfered pistol once more, she clutched it in her hand, prepared to fire should the need arise.

The crunch of hurried footsteps approached, and she stiffened.

Another shift in movement came from behind her, and she inwardly cursed. Her cousins stopped at the sound.

"She's not alone," Miles said. "It's a trap."

Francis cursed. And they ran.

Clambering from her hiding spot, Juliana rose to her feet and gave chase. She and her friends, Maria, Heather, and Grace, darted for the gate, while Jasper and Leo followed her cousins over the wall.

The close was dark, the ground glimmering with something slick beneath her half boots. Her breath fogged around her face, trailing behind her as she ran.

Footfalls and heavy breathing echoed around her, the sound barely audible over the throb of her heart in her ears.

"Where did they go?" Maria asked, winded.

Juliana shook her head. The men had vanished. There was no time to waste, however, so she let her instincts lead her and broke into a run. Soft footfalls followed her as she darted down the close toward Crown Court.

Men shouted somewhere ahead of her and to the right, and she called back to her friends. "Toward Drury Lane!"

She turned down another close, hoping to intercept the men. And all of the sudden, she was very aware that the only sounds she could hear were her racing pulse, her own breathing, and one set of footsteps. She was alone.

Turning, Juliana gazed through the darkness behind her. Heather and Maria were indeed gone.

"I finally have you to myself," a winded voice said, echoing off the walls of the close and seemingly coming from all around her.

Juliana spun, but couldn't see him through the darkness. Wherever he was, he hadn't allowed himself to be silhouetted against the light at the end of the close.

"Not for long, Miles," she warned, lifting her pistol and aiming it blindly. "Soon, you will be put on trial for your crimes...if my bullet doesn't kill you first." The words were all bravado, and she hoped that he didn't test her.

He laughed, the sound low and grating, and a cold sweat broke out between her breasts.

"Why does the title mean so much?" she asked.

"It rightfully belongs to Francis."

Juliana shook her head incredulously. It was the same argument from their childhood. There was no sense in attempting to clarify the entailment to the man, for he would never listen. "Had you been successful, you would likely be hanged for murder, and your entire plot would be for naught. Why are you willing to take that risk? What purpose does it serve but to cast you in the role of villain?"

His hiss echoed off the stone walls of the close. "Your brother doesn't deserve the dukedom, and you're just his half-sister bitch. Everyone will be pleased once you both are gone. Francis and I will be lauded as heroes."

Juliana moved her aim further to her left, following the sound of his voice and soft movements.

Another shout rose up from the direction of Drury Lane, and Juliana silently hoped that Francis was being apprehended.

Despite the opaque close and the darkness of her green cloak, Juliana was certain that Miles could see her. That put her at a distinct disadvantage. Could she run from him, or would he shoot?

Realization dawned then, and renewed hope bloomed in her chest.

"You haven't a loaded weapon," she said with returning vigour. "I have the advantage."

"No one has the advantage over me," he snarled.

Crack! A gunshot reverberated along Bow Street, the noise bouncing off every building, and for a moment, Juliana's breath caught in her throat. Who had fired the gun? Was someone hurt?

"Francis!" Miles called.

"Stop, or I'll shoot!" Juliana shouted at him.

His frantic footfalls raced toward the noise, and Juliana's heart skittered. She couldn't allow him to get away!

Just as his dark silhouette was framed by the entrance to the close, Juliana aimed and pulled the trigger.

Crack! The sharp blast of the pistol firing echoed off the walls of the close and rang in her ears. And Miles fell to the cobblestones.

Not knowing what else to do, Juliana hurried painfully to his side.

He groaned and cursed, moving to rise, despite the fresh wound in his calf.

"No!" Juliana held him down with her hands and pressed one knee into the small of his back. "You're not going to get away, Miles."

"*Juliana*!" Maria gasped as she and Heather entered the close.

"Here!" Juliana called. "Please help me keep him down."

"Good show, Juliana!" Heather clapped her on the back before staying Miles' arm. "Your brother was shot."

"Hsst, Heather!" Maria hissed. "It was merely a graze, Juliana. Do not let Heather alarm you."

The odd timing notwithstanding, Juliana felt a moment of wistfulness. She had missed her friends dearly, and was so grateful to have them at her side once more.

"Is Leo—?" Juliana began.

"La, what a handsome man, Juliana." Heather whistled. "Better lure him to your bed before some other lady nabs him."

Miles grumbled several choice words before struggling fruitlessly against their hold.

Juliana's lips quirked. "As a matter of fact, Leo—"

Heavy footsteps raced toward them, halting her words. A large figure stopped mere paces away.

"Juliana!" Leo's relieved voice came before he approached. "*Christ*, but I'd worried that you'd been hurt."

He unknotted his cravat and slid it from around his neck.

"What of Francis?" Juliana asked breathlessly, still focusing her energy on restraining Miles.

"Apprehended." Leo gave a nod while he tied Miles' wrists

behind his back. "Miss Huntsbury and your brother have him in hand."

Swift relief hit Juliana like a wave crashing in the ocean. It was finally over.

Voices faded into the Bow Street building's foyer, leaving Leonard and Juliana blissfully alone in the parlour. He'd been waiting for the opportunity to speak with her privately; and, this was it.

"Jasper will be well," Juliana said softly. "The ball grazed his ribs."

Leo nodded. "Will you stay with him while he recovers?"

"No, but I will visit." Juliana stepped closer. "*This* shall be my home."

Or you could stay with me.

He cleared his throat, his hands trembling as he reached out and pulled her against him. "I cannot tell you how relieved I am that you are safe."

"Did you fear that my plan would fail?" she asked with a taunting grin.

"Never. I worried over your safety in such a vulnerable circumstance, but I had every confidence in you. My—" He swallowed past the lump that had abruptly formed in his throat. "I simply cannot countenance a day without you in my life."

Her glistening green-and-slate gaze raked over his features, her dark curling hair falling chaotically—and endearingly—out of its pins to encircle her face. The hint of a smile played over her lips, teasing him in his desire to taste them. But first, he must speak his truth.

"I love you, Juliana."

Heat bloomed in Juliana's chest, and twin prickles of nervousness raced down the backs of her legs. *Leo loves me!*

Suddenly, her fears surrounding the reasons for his proposal seemed cruel and unwarranted. He mightn't have asked with prose and professions of admiration, but the depth of his feelings meant more to her than flowery words.

Her pulse thrummed rapidly, and her abdomen hummed with energy. She clasped his lapels. "I love you, too, Leo."

With a low groan, he pressed his lips to hers in a smouldering kiss.

"Please, Juliana," he growled, trailing his lips along her jaw to her earlobe. "Please say that you'll accept this reformed pirate as your husband."

The breath rushed from her lungs with an audible *whoosh*. "Yes, I—"

Her words were cut off as he crushed his lips to hers once more. A laugh bubbled out of her, joyful, light, and entirely freeing, as though those few words of his had lifted a weight from upon her heart.

There was naught to fear any longer; Miles and Francis had been brought to the magistrate and locked in gaol, and she'd successfully completed her first test to become a Bow Street runner.

"Oh," she breathed, pulling away slightly. "What will Elizabeth think? Do you know if she is returned to Woodhaven Hall?"

A grin tugged at Leo's lips. "She is not. Percy brought her to London—for reasons he has yet to tell me."

Juliana's eyebrows lifted in response.

"Indeed. And rest assured, Lizzy is tremendously excited to have you in our family. I can only imagine how proud she will be once she learns of your position as a runner, solving problems and seeking justice."

Another wave of warmth washed over her at the praise, and her smile grew. "And *you*, Leo? If my place is in town, where will yours be?"

"My place will always be next to you." He squinted one eye in a cringe. "So long as you do not mind the gossip."

Juliana huffed a laugh and raked her fingers through his shortened blond hair. "Love, I'm the daughter of a duke working on Bow Street. I am not worried about gossip."

"My perfect match, then."

She hummed and pressed a kiss to his jaw, the day's growth of beard prickly against her lips. "Perfect, indeed."

EPILOGUE

"**I** am returning home, Grace," Juliana said, rising from her new desk in the Bow Street house and striding across the room. "The paperwork for the Weston case is completed and ready for filing. I shall be ready for the next on the morrow."

"Capital, Juliana." Grace smiled. "Good evening to you."

"And you," Juliana called as she quit the room, donning her bonnet and gloves as she passed through the foyer.

Crisp early spring air encircled her, and she breathed it in deeply. As was the usual, the Livingston carriage awaited her out front. She waved to the driver and smiled at the footman as she entered. The ride was smooth, though her thoughts grew increasingly tumultuous.

It had been two months since her cousins had been apprehended, and one long month spent enduring a public trial and sentencing. But today, her cousins faced the hangman, and she could scarcely countenance it.

The carriage rolled to a halt, and she took a slow, deep breath before disembarking. Their home matched those along the row, but to her it stood out as the most beautiful. It was where love grew, and where their family took shape: her, Leo, and young Lizzy.

The past months had given them so much joy, and to Leo's surprise, society rather adored their notoriety. They had not only accepted him but extolled his virtues after the story of their misadventure came to light. They thrived on the tale of the duke's daughter finding unlikely aid in a reformed pirate hidden away at a snowy estate. The tale had brought in many clients for the Bow Street offices, as well.

She greeted the butler, handing him her bonnet, gloves, and cloak before following voices upstairs to the nursery. Her steps were muffled on the carpeted runner, and the moment she reached the doorway, she was grateful for her silence.

Inside, her dear new husband, Leo, and their niece, Elizabeth, sat upon the floor, sipping tea from miniature teacups and conversing about the latest fashions. Juliana's heart swelled with affection, and her worries fell away.

The scent of cinnamon, coconut shaving soap, and trees teased her senses, and she sighed happily. She was home.

"Aunt Juliana!" Elizabeth exclaimed, rising and rushing forward for an embrace.

Juliana caught the sprite in her arms and bussed her blonde ringlets affectionately. "Have you had a pleasant morning, Lizzy?"

"Yes!" She bounced on her toes. "Won't you join us for tea?"

With a grin, Juliana followed her to the service and accepted a miniature cup.

Leo placed his hand upon hers and caressed the back of her knuckles with the pad of his thumb. "Are you well, my love?"

She nodded, her lips thinning, and something sharp twisted in her abdomen. Her nightmares had been particularly fierce the previous night, and she'd been so grateful to have Leo there to sooth her afterward.

"Jasper will see it through."

"I know he will." She turned her hand in his and gave it a gentle squeeze. "I am precisely where I am meant to be."

Bodies jostled against Jasper as he kept his place among the milling crowd on Newgate Street. He'd never understood society's fascination with public hangings. They even went so far as to cheer, and have vendors selling their wares. It was morbid. But he needed to see this through. He didn't wish death upon his cousins, but a part of him was darkly relieved to have his fear and anxiety released.

Apparently, his cousins had committed several heinous crimes in addition to their attempts on his and Juliana's lives, and the ruling had been swift and formidable.

Cheers rose up among the crowd, and another person bumped his side. Lord, but the stench of unwashed bodies, urine, and manure was bloody overwhelming.

Three men were at last ushered along the end of the walk toward the gallows, their heads covered by rough hoods. He immediately recognized one man's gait, but the other two were unfamiliar.

Jasper frowned, his gaze sharpening on the men as a cold chill rippled down his spine. They marched up the steps of the wooden platform, and his gut churned.

"*Stop!*" Jasper stepped forward. "Sir! Executioner!" He waved to get the man's attention before he made any announcement to the crowd.

But the blasted man couldn't hear him over the din, and every sodding man, woman, and child was waving their arms. Jasper had no choice.

With an internal grimace, he pushed past the crowd and into the clearing as the nooses were being tightened around the men's necks.

"*Stop!*" Jasper hollered.

Two guards made to approach him, but the executioner saw him, at last.

"I am the Duke of Derby," he announced over the din, "and I demand to see the faces of those men!"

"What is the meaning of this?" the executioner returned.

Jasper listed his cousins' names, their trial, and the crimes for which they had been sentenced to hang. "One of those men is Miles Sinclair, but I can assure you that his brother Francis is not among them."

A gust of chilled wind blew past them, ruffling the executioner's hair as he chewed on his bottom lip. After a moment's consideration, he jutted his chin toward the man tightening the last noose.

One at a time, the hoods were removed from the heads of the doomed men. And Jasper's suspicion was confirmed. The crowd jeered and hooted.

Miles spat upon the wooden platform, his face mottled but defiant, and oddly euphoric. "Francis is coming for you, Jasper! Francis is coming!"

His maniacal laughter was cut off when the hooded man flipped his switch. Jasper couldn't watch. He turned on his heel and made his way through the crowd and down the street to his waiting carriage. The magistrate—and the runners—needed to hear of this. *Christ*, what would happen to Juliana and her new family? It wasn't to be borne. His pulse sped and his mind whirled.

Francis is coming for you, Jasper...

SECRETS AND SIN

An Excerpt

SECRETS AND SIN—PROLOGUE

London, May 1807

GLITTERING CHANDELIERS HUNG HIGH OVERHEAD, casting light upon the swirls of colour below. Miss Maria Roberts flipped open her fan and waved it before her rhythmically as her stomach swooped in anticipation. Music filled the grand ballroom, and hope swelled in her chest.

The ballroom was large and full, the air fragrant with perfume and heavy with humidity. It was utterly delightful.

She scanned those in attendance, enjoying the bustling activity and high energy, and her gaze irrevocably slid sideways toward a group of young men. Despite her best efforts to the contrary, she frequently found herself watching the handsome profile of Jasper Sinclair, the future Duke of Derby.

The young man was the focus of all the society mamas, who were no doubt studiously directing their newly out daughters in the art of fan flirting in his direction—a practice which continued to mystify Maria. He was charming, affable, and knew precisely what to do to get a woman's heart fluttering.

Her stomach twisted in knots, and she suppressed a sigh. With every one of the man's breaths, he stole hers away. With every flash of his single dimple, tingles skittered over her skin. And, Lord help her, with every word he spoke, her belly trembled. His hair was black as pitch and appeared feathery to the touch—heavens, but she wanted to touch it—and his eyes...

"Have you any names on your dance cards?" her dear friend Lady Juliana Sinclair asked, jolting Maria out of her ill-timed musings about the woman's brother.

The third of their trio, Miss Heather Morgan, shook her head. "I do not expect to receive any. My aunt says that I ought instead to focus on—"

"Come now, dearest," Juliana murmured, a delicate frown puckering her brows. "You ought never to take what she says to heart. Your aunt's treatment of you is abysmal. You may set your heart on whomever or whatever you desire. And I daresay you should."

Heather nodded. "Yes. Of course you're right, Juliana."

"Indeed." Juliana turned her gaze to Maria. "And you, Maria? Have you any names on your dance card?"

"No." Her stomach gave a sad wobble. "We are only in our second season; not on the shelf *already*."

"I should say not," Heather mused, her expression rueful. "It would appear, however, that we *are* wallflowers."

"*Wallflowers*." Juliana scoffed. "Surely not! You two are lovely, and I'm... Well, you two are very pretty."

Hiding a perplexing flinch at being called *pretty*, Maria gently chided her friend. "Oh pish. While our intelligence might be intimidating for men—and therefore *must* be disguised—our beauty is undeniable."

Juliana mightn't believe it, but she *was* beautiful: tall and shapely with stunning hair. And, for pity's sake, she was the daughter of a duke! It seemed impossible that men would not line up for the opportunity to dance with her. But her friend had experienced several disheartening encounters with disingenuous men and fortune hunters—and was, Maria knew, understandably jaded.

Dancers whirled past, and Maria watched them with longing. How odd that she'd never been particularly fond of dancing, and yet she now found herself missing it.

"Besides, how handsome a woman is scarcely determines how marriageable she is. One must also consider their breeding," Heather mused, listing the items on her fingers, "the suitability of their relations, or whether madness runs in their blood—" Her eyes flashed wide. "Oh Maria, I'm sorry. I—"

Maria waved a gloved hand through the air, her empty dance card dangling limply from her wrist. "I know that you meant no harm by it, Heather."

"Your brother is a genuinely lovely person; not mad, at all," Juliana put in. "I fail to comprehend society's lack of acceptance."

Maria nodded. "Thank you."

"Nevertheless," Heather continued, "we are undeniably wallflowers."

"I daresay it matters naught…"

Her friends' discussion continued as they strode to the refreshment table, giving Maria an opportunity to gather herself. All the while, her thoughts turned inward. Her brother, Thomas, was indeed wonderful. And Juliana was correct: he was by no means mad. With the *haut ton's* skewed definition of madness, however, Thomas was forced to—

Maria discreetly cleared her throat in an attempt to dislodge the lump that had abruptly formed there. Thomas wasn't the only reason she was a social pariah. It was also because of her boisterous and overbearing mother, her too-familiar father, and her own…peculiarities.

A heavy sigh escaped her.

She looked downward at her attire. That evening, she wore white, like the other debutantes of the *ton*. Her bodice was modest, her sleeves capped, and her brown hair done fashionably high. Her gown wasn't threadbare or out of style, but for some reason she felt mundane, and wished she were permitted to wear a colour that brightened her grey eyes and detracted from her too-strong jaw.

No, her inner voice challenged. She didn't just feel *mundane*. Today, this dress felt...*wrong*. Mayhap it didn't perfectly suit her body—despite the modiste's assurances to the contrary—or perhaps the lack of colour made her look drawn. But whatever the reason, the wrongness itched along her spine and curdled high in her belly.

And yet... She still wanted to dance.

Raucous laughter erupted from several paces away, drawing Maria's attention to the group of handsome young men gathered around Jasper. The young pups gazed at him in admiration, clearly pleased that they'd been included among his circle.

Maria angled her slender neck, notching her chin higher in the hope of making her jaw appear less harsh should one of them deign to look her way. *Please let it be Jasper.* She shifted her stance near the wall, affecting nonchalance in an attempt to lure the men toward her. Would that they asked her to dance!

"It's unfortunate, really," one man said mockingly.

"Indeed not," another young man replied. "It's their own fault."

Maria stilled. Did men gossip? She trained her ear on them while she focused her gaze on the dancers.

"How so?" Jasper asked, sipping on his champagne.

"If," the man responded, "they truly intended to attract a husband, they would lower their necklines and fix their flaws.

And, of course, one cannot go wrong with allowing a man some liberties."

The men laughed again, and Maria pursed her lips.

"You just want to get under their skirts, Billingsly," the first man said with a superior sniff.

"Doesn't every man?" drawled another.

More laughter erupted, and Maria's stomach dipped unpleasantly.

"But one must have standards," Jasper interjected. "Unlike Billingsly, of course."

The man named Billingsly lightly shoved Jasper with his elbow. "Sod off, Sinclair. I wager that even you haven't the cods to seek a dance with a wallflower."

"And your sister doesn't count," another young man put in.

Sounds of discreet interest and boorish delight surrounded the men, and Maria set her jaw against a scowl. Outrage, affront and, she was ashamed to admit, *hurt* pulsed through her with every beat of her pounding heart. How could men speak thusly about women? They ought to know that she and the other wallflowers were not truly out of the range of hearing—though perhaps that was their wish, for they'd not attempted to lower their voices despite their proximity to the outskirts of the ballroom. She'd not imagined Jasper would be capable of something so...so *crass*.

Indeed, not the Jasper she knew.

"A wager?" Jasper asked.

"I do love a wager!" another man interjected, interest and devilment ripe in his voice. "What are your terms, Billingsly?"

There was a moment of silent interest while the swirling dancers and the overwhelming scent of candle wax, sweat, and perfume dizzied Maria.

"If we're wagering, I'll make this interesting," Billingsly

urged. "If you can encourage a wallflower to fall in love with you, then snub her, I'll give you ten quid."

Maria's eyebrows rose and her heart stuttered at both the large sum and the abhorrent terms.

"Because I'm charitable," Billingsly continued, "I'll give you ten shillings just for asking the ugly wench to dance, and another seven if she accepts."

Out of the corner of Maria's eye, the smug, challenging smile on Billingsly's face was almost menacing. Surely Jasper would not accept the wager. He was Juliana's brother, after all, and Juliana was among the wallflowers that the other man found so distasteful.

Maria refused to believe Jasper capable of something so hateful. He'd joined in their discussion, but he would refuse, of course. He would defend his sister's honour, and would unquestionably not ruin a woman merely for the sake of a wager.

Struggling to keep her breathing slow and even, the din around her was drowned out by the rush of blood in her ears. Out of the corner of her eye, she could see the men gesturing, but could no longer hear their conversation. *Jasper will refuse.*

Abruptly, he moved. Dragging his fingers through his hair and straightening his coat, Jasper sauntered toward the wall of women.

Sharp pain burst beneath her sternum as her heart broke. The ache spread over her chest and tingled down her arms. *No, Jasper. Don't do it.*

Then he stood before her, his two-toned blue-and-brown eyes glittering with false appreciation, his smile broad and gleaming. He appeared for all the world like a young man in earnest as he bowed. And it hurt her all the more.

"Good evening, Miss Roberts," he said charmingly.

Maria was very aware of the other wallflowers' awe at his presence. But all Maria felt was a mix of indignation, disappointment, and…anguish. The man had let himself down with this barbaric choice.

She nodded coolly and dipped into a shallow curtsey, deliberately leaving off his title as she replied. "Good evening."

His smile deepened, and she was struck by his ability to be so affable to a woman's face and yet so dismissive and cruel behind her back.

"Might I claim the next waltz?"

A waltz. The most intimate of dances. Her chest clenched. He'd accepted the larger wager, then—to make her fall in love with him. Another twist of the proverbial knife to her heart, to be sure.

Well, she would not give him the satisfaction.

"I thank you for the request, but I am otherwise engaged."

He blinked, his gaze sliding downward toward the empty dance card dangling from her wrist. Maria indiscreetly hid it among the folds of her skirts.

"Brother!" Juliana exclaimed delightedly, drawing nearer with Heather at her side.

The strains of another quadrille echoed through the ballroom from the orchestra's balcony, and a flurry of motion and swirls of hot air filled the space. Maria could not countenance another moment. Her heart ached and her stomach churned.

"Please excuse me," she muttered. Ignoring the surprised —and penetrating—glances of all those around them, including the dishonourable Jasper, Maria spun on her heel and strode determinedly toward the refreshment table.

If that *gentleman* and his friends were representative of her choices for a marriage, Maria wanted nothing to do with it. She would find a way to support herself in the future without relying on a man. Indeed, from that moment forward, she would gladly accept—nay, *welcome*—her role as a wallflower.

*L*ondon, Spring 1817

BODIES JOSTLED against Jasper as he made his way out of the crowd on Newgate Street. Morbidly energetic cheers rose up around him. The elbow of a man pumping his fist into the air narrowly missed Jasper's temple as the dying struggled for breath.

Francis is coming for you, Jasper. Miles' chilling last words raced through Jasper's mind, and his pulse rushed dizzyingly through him.

Francis had not made it to the gallows. But why? *How?*

Dazed from the stench of unwashed bodies, urine, manure, and the dreadful reality that his cousin was loose, he made his way out of the crush and down the street to his awaiting carriage.

"Home," he called to the coachman as he entered.

He settled back just as the carriage jolted into motion. He

would have to warn Juliana and her new family. Sending them away would be the safest option, of course.

Christ. She'd want to help him again. She and her friends had become runners for Bow Street, of all things. Jasper had indulged their fantasy, but what could they truly accomplish facing off against Francis? The man was utterly mad. And while they'd been successful in capturing his cousins once before, he simply couldn't risk their lives on luck.

And Maria, his inner voice whispered. She would wish to help, would put herself in any amount of sodding danger just to ensure that Francis was found and dealt with. Jasper's chest squeezed disconcertingly. She cared for others far too damned much.

The carriage jolted, and someone shouted. Jasper's stomach churned.

Francis was hungry enough for the dukedom that he would not simply murder those who posed a potential threat; he would eviscerate them with excruciatingly slow assaults on their sanity. The man had already made attempts on Jasper's life, for pity's sake, took pleasure in inspiring fear in others and would, therefore, use any means to frighten Jasper.

During the trial, Francis and Miles' smug determination to prove Francis' legitimacy and—outrageously—to assert that Jasper's father was somehow responsible for their sister Jean's death was unhinged.

The fact remained that while Jasper's uncle—Francis and Miles' father—was older than Jasper's pater, he would never have become duke. And, therefore, *Francis* would never become duke.

Even skewed as the judicial system was when it came to the peerage, Francis' father was illegitimate, and couldn't benefit from such inequality. So what could possess Francis to believe that, after all he had done, he could still attain the dukedom?

The man had never truly been logical when it came to his wants and desires, but this…

A grunt of irritation escaped Jasper.

Now that Miles had been hung, Francis was alone in the world. And more dangerous than ever.

The carriage pulled up to his house, and he disembarked before it had completely rolled to a stop, his senses on high alert. The sky overhead had darkened, threatening a sudden spring rain and casting disquieting shadows along the streets of Grosvenor Square. A thread of unease tightened his gut, propelling him toward his front door. Which failed to open as he approached.

With a frown, Jasper pressed the latch and entered. "William?" His voice echoed in the stark, grand foyer.

There was a moment of absolute silence, then with crisp finality, the door slammed shut behind him. *"Sodding hell!"* Jasper exclaimed, gripping his chest as he spun.

His butler's clipped footfalls approached from the kitchens before the man appeared at the far end of the foyer. Jasper's pulse gradually returned to normal as he noted the shuffle of movement from his maids and footmen abovestairs and the off-key humming of his housekeeper.

"My humble apologies, Your Grace," William breathed as he accepted Jasper's hat and gloves.

"Not at all." Jasper's lips quirked in a tight smile. "I'm to pen an urgent missive to the magistrate then call on the Marchioness of Livingston. Please have the carriage ready." He stepped away, but turned back to the man. "And do not permit callers, William. My cousin has escaped the noose, and I'll not risk the safety of the staff."

"Of course, Your Grace."

With a nod, Jasper crossed the foyer and strode to his study. A fire was lit in the hearth but, despite the warmth to the room, a chill danced down his spine. He turned to close the door and his heart all but stopped in his chest.

There, jutting from the wood of the door was a dagger piercing a folded piece of parchment with his name penned on the front.

His pulse tripped, and he leaned forward to inspect it. He knew that slanted, untidy penmanship.

Inhaling deeply, he prepared to call out for his butler. But an odd fragrance stopped him. Cautiously, he sniffed at the paper. *Bitter almonds*. Jasper reared back in alarm and hastily retrieved a spare set of gloves from the drawer of a side table.

With a muttered curse and trembling fingers, Jasper donned the gloves and tugged the note free, striding toward the hearth.

*Thou a**R**t a boil,*
> *A plague-sore or embossèd carbuncle*
> *In my corrupted blood.*

Jasper's skin grew cold. Francis had been inside his sodding house. And damn, but the quote was familiar, but he couldn't bloody well place it. It sounded like Shakespeare...

With a slight hiss, the parchment caught as he tossed it upon the fire. Then Jasper looked at his leather gloves. If Francis had meant to poison him through contact with his skin, his gloves were unquestionably soiled. He sighed. Damnable loss. Carefully, Jasper plucked at the fingertips of both gloves until he was able to flick them into the fire.

Whomp. Bright flames warped the leather, curling and distorting them until naught was left but a charcoal mass.

❦

With a final scratch of her pen, Maria sat back in her chair and revelled in the success of completion. Warmth spread across her chest and a little bubble of happiness filled her abdomen. It did not matter how many articles she had written over the past years, she still felt the same upon their conclusion.

Someone rushed past, the movement rustling her parchment. Maria glanced up. The newspaper offices were bustling with activity. Some men sat writing news articles behind three neat rows of two small desks, while others went about their business, hurrying between the desks or out to the main corridor.

The wood-panelled walls were dark and confining, but two large windows along one side of the room flooded the space with natural light.

"Is that the article for this week, Mr. Robertson?" a young paper boy asked, suddenly appearing at her side.

Maria nodded, and replied in her practiced deepened voice. "Just finished." She handed the parchment to the lad with another nod, and he scampered to her superior's office.

With a flourish, she rose and lifted her coat from the back of her chair, smoothly sliding her arms through the sleeves before straightening the cuffs. It was her final day in the office that week, and she could scarcely countenance another moment away from her apartments.

How does Juliana fare? The thought ran through her mind, as it had all day. Juliana's cousins had been hanged that morning; Maria could only imagine that Juliana would need comfort at such a time. Mayhap she ought to fetch Heather, and they three could sit for tea. Although, she supposed Juliana *did* have her husband now.

Raised voices came from the building's foyer, causing Maria to pause in the act of putting on her hat. She trained her ears.

"…wasn't the right man!"

"This is a story; someone start writing!"

"Fetch Mr. Balfour; this ought to be tomorrow's headline!"

Along with several of her fellow writers, Maria rushed to the foyer.

"What has happened?" one man asked.

"The hanging!" a man replied breathlessly. "Francis Sinclair was not there!"

A shard of ice lodged itself in her chest, and tingles of unease raced down her gloved fingers.

Her colleagues dashed about, no doubt preparing an article for tomorrow's paper, but Maria was stuck. Francis hadn't made it to the hanging. Lord, but the man was vile, capable of any number of cruelties, and he would undoubtedly seek revenge on Juliana and Jasper.

No, indeed, she reminded herself. He would no longer come for just Juliana and Jasper. After the events of the past months, Maria knew the bestial, brutish games of which Francis was capable, and he would not limit himself to just his cousins. He would target anyone with whom they associate. That put Maria squarely in the line of his ire.

"Oh! Duncan—er, Mr. Robertson—I've a missive for you."

Maria blinked, the secretary's voice jolting her out of her reverie.

"Good day, Cordelia," Maria said, doffing her hat and offering a short bow at as she neared.

Maria felt a connection to the woman, who regrettably knew only one side of Maria. She grinned and accepted the folded piece of parchment. "Thank you. How was your day?"

Cordelia's auburn eyebrows bunched together in consternation, and she lowered her voice to a whisper. "I fear our superiors must be displeased with me. I'm absolutely certain that I've done nothing incorrectly but, as you know, they've recently requested that I replace Higgs in bookkeeping—in addition to continuing my position here." Her lips thinned and she leaned closer. "Well, I was double-checking the cost of ink—to ensure we weren't overcharged in our recent order, you see—and I happened to note that Higgs had been paid thrice my current wages, for just the one job."

Maria's heart sank as she watched worry and dejection swim in her friend's green eyes. While Maria knew about the disparity in men and women's wages, it hurt to know just how much it impacted Cordelia.

Perhaps...

"Have you considered," she began in an undertone, "an alternate vocation?"

Cordelia shook her head with a pained grimace. "I wish that I could, but I can ill afford to lose this position."

Tapping her gloved index finger on the desk, Maria made a swift decision. "Allow me to think on it. I might be able to offer my assistance."

"Truly? Oh, thank you!" A bright smile lit Cordelia's features as she waved Maria off.

Stepping out onto the sidewalk outside *The Morning Herald* offices, Maria lifted her arm to hail a hack, the motion pulling on the binding tightly wrapped around her breasts. By the end of the work day, the blasted thing grew tiresome. But it was necessary.

A gust of cool wind tugged at her coat and her queue, the darkening grey sky threatening rain. With a hearty *clip-clop* and the clatter of wheels on cobblestone, a hack stopped. Maria gave the driver the direction, and entered, more than content to finally be on her way home.

Flipping over the parchment in her hand, she glanced at the direction and instantly recognized the halting scrawl. Eagerly tearing open the seal, she scanned the first sentence.

. . .

The lagoon was warm and deep, the water an almost opalescent blue, somehow reflecting the sun even from within the cave...

SHE SIGHED. It was perfect. Her friend had answered her question and confirmed her research. They'd met at the opera years ago, when the woman and her brother had journeyed from Gibraltar to visit a Spanish uncle who had purchased a home in London. Before they returned home, she and Maria had exchanged directions and frequently corresponded.

But *this*. This information was precisely what she required to conclude her next chapter. Despite the dangers—and the tides—her principal character would secret treasure away deep in a lagoon... Her next chapter, however, would have to be delayed until Maria had spoken to Juliana and sorted out the business of Francis' escape from custody.

Her abdomen buzzed with trepidation, and she silently urged the driver to increase their pace.

Undoubtedly, their offices on Bow Street would hear the news of Francis Sinclair before the article was printed on the morrow. Maria had been welcomed in by Grace Huntsbury— the woman behind the business—but had not yet been given command of her first assignment. Would capturing Francis and returning him to gaol be her first? What would Jasper think of her involvement?

She clucked her tongue, the sound scarcely audible over the thundering of horses' hooves and the rattle of the hack's wheels on the cobblestones. Jasper would berate her, as usual, but beneath it all, he would be frightened. That underlying concern for her safety, and the safety of others, was what redeemed him during those irksome moments. Drat the man.

Another deep sigh escaped her. He'd surely been there to witness the hanging of his cousins and secure himself a sense of conclusion. How had he taken the news of Francis' escape?

The hack jostled around a corner, and Maria put a hand out to stabilize herself. They turned off Wafting Street onto Bread Street, and she drummed her fingers on her thigh. It was at this time that she ordinarily felt the buzz of anticipation in her middle, but today was different.

Voices rang out around her: the bartering of goods, tittering of young women, trotting of horses' hooves, rolling carriage wheels, and the faint wails of newly born babes.

Upon rocking to a halt, Maria quit the hack and paid the driver, breathing deeply the scent of horses, coal smoke, and manure. The buildings lining the street were coal-darkened and ever so slightly crooked. And she adored it.

Home.

Her apartments were on the third floor of a building with a cobbler as its ground floor shop front. Maria did so adore her home in Cheapside, and she rather lamented the fact that she had to return to her parents' house every eve. Would that she could live here with Thomas, regardless of the perils of Cheapside at night.

Snick. The lock slid open, and she burst through the door into her familiar space. The door opened onto their large sitting room furnished with overstuffed armchairs, a settee, and a chaise, all upholstered in rich purples and blues. A fireplace was set into the wall on the left side of the room, while the entire back wall was covered with custom-built bookshelves that wrapped around their tall windows. The door nearest the fireplace led to the kitchens, and on the right wall sat her writing desk, a piano, and the corridor that led to their bedchambers.

Pride swelled in her chest—as it did every time she entered her home—even while urgency flooded her.

"Thomas," she breathed.

"Maria!" Thomas Roberts rose from his armchair by the fire and set his book aside. "You're home earlier than I'd expected."

"The news has not yet broken, brother." Maria locked the door and rushed through the sitting room to her bedchamber. "Francis Sinclair did not appear at his execution."

"No?" he called through her slightly opened door. "Blimey. What does this mean"—he paused to release a throaty grunt—"for the duke and Juliana? And for you?"

Maria laid the walking dress that she'd worn that morning upon her never-used bed, then swiftly unfastened her waistcoat buttons and cravat. "I imagine that the duke's cousin will seek revenge."

Grunt, click. Another of Thomas' habitual spasms echoed down the short corridor. The spasms were as much a part of him as the colour of his eyes. But far too many people couldn't see past his uncontrollable sounds and movements and recognize the kindest, dearest man in London.

"You'd best act fast," he said. "Francis must be brought back before the magistrate and—*grunt*—pay for his crimes." He paused, and there was a muffled *thump* before he continued. "The duke, Juliana, and her new family must be protected. And no doubt *you* will be a target now, as well."

"In that you're correct." She stepped into her frock and slid her arms through the sleeves. "But I daresay we've bested the man before, and we can do so again."

Grunt.

"Please lace me?"

He strode into the bright lilac-and-white bedchamber, his face in a contorted grimace.

Maria laughed softly as she reached to smooth the hair over his furrowed brow. His spasms came more frequently when he was under stress. "How was your day?"

Grunt, grunt. "Well enough."

He rounded behind her and tugged at the laces of her stays.

"Did Mrs. Fredrickson—dear me, not so tight, please!—come to prepare meals?"

Thomas sighed. "Yes—*click*—she did."

"And the maid? Did she—"

"For pity's sake, Maria," he groaned, moving his attention to her walking dress. "You're less than a year younger than me and yet you flutter about—*grunt, grunt*—l-like—" He huffed in agitation as he struggled to get the words out. "You needn't —*grunt, click*—worry about me."

"It isn't worry; it is love," Maria assured him.

He groaned again, and fastened the last hook on her frock. "Are you intentionally trying to guilt me, sister?"

Maria spun to face him with a small laugh. "I am doing whatever you wish for me to be doing." She pressed a light kiss to his whiskered cheek. "Thank you."

"What would you do if I was not here to attend you while you changed personae?"

In her early days of embracing the side of her that was *Mr. Duncan Robertson*, she'd discreetly paid a courtesan to aid her, but that had not lasted long. Almost immediately after securing work and a home for *Duncan*, she had posed as a distant relative of Thomas' and removed him from Bedlam. They had been so close as children; it had nearly broken her when their parents sent him away.

A wave of sorrow swept through her, but she disguised it with a smirk.

She moved to her dressing table and removed the tie for her queue. "I would scandalize the general populace by walking about half-dressed, for certain."

Making swift work of her brushing, Maria hastily knotted her hair at the base of her head and began applying pins.

"Ah." Thomas caught her gaze in the mirror while he thumbed her missive. "You've received—*grunt, click*—word from your piratical friend."

Her grey eyes lit with anticipation. "I have. Right now, however, there is a more pressing matter at hand."

Grunt. "Correct. You must aid in the tracking and capturing of a madman." Thomas leaned a hip against her chest of drawers and crossed one ankle over the other, his face twitching into a grimace. "You've been among the ranks of the women of Bow Street for above a month but have yet to take charge of your own assignment. Tell me, h—" *grunt.* "—how do you plan to undertake such an ambitious task?"

Want to read more of Maria and Jasper's story? Pick up Secrets and Sin, Book 2 in the Bow Street Wallflowers trilogy.

ABOUT THE AUTHOR

Award winning queer and autistic author of steamy and suspenseful historical romances. Cheri began writing as a child and fell in love with historical romance as an early teen. Finally, she combined her two passions and started writing heart-pounding historical romances full of danger, spice, and a guaranteed happily-ever-after.

She lives in BC, Canada with her high school sweetheart husband, their four neuro-spicy children, and their dogs. She/they.

Readers can find Cheri on TikTok, Instagram, Discord, Bluesky, Threads, Lemon8, and Rednote. Links are available on Cheri's Linktree via her website: www.cherichampagne.com